THE GOOD PLAIN COOK

THE GOOD PLAIN COOK

Bethan Roberts

WINDSOR
PARAGON

First published 2008
by Serpent's Tail
This Large Print edition published 2009
by BBC Audiobooks Ltd
by arrangement with
Profile Books Ltd

Hardcover ISBN: 978 1 408 41501 6
Softcover   ISBN: 978 1 408 41502 3

British Library Cataloguing in Publication Data available

Printed and bound in Great Britain by
CPI Antony Rowe, Chippenham, Wiltshire

For the good, lovely Hugh
and in memory of Evelyn Dix

Surely there could be no more fitting medium of individual expression for women than fashioning something of loveliness.

The Big Book of Needlecraft (c.1935)

Sussex, 1936

ONE

WANTED—*Good plain cook to perform domestic duties for artistic household. Room and board included. Broad outlook essential. Apply Mrs E. Steinberg, Willow Cottage, Harting.*

It was the third time since breakfast that Kitty had read the notice she'd cut from the *Hants and Sussex Herald*. Folding the slip of paper back into the pocket of her raincoat, which she'd belted tightly because her waist—as her sister Lou often pointed out—was her best feature, she walked along the slippery grass verge towards her interview at Willow Cottage. Beneath her blue beret, the ends of her hair were beginning to kink in the mist of spring drizzle.

Lou had told her that the cottage was now in the ownership of an American woman, and that she lived with a man who was, apparently, a poet—not that you'd think it to look at him; he was quite young, and didn't have a beard. No one was sure if the poet was the American woman's husband or not. 'No one else will answer that advert, knowing who *she* is,' Lou had said. 'And I'll bet they want one person to do it all: cooking and skivvying both.' But Kitty had had enough of living with her sister, despite all the modern comforts laid on at 60 Woodbury Avenue, and so she'd written, not mentioning that she'd no experience as a cook. At the last minute, she'd added the words, *I have a broad outlook*.

She turned into the lane which led to the gravel driveway. The cottage was just off the main road out of Harting and was the largest in the village. Through the dripping beech hedge, she caught glimpses of the place. It was red brick, and had exposed beams, like many in the village, but the front door was crimson, with a long stained-glass panel of all colours, much brighter and swirlier than anything Kitty had seen in church, and obviously new. There was a large garage at the end of the drive, from which a loud *chuck-chuck* noise was coming. Kitty recognised the sound: there'd been an electricity generator at the Macklows' too, where she'd worked as a kitchen maid after leaving school.

As she approached the house, Kitty noticed a woman's round-toed shoe on the front lawn, its high heel skewed in the mud. Bending down, she tugged it free. It was quite large for a woman's shoe, and the sole was shiny with wear. The inside was soft cream leather, the outside brilliant green and scuffed. She tapped it on the stones to remove some of the mud, then walked around to the back of the house.

Squinting through the rain, Kitty could see a stream and a line of willow trees at the end of the garden, before which was some kind of building that looked like a tiny house. Plants seemed to be everywhere, spilling over the paths without any apparent order; the large lawn needed a cut. Amongst the daffodils, Kitty caught a glimpse of a woman's rain-streaked backside, sculpted in stone.

She adjusted her beret, tried to comb out the ends of her hair with her fingers, and knocked at the back door.

Immediately there was a series of high yaps, and when the door opened, a little grey dog with large

4

ears, a straggly beard and black eyes jumped at Kitty's legs. Kitty stooped to scratch its head. When she was very young, her father had owned a docile Jack Russell, who'd never minded the sisters dressing him up in bonnet and bootees. The grey dog caught hold of Kitty's cuff and gently licked the rain from its edge.

'Don't mind Blotto, he gets excited with strangers.' A tall girl of about twelve stood in the doorway, chewing a piece of her long blonde hair. 'Who are you and why didn't you knock on the front door?'

Kitty straightened up and held the shoe behind her back, suddenly worried that the girl would think she was stealing. The rain was coming down harder and she hadn't brought her umbrella. Her beret must look flat and ridiculous by now, like a wet lily pad on her head.

'I've come about the position, Miss.'

'Position?'

'Is your mother—is Madam in?'

'Who?'

'Madam—Mrs Steinberg, Miss.'

The girl frowned and chewed. 'I don't know,' she said, not letting the strand of hair drop from her mouth. 'What have you got behind your back?'

Kitty glanced down at the girl's dirty knees. She was wearing a very short and ill-fitting tulle skirt with an orange cardigan.

'I found it on the front lawn, Miss.' Kitty held the shoe out to the girl, who shrugged.

'That's been there for ages,' she said.

Kitty let her arm drop. 'Have I come to the right place?'

'*I* don't know.' The girl bent down and scooped

5

up the dog, which buried itself in her hair and began licking her ear.

'There was a notice, in the *Herald*. For a plain cook, Miss.'

Rain was dripping into Kitty's collar now. She tried to see into the kitchen, but the girl shifted and blocked Kitty's view.

'Ellen never said anything to me.'

'Perhaps I'd better be going.'

The girl stared at Kitty for a moment. Her eyes were startlingly blue.

'But then, she never tells us anything, does she, Blotto?' She kissed the dog on his nose and was licked right up her forehead. 'My name's Regina, but that's horrible so everyone calls me Geenie, and this is Blotto, he's a miniature schnauzer, which is a very good breed of dog.'

'I think I've made a mistake.'

She'd be dripping all the way back on the bus by the time it came.

'Geenie! Who's there?'

So she *was* American.

'She won't tell me her name and she's got your shoe.'

A tall woman came to the door. She was wearing an embroidered red jacket and wide-legged mauve slacks. Her hair waved above her high forehead and was the colour of brown bread. She wore no jewellery. Her nose was huge; the end of it looked like a large radish. She blinked at Kitty.

'What's your name, please?'

'Allen, Madam, Kate—Kitty—Allen. I've come about . . .'

The woman stuck out a hand and Kitty met it with the shoe.

6

'What's that?'

'It's been on the lawn for ages,' said Geenie. 'I wear it when I'm being Dietrich.'

The woman ignored this. 'Is it Kate or Kitty?'

At the Macklows' she'd been plain 'Allen'.

'Kitty, Madam, please.'

'I'm Ellen Steinberg. Do come in. You could have used the front door, you know, this isn't London, and it's only a cottage.'

'Yes, Madam.'

'Get out of the way, Geenie, and let the girl through.'

Geenie ducked under Mrs Steinberg's arm and fled, taking the dog with her.

'You'll have to excuse my daughter. I'm afraid she's always been highly strung.'

Kitty followed the woman into the cottage, still gripping the sodden shoe in one hand.

*　　　*　　　*

There was no fire in the sitting-room grate. Ashes floated in the air as Mrs Steinberg walked past the enormous fireplace, dropped into a velvet armchair, and drew a fur rug across her knees. 'Take a seat, please, Kitty.'

Kitty sat on the sofa, which was covered in a tapestry-like fabric, threaded with gold. She thought about putting the shoe on the floor, but changed her mind and folded her hands around it in her lap. Then she looked up and noticed, above the armchair where Mrs Steinberg was sitting, a hole in the wall. It was as big as the woman's head, and its edges were ragged.

Mrs Steinberg twisted around and looked at the

7

hole too, but said nothing.

Kitty let her eyes wander over the rest of the room. The walls were all white, except for one which was covered in wooden racks filled with records. The floorboards were bare, apart from a red rug in front of the hearth. The curtains were pink and green chintz, lined with purple satin. On the mantelpiece was a large bunch of irises and daffodils, stuffed into a blue ceramic jug. The flowers were interspersed with long blades of grass.

'Mr Crane loves grass,' said Mrs Steinberg.

Kitty dropped her eyes.

'He says the grass of Sussex is the best in the world. He's worked wonders with this place; it's really all his doing. He's an absolute whiz with interiors. We're both very keen on modernisation. But it's still damned icy, don't you think? And the rooms are ridiculously small.'

The woman's voice was strange—not as American as Kitty had imagined, and high-pitched, like a girl's. Kitty shifted her feet. Mrs Steinberg had hung her raincoat and hat to dry in the kitchen, but her shoes were soaked.

'However. We *have* got gas *and* electricity, Kitty! A very recent addition out here in the wilderness. So it will be easy for you—in the kitchen. And music. We've got plenty of music. I hope you like music?'

'Yes, Madam,' said Kitty, wondering what music had to do with anything.

'Excellent. Geenie's never been musical and Mr Crane is hopeless. He thinks brass bands are a good thing! So, you see, I need an ally.' She adjusted the fur rug and stretched out her feet.

8

Her shoes were made of a soft material, gathered in a visible seam around the sole; to Kitty, they looked like a pair of man's slippers.

'Every woman needs an ally in the house, don't you think? It's no good just having men and children. You must have dogs, too, and other women.'

Kitty plucked at her skirt. She'd worn her best— blue boiled wool with a pleat at the side—and now it had a damp patch on the front from the wet shoe.

'How old are you, Kitty?'

'Nineteen, Madam.'

Mrs Steinberg frowned. Kitty wasn't sure if she was too young, or too old, for the job. At the Macklows', all the girls had complained about this problem: when you were young they didn't want you because you'd no experience, but as you got older they were reluctant to promote you for fear you'd go off and get married.

'And what was it you did before?'

'I'm a cleaner in the school, Madam, at the moment. But before that I did a bit of cooking for a lady in Petersfield.' In reality, she'd scrubbed the zinc, laid out the cook's knives, and fetched, cleaned or carried anything she was told.

'Are the schools here awful? The ones in London were really dreadful. Geenie was very unhappy in all of them. The English seem to believe children can learn only through punishment.'

Kitty thought of her school, of the hours spent copying words and numbers from a blackboard, the dust that gathered in the grooves of her desk, the teacher who used to pick the boys up by their

9

collars and shake them. 'I—wouldn't like to say, Madam.'

'Can you brush hair?'

'Yes, Madam.'

'Because Geenie's hair needs a lot of brushing and although I don't expect you to be her nanny there will be times when I may need help—'

'Oh.' Kitty grasped her knees. 'I hadn't realised . . .'

'Our old nanny, Dora, left us recently. Geenie was far too attached to her, so in the end it was all to the good.'

Mrs Steinberg fixed Kitty with her grey eyes, which seemed to be smiling, even though her mouth was not. 'So. Tell me. What can you do?'

Kitty wanted to ask about the times when Mrs Steinberg would need help with the girl, but she'd been rehearsing her answer to this question, so she replied, 'I'm schooled in domestic science.'

It was what Lou had told her to say, insisting it had enough meaning without having too much. She'd read about it in one of her magazines.

'Whatever does that mean?'

A sharp heat rose up Kitty's neck. Her mouth jumped into a smile, as it always did when she was nervous.

Mrs Steinberg laughed. 'Do you mean you can cook and clean?'

Kitty nodded, but couldn't seem to find enough breath for words. Her feet were numb with cold now, and she was beginning to feel awfully hungry.

Mrs Steinberg waved a hand in the air. 'So what can you cook?'

Kitty had prepared an answer to this as well. She'd always cooked for Mother, and had seen

10

enough, she felt, in the year she'd spent in the Macklow house to know what the job was. The most important thing seemed to be always to have a stockpot on the go.

'Meat and vegetables both, Madam. Savouries and sweets.'

Mrs Steinberg seemed to be waiting for more.

'I can do meat cakes, beef olives, faggots . . . And castle pudding, bread and butter pudding, and all of that, puddings are what I do best, Madam.' She could eat some bread and butter pudding now, with cold custard on it.

Mrs Steinberg's face was blank. 'Anything else?'

Perhaps they were vegetarians. Lou's husband Bob said that some of these bohemians were. 'Fruit fritters . . . and, um . . .'

'Nothing more . . . continental, Kitty?'

'I can do cheese puffs, Madam.'

Mrs Steinberg laughed. 'Well. Never mind. I hope you won't mind doing some housework, too. I'm not very fussy about it, but there'll be a bit of sweeping and dusting now and then, keeping the place looking generally presentable.' She twisted round in her seat and looked again at the hole above her head. 'It will be easier for you when Mr Crane and Arthur have finished knocking these two rooms together, of course. One large, light, all-purpose room, that's what we want. I don't believe in all this *compartmentalisation*, do you?'

'Yes, Madam. I mean, no, Madam.'

'Stop calling me that. It makes me sound like a brothel-keeper. You can call me Mrs Steinberg.' The woman's long fingers rummaged at her scalp as she spoke. 'Now. Would you like to ask me anything?' She perched on the edge of the

11

armchair and held the wave of her hair back from her forehead with both hands. 'Anything at all.'

Kitty looked at the woman's clear forehead for a moment.

'Anything at all, Kitty.'

'Are there any other staff here, Mrs Steinberg?'

'Just Arthur, the gardener and . . . handyman, I suppose you'd call him. He doesn't live with us, but he's here most days.'

Kitty shifted in her seat. 'There's no housemaid or parlour-maid?'

'You won't be expected to wait on us, Kitty, if that's what you're worrying about. We don't go in for all that.'

'No, Madam.'

There was a pause. Kitty squeezed the green shoe in her hands.

'Are we settled, then? Could you start next week?'

She must ask it. 'Will I be expected to—what you said about when you're not here . . . your daughter . . .' She mustn't be the nanny. That was not what the notice said. 'What I mean is, what will I be doing, exactly?'

'Kitty, I'm probably the only bohemian in the country who likes order.' Mrs Steinberg smiled and widened her eyes. 'Let's see. Start with the bedrooms. There are four rooms, one for myself, one for Geenie . . . And one for Mr Crane, of course.' She paused. 'Then a guest room. And, downstairs, sitting and dining room—soon to be one—bathroom, a cubby-hole that's supposed to be a library, but you don't have to bother with that: only I go in there. So it's not very much. A little cleaning and polishing, fires swept and laid when

12

it's cold, which it is all the damn time, isn't it? And the cooking, of course, but we quite often have a cold plate for lunch, and only two courses for dinner, unless we've got company. Geenie eats with us; we don't believe in that nonsense of hiding children away for meals. And we don't go in for any fuss at breakfast time, either. Toast will do for me, but Mr Crane does like his porridge.'

Kitty blinked.

'He has a little writing studio in the garden, you probably noticed—it's where he works. But, if you'll take my advice, you won't go in there. The place is always a mess, anyway, and he hates to be disturbed. He's a poet, but at the moment he's working on a novel.' Here she paused and smiled so brilliantly that Kitty had to smile back. 'I'm encouraging him all I can. That's why he's living here, you see; it's a vocational thing, really; if one has artistic friends, one must help them out.'

Kitty looked about the room for a clock but couldn't find one. How long had she been here? Her stomach felt hollow. She thought of sausage rolls, of biting into the greasy pastry, the deep salty taste of the meat.

'And then there's Geenie. Well, of course, I would really appreciate it if you could keep an eye on her occasionally but she's my responsibility now.'

If Kitty didn't move, her stomach might not growl.

'Children need their mothers first and foremost, don't they?'

Kitty nodded, relieved. 'Oh yes, Mrs Steinberg.'

There was a pause. The growl was building in Kitty's stomach, pressing against her insides as if

13 Ⅹ

some creature were crawling around the pit of her.

'So. Can you start next week?'

As she nodded, Kitty's stomach gave a long, loud rumble. Mrs Steinberg raised an eyebrow and smiled. 'It's lunchtime, isn't it? Yes. I must let you go.' She clapped her hands together. 'Kitty, I think you'll do nicely. Forty pounds a year, and two afternoons off a week, all right?'

'Thank you, Mrs Steinberg.'

The woman stood, and Kitty followed.

'Are you still holding that shoe?' Mrs Steinberg laughed. 'Why don't you keep it? As a welcome gift. We might even be able to find the other.'

Kitty looked at the sodden shoe. It was at least two sizes too big for her. 'Thank you, Mrs Steinberg,' she repeated.

TWO

Geenie walked into a sitting room full of dust. Her shoes made a strange scrunching noise on the floorboards and she could taste something in the air: a cloud of powder, like the stuff Ellen threw about her face every evening.

Her palms were still smarting from gripping the willow tree in the back garden. It was a new game: holding on to the ridged bark with all her strength, digging her nails in, seeing how much matter would lodge beneath her fingertips, then going in the house and telling Ellen that she'd fallen. Showing the marks on her palms, she usually got a frown from her mother. Just occasionally, though, she was rewarded with a short spell on her lap, which,

14

although not wide, was always warm, and she could run her hands along the smooth skin of Ellen's knees and listen as she breathed close to her ear. 'You're too old for this sort of thing,' her mother would say. 'Girls of eleven shouldn't be sitting in their mothers' laps.'

Blotto trotted behind as she walked into the sitting room. 'Ellen!' she yelled. 'Ellen!'

The dust fell. Blotto sniffed the air.

Then she saw it. A hole right through to the next room. Pressing her palms together, she approached, and Blotto followed. She stood for a minute, examining the gap where wall had once been. The dog sniffed the pile of rubble at her feet and gave an interested half-bark. Geenie ignored him and pushed a finger into the damaged brick. A few crumbs fell on her shoes and she smiled. Now they would be scuffed, but it wasn't really her fault, because there was a hole in the wall. She pulled a loose bit of plaster away and a cascade of brick dust covered both shoes. Again, not her fault, and more interesting, even, than the willow tree game. Brick made a greater imprint than bark, and the sound of it falling around her bare legs distracted her from the familiar afternoon noises that had begun to seep from her mother's bedroom.

Blotto sniffed at the new pile of debris, whimpered, then retreated.

After a bit more working, her knuckles scraping on the rough brick until they were peppered with blood, the hole was big enough for Geenie to put a leg through, so one patent T-bar shoe touched the floorboards in the dining room, whilst the other remained in the sitting room. The broken brick dug into her inner thigh as she shifted her leg until

15

her foot was planted firmly on the floor. She tried to imagine what it would be like to live between two rooms like this: one foot always in the sitting room, the other in the dining room. If the hole were large enough to walk through, they could have their dinner and Blotto need not be shut in the other room, because there would be no other room. That would be good. But it would also be bad, because she wouldn't be able to shut herself in the dining room as tightly as she liked. There was a particularly useful cupboard in the corner of the dining room, which smelled of sherry and dust, whose door made a lovely clunkety-click noise when opened or closed. The bottom shelf was big enough for Geenie to curl into, and if she hooked her finger round the knot of wood by the handle in the right way, she could hold the door almost closed and breathe its dark sherry air and no one would know she was there. Then she could listen to George and Ellen as they argued or kissed, and she could think of the times when Jimmy, who was gone now, had read to her whilst they sat together in the cupboard under the stairs in their London house, eating sherbet.

The familiar noises from her mother's bedroom had become more drawn out. Geenie called for Blotto. If the dog came back, they could howl together, and then she wouldn't have to listen to the bedroom noises. She called him again, and waited for the tick-tick of his claws on the floor. But the dog did not come.

She looked at the pile of rubble by her sitting-room foot and noticed the wooden handle of the lump hammer amongst the destroyed brick. She reached down, her dining-room leg catching on the teeth of the hole, and ran a finger along the hammer's cool head. Bringing her finger to her face, she considered the dust there. It had lodged in all the ridges of her skin. If she were to pick the hammer up and then drop it on her shoe, she would probably break her toes, like the Chinese women who had their feet smashed and bound so they could wear small shoes. Ellen often said she wished a kindly aunt had broken and bound her own nose when she was younger than Geenie, so that one marvellous day she might have unravelled the bandages to reveal a tiny nose, *tip-tilted like a flower*, which is what it said in the Tennyson poem, and what Geenie's nose was like.

If she dropped the hammer, it would make a noise so loud that Ellen and George might run downstairs. They might stop kissing, or arguing, and rush to her aid, because they would hear a loud noise and not know what it was, and a loud noise meant trouble.

Geenie twisted her body so that she faced the sitting room. She picked up the hammer and held it in both hands. She lifted her arms above her head. Breathing out, feeling the stretch in her muscles as her dining-room leg struggled to remain planted on the floorboards, she stayed still for at least a minute, focusing on the middle pane of the front window. This was necessary in order to concentrate on the banging coming from above. It was becoming more insistent, and there was now a low grunt accompanying every bang. Still Geenie held the hammer above her head and waited. Her arms began to ache. Then it came, familiar and awful: her mother's long 'yes'.

As the 'yes' grew louder, Geenie swung her body

17

round and slammed the hammer to the wall with all her strength.

THREE

Mrs Steinberg had told her to make herself at home, and said they would like lunch at half past twelve, if she could manage it. She hadn't said what they would like for lunch or how Kitty was to prepare it. They'd walked through the kitchen— they had to, to reach Kitty's room—but the American woman hadn't mentioned anything useful, such as where the pans were kept, where an apron might be, or what was in the larder. She'd just waved a hand and said, 'Isn't that lantern absolutely beautiful? My first husband brought it back from China. But everything else is brand new.' The lantern, hanging over the central table, was made of red silk; a greasy yellow tassel trailed from its base. The tassel was so long that it almost brushed the tabletop, which couldn't be hygienic.

Mrs Steinberg had been very generous, though, Kitty reminded herself as she looked around her new room: forty pounds a year was more than she'd ever been paid before, and the room wasn't bad, either. There were a couple of small multi-coloured woollen rugs for the tiled floor; a chest of drawers; and a wardrobe, so Kitty didn't have to hang her clothes on the back of the door. Mrs Steinberg had also provided a picture above Kitty's bed of a naked woman beside a waterfall, at which Kitty now stood and stared. She hadn't liked to look at it too closely when the other woman was

18

in the room, but her initial impression had been right: the woman's flesh had a greenish tint, and was full to bursting. Her neck seemed unnaturally long, and her head twisted to the side as if she'd just heard a stranger approaching through the ferns. Kitty imagined the woman was thinking about plunging in, but had first to pluck up enough courage to submerge herself in cold water.

The first thing Kitty did was place the framed photograph of her mother and father, sitting very upright, on the chest of drawers. Her mother's gaze was steady, her mouth fixed; her father looked off to the side, as if he were about to move. They must have been quite young when it was taken, as her father had died in his early thirties, when Kitty was five, but to Kitty they already looked unreachably old. Perhaps it was something to do with her mother's high lace collars, which she would sew on to make an old dress new. Kitty had mended those collars herself during her mother's illness, spending hours darning them with her finest needle.

Opening the wardrobe, she was surprised to smell not mothballs but perfume: something powdery and sweet, like cinnamon. Onto the top shelf she bundled her cloth bag of scraps. Then she took up her wooden work-box, sat on the narrow bed, and opened the lid.

Now she was going to live in this new place, it was important to see that everything was there, all the things she'd carefully collected together over the years. She brought out the odd pink suspender clasp (had it been Mother's?); the paper packets of sharp and between needles; the dirty lump of beeswax, deeply scored; the scissors with the tortoiseshell handles which she saved for her embroidery; her other, sharper scissors, for cutting out; her star-shaped cushion, studded with steel and ribbon pins; her woollen strawberry, for cleaning needles; several reels of cotton of differing thicknesses; a card of hooks and eyes; a smooth copper thimble, which she hated using but kept anyway; and buttons of various shapes and sizes. The buttons were the most precious items in Kitty's work-box. Her favourite had always been the large lilac one with the wooden surround, but she'd recently come into a set of four tiny mother-of-pearl buttons which Lou had cut from a nightie before shredding it for dusters, and it was one of these that she now rubbed along her bottom lip, relishing its smoothness.

There was a knock on the door.

It was too late to put the sewing things away in the work-box, so she stood in front of the bed, hoping to conceal them.

'Come in.'

Geenie loomed in the doorway. She was wearing a long white cotton robe with wide sleeves and a square neck, together with a thick gold necklace. Her large eyes were rimmed with black kohl. 'What's for lunch today?'

Kitty stared at the girl, trying to make sense of her appearance. The girl stared back.

'I—don't know, Miss.'

'I hope it's not salad.'

The kohl had left a black smudge in the corner of the girl's eye, like a piece of soot. Why was the child dressed like that, at half past ten on a Monday morning?

'I need to speak with your mother,' said Kitty.

'It's up to her, Miss.'

'Dora used to decide for herself, and she always made me plain omelettes.'

'Well. I'll ask your mother what she thinks . . .'

Why wasn't that girl at school?

Geenie stepped into the room. Pointing to the bed, she asked, 'What's that?'

'It's my work-box. I was just looking at it. Sorting it, I mean.' Kitty started gathering up the sewing things and putting them back in the box.

'Let me see.'

The girl was close to her now; she had an earthy scent. It was what Kitty had noticed about the children at the school where she'd cleaned—the smell of them, warm and yeasty, like the scent of excited terriers. But this girl smelled fresher than that.

Geenie sat on the bed. Her white robe rustled as she bent over the box and peered inside. She picked out a large cardigan button. 'What sort of wood is this?'

'I don't know, Miss.'

The girl tossed the button back into the box. Then she rummaged again and found the cut-glass button from Lou's wedding dress. Bob had paid for everything, even tea at the White Hart Hotel, and he hadn't allowed his bride to have a home-made dress run up by her sister.

'This one's pretty.'

'Yes.' Kitty smiled. 'It's from my sister's wedding dress.'

Geenie ignored this. 'Is it the kind of thing Cleopatra would wear?'

'I don't know, Miss. Possibly.'

'I'm Cleopatra today.'

21

'Are you, Miss?'

'Do you think I make a good one?'

Kitty hesitated. She knew she should say yes, but she wasn't really sure what a good Cleopatra should look like.

'You look very pretty, Miss.'

Geenie looked at Kitty. 'Do you like pretty things?'

'Yes Miss,' said Kitty. 'Everybody likes pretty things, don't they?'

The girl lay back on the bed. 'My mother says pretty's not enough. Things ought to be beautiful.'

There was another knock at the door. Before she could answer, Mrs Steinberg was standing on the rug.

'What are you doing here?' she asked Geenie.

The girl did not sit up or reply.

Mrs Steinberg straightened her navy blue jacket and stepped towards the bed. 'I suggest you stop bothering the cook. She's got a lot to get on with.' She pulled her daughter up by one arm. Geenie dangled before Kitty, her feet hardly touching the floor.

'May I show you to Mr Crane before lunch, Kitty? He's got a gap in his writing schedule and has asked to meet you.'

Kitty closed the work-box.

*   *   *

'The writing studio,' said Mrs Steinberg, opening the door to the little house at the bottom of the garden. 'Kitty, this is Mr Crane.'

The room smelled of flowers, gas and dog. On the windowsill, a row of hyacinths bloomed in glass bowls, their flowers stiff and bright, like the coral Kitty had seen once, in the aquarium at Bognor. The curtains were flame yellow, and in the corner of the room a gas burner sputtered. Beneath the window, there was a desk strewn with papers, amongst which was an old typewriter. Under the desk was a pile of dirty blankets.

'Pleased to meet you, Kitty.'

He was tall and his nose was long and straight, but his left eye drooped a bit, making his face seem slightly lopsided. His clothes were too large for him, his long green cardigan patched at the elbows. As Lou had said, he didn't look like a poet. Not that Kitty knew what poets were supposed to look like. The only picture she'd seen was a painting of Byron in a schoolbook, and he wore a very white shirt and had lots of unruly hair. Mr Crane's hair was dark and quite neat.

For a brief moment, Kitty thought she should bob, but Mr Crane's firm handshake kept her upright.

'Kitty's going to be our new help, George. She's a plain cook.'

He touched his forehead, as if considering the situation. His sleeves were pushed up his forearms and Kitty saw lines of flat dark hair and an ink stain on his wrist. It was an elegant wrist, with a prominent, rounded bone.

'Isn't it wonderful? She's been cleaning at the school until now, but she loves music and she's got a broad outlook, haven't you, Kitty?'

'Yes, Madam.'

'I've told her not to call me that, George. And I've told her there's no need to come in here.' Mrs Steinberg walked across to the desk, trailed

23

her fingers along the typewriter keys and leaned back on Mr Crane's chair, one leg crossed over the other. 'He *hates* to be disturbed, don't you, George?'

Mr Crane didn't reply. He was still holding his forehead and looking at Kitty.

'He loathes it. Particularly if he's reading Karl Marx.'

Mr Crane gave a short laugh. 'Welcome to Willow Cottage, Kitty. I hope you'll be happy here.'

'Thank you, Sir.' She did bob, then, without meaning to; her knees bent and she cast her eyes to the floor.

He touched her elbow as she came back up. 'Don't,' he said. 'Don't do that, there's really no earthly need ever to do that, and please don't call me Sir.'

She looked at the place where his long fingers had been on her arm.

'Please. You can call me—'

'Mr Crane,' said Mrs Steinberg, showing Kitty the door.

*   *   *

The kitchen smelled of coffee and Blotto, who was snoozing under the large table. She slipped the apron that was hanging on the back of the door over her head and buttoned the straps. She was already late getting on with the lunch, and she'd have to work fast if she was going to have anything ready on time.

Geenie skipped ahead and sat at the table to watch with her blackened eyes.

24

'Excuse me, Miss, but don't you go to school?' asked Kitty.

The girl shook her head. 'George says he could teach me at home but Ellen says he should be working on his book.'

She seemed to draw her lips inward as she gazed at Kitty, as if keeping something close.

'Your mother doesn't mind?'

The girl shook her head again. 'What are we having for lunch?'

Kitty walked to the larder without replying. Perhaps it would become clear what she was to prepare once she was inside. Mrs Steinberg may have left a note, or a particular set of ingredients might have been set aside. There was no need, no need at all, to panic. She closed the door behind her so the girl couldn't follow.

In the larder, she was greeted by bottles and bottles of wine, stacked all around the walls, beneath the lowest shelf. At least a quarter of them were empty. She brought one to her nose and sniffed. Vinegar. Raspberries. Something burny, like medicine. On the shelves were three bags of sugar, a sack of flour, and at least a dozen bottles of oil, all with labels that seemed to be in French; there were jars of lobster and cockle paste, and jam. One was open and had crumbs in it. There were two jars of something black that looked like Bovril but wasn't. In the corner, a refrigerator—bigger than the one Bob had recently bought for Lou—hummed. Kitty opened the door: a dozen eggs, a packet of butter and bottle of milk, but no cheese.

The larder door opened.

'Can I have an omelette?'

Kitty could scramble, poach and boil eggs with confidence, but her omelettes were always flat.

'Just a minute, Miss.'

She closed the door and stood biting the skin around her nails. What could she make from eggs and quarter of a loaf? Was Mrs Steinberg expecting her to go into Petersfield to fetch some groceries? Kitty hadn't asked about the time of the deliveries. It was already eleven o'clock, and even if she managed the eleven-thirty bus she wouldn't be back before one.

She did another circuit of the larder, opened a jar of the black stuff that looked like Bovril and sniffed. Sardines and mud.

If Lou were here, she'd have asked Mrs Steinberg outright, first thing. *What should I make for lunch, Madam?* It would have been easy to ask the question when the woman was showing Kitty her room; it would have been easy, if she hadn't been too busy not looking at the awful painting of the naked woman to think straight. Why hadn't she spoken up, then and there, and got it over with?

She opened the larder door, took a step back into the kitchen, and almost walked into him.

'Sorry to startle you,' the man said, looking her up and down. He stood firm, with his legs apart and his feet planted evenly on the floor, as if he'd been rooted there all the time she'd been in the larder. His mouth was set in a peculiar shape. Was he chewing on something?

Kitty held on to the door handle and tried to arrange her smile in the right way. She looked around the kitchen: no sign of the girl. She must have got bored of waiting and gone outside.

There was a clicking sound as the man rolled

26

whatever was in his mouth from one side to the other, making his neatly trimmed moustache twitch. His cheeks looked weathered but his eyes were bright, the skin around them unlined. 'I do the garden and that.'

Kitty nodded, still holding on to the door handle.

'And look after the beast in the garage.'

'The beast?'

'Mrs S. asked me to fetch you these.'

He brought a bunch of carrots, already cleaned so they were gleaming yellow, from behind his back. His hands were large and tanned. Then he swallowed, and Kitty smelled aniseed.

'She said something about soup.'

Kitty looked at the trailing ends of the vegetables. 'But I haven't any stock.'

'And these.' He produced a bundle of onions. 'I keep all the veg in the shed.'

Kitty let go of the door handle. She walked past him, sat at the table and pressed a hand to her mouth. Crying was not what a new cook should do on her first day, not in front of this man with his big hands and his low voice.

The man placed the vegetables on the table. Then he produced a penknife from his pocket, divided the carrots into three piles, and deftly sliced the tops from them.

After a minute she heard the rustling of a paper bag. 'Want a sweet?'

She hated aniseed but she took one and held it. The man had left his boots at the door, and his thick sock had a hole in it, Kitty noticed. A long nail was pointing in her direction.

'Sorry,' she said, rolling the sweet between her

27

finger and thumb. 'I'm not quite . . .' she took a breath. 'I'm Kitty.'

'Arthur.'

Kitty rose from her chair. 'I ought to get on— the stockpot . . .'

'Sit down, don't bother yourself.'

She sat, and Arthur stood over her, stroking his moustache. How old was he? Probably not yet in his thirties, but that moustache made him look older.

'All right?'

She nodded.

'I'm making myself a cup of tea. I daresay you'd like one.'

Once he'd turned his back to her and was filling the kettle, Kitty slipped the aniseed twist into the pocket of her apron.

He wasn't tall and his shoulders were bulky, as if he had a lot of clothing bundled under his jacket. His wavy hair looked a bit like the woollen fur on a toy bear she'd had once.

She watched him as he fetched the pot and cups in silence. The pot was light green and strangely angular. There was no cosy. He measured out the tea carefully, tapping the spoon on the side of the caddy to even it out before he tipped the contents into the pot. Then he went into the larder and Kitty rubbed at her cheeks and straightened her apron.

Arthur set the pot on the table. He'd poured the milk into a jug and found the sugar basin. 'Always have tea at eleven,' he said, pouring two cups.

Kitty looked at his face as he spoke. His teeth seemed set deep inside his mouth, a long way back from his lips.

'Where were you before?' he asked.

'At the school,' she said. 'And I was a—cook, a plain cook, for a lady in Petersfield.' She wasn't sure why she'd lied to him. He looked like you could tell him the truth and he wouldn't mind.

'You'll soon settle.'

Some tea had slopped over the edge of his cup and he scraped its bottom along the edge of his saucer before pouring the spill back. Then he took a slurp, swallowed, and sighed. He held his cup with both hands and stared into space for a long time before speaking again. 'The girl before you didn't stay long.'

'Dora?'

'That's her.'

'Why did she leave?'

'The usual.'

Kitty waited for more, but he was staring into space again.

'What are they like?' she asked, being careful not to look at him too closely.

'Mr Crane and Mrs S.?' He swilled his tea around the cup. 'He's all right. Bit wet, but not afraid to get his hands dirty.' He took another slurp.

'And her?'

He drained his tea. 'She's—all right.'

There was a silence. Arthur began to clean his fingernails with the end of his penknife.

'How long have you been here?'

'Since before they came, end of last summer. I worked for Mr Jacks, whose house it was. So I stayed with the house. Part of the furniture, you could say.' He frowned and studied his own hands, which he'd spread before her on the table. They were, Kitty noticed, completely hairless. The muscles at the base of his thumbs bulged as he formed, then released, fists. 'They wanted it all different, of course.'

Kitty tried a smile.

Arthur looked at the clock. 'Best get on.' He flicked the penknife closed and tucked it in his top pocket. 'The beast will need stroking.'

He stood up and flexed his fingers. 'Like I said, veg is in the shed. Help yourself.'

She watched him as he pulled on his boots, noticing the way he stooped over the laces and tightened them with some effort.

'Sorry,' she said, 'but where did you say the shed was?'

Without a word, he opened the back door, stepped outside, and motioned for her to follow him.

They walked along the gravel path at the back of the cottage, Kitty watching Arthur's broad back. He walked swiftly, swinging his hands by his sides. He pointed to the garage. 'Beast's in there. Useless thing, electricity, if you ask me. Lights go off all the time. Don't know why they don't have gas,' he said. 'And my shed's there.' He stopped and nodded at a one-windowed wooden hut, covered in ivy and almost hidden behind the garage.

Kitty looked from one to the other and swallowed. 'Right.'

'Leave you to it, then,' he said, disappearing into the garage.

When he was gone, Kitty stood for a moment, staring at the shed door, before hurrying back to the kitchen. It would have to be omelettes. They would have to be flat.

30

FOUR

'Come on, Flossy,' said her mother. 'Nothing really matters if you're naked. Remember what Jimmy used to say, darling? *Nudity is the magician of the genders.* He was right, wasn't he?'

Geenie's toes were cold, even now. It was Sunday afternoon, and it had begun to warm up outside, but she was still wearing her orange cardigan with the flower buttons, knitted by Nanny Dora. Now Dora was married and living with her husband in London. Ellen said it was for the best, because Dora had her life and they had theirs. But Kitty was not the same at all. She was not nearly so pretty. Everyone said that Dora was more like a Gaiety girl than a nurse, with her plump little figure and her budding lips. Kitty was short and wiry-haired, never took her apron off and hadn't shown any sign of knitting.

'What if someone sees?'

'Who's to see, apart from George? Kitty and Arthur are both off this afternoon. And who's to care, anyway?'

Ellen had already removed her own short-sleeved turquoise blouse. She rubbed the military-style shoulders together as if trying to get rid of a stain. 'Rather manly, isn't it? Better to take it off,' she said, opening her fingers and letting the blouse fall to the ground. The buttons clattered and, beneath the table, Blotto stirred. 'It's not as if you've got much to show, anyway. Nothing to make a fuss about. If I can do it, you can.'

Geenie looked down. It was true: nothing

31

interrupted the view to her sandals. There was no bosom, stomach or thigh to upset the straight plane of space between her nose and her toes. But she knew that, underneath the orange cardigan and sundress, her body held secrets. The faint lines of a few pubic hairs, for instance, disturbing the smoothness of her own skin. When she was in bed at night she sometimes put a hand there and stroked them.

Her mother crouched down and looked into her face. 'When you've got something, I'll be the first to notice.' She paused and licked her lips. 'And then we can take action. It's no good being shy about these things.' She touched Geenie's cheek and lowered her voice. 'God knows, I thought of sex as the most awful ogre until I met your father. Can you imagine? I was twenty-three! A scandalous age to be a virgin. But he enlightened me. It was really nothing to worry about, nothing at all. In fact, he was more worried than I was, when I'd finished with him.'

Ellen straightened up and undid the buttons on her skirt, which shot to the floor, turquoise stripes concertina-ing before Geenie's eyes.

'Is George going to sunbathe?'

'George is writing, darling. I'm sure he won't be interested in sunshine. Or, for that matter, in naked females.' As she spoke, her mother pulled her ivory petticoat over her head and her thick hair crackled. Geenie could see the brown strands standing up on the crown, like skinny twigs.

'Are you still in that damned dress? The sun will be gone by the time you get out there. This is England, Geenie. You have to make the most of these days of grace. Unhook this for me.'

32

She knelt down to allow her daughter to reach the hook of her bra. Geenie hesitated before facing the bunched-up skin around the straps of the device. She particularly hated the way it bulged over the hooks, and wondered how her mother could stand this cage of rubber, ribbons and gauzy cotton. It was something like the tents Dora used to use for spotted dick and other steamed puddings.

After a small struggle, she unhooked the bra, and felt the relief of her mother's flesh as it was released.

Ellen bent over and stepped out of her knickers. Geenie decided to stare at the sink.

'Still not ready?'

She shook her head.

'All right. But you'll regret it. It'll be wonderful out there. The sun on every part of you. There's nothing more natural than that, darling. Nothing more natural than the sun on your own skin.'

As Ellen opened the back door, Geenie caught the smell of her mother: something sharp but spicy, like dandelions.

When she'd gone, Geenie took off her cardigan and put her chin on the edge of the sink, letting the enamel cool her jaw. She could hear her mother humming and flapping out a towel. With one hand, she gathered up the hem of her sundress and hooked it beneath her chin. Then, staring at the taps, she circled a finger around the slight swelling of her nipples, first one, then the other. The skin there was like the lamb's ears Arthur grew in the garden, all velvet springiness. She raised her chin from the sink and pulled the dress over her head. Cupping a hand beneath each nipple, she hunched her shoulders and thrust the flesh on her chest upwards in an effort to make a cleavage. But Ellen was right: there was nothing to make a fuss about.

Clutching her sundress, Geenie tiptoed to the back door, which was still slightly ajar, and peeped out of the crack. Her mother was reclined on a white towel in the centre of the lawn. Apart from her sunglasses, she was totally naked, and she was tapping her nails on one thigh, bouncing them off the flesh.

The door to George's writing studio, Geenie noticed, remained closed. A few weeks ago, Geenie had peeked through the studio window and seen a piece of paper scrolled into George's typewriter with the words LOVE ON THE DOWNS typed at the top. When she'd peeped again yesterday, that piece of paper was still there, with nothing else added. But, as Ellen often pointed out, George was very busy. He was making the cottage into a modern home so they could be a real family. Which was why Geenie shouldn't go around knocking holes in walls, even if they were already broken and rubble was all over the rug, and why her mother had told her to stay in her room and miss supper last week. It hadn't been too bad, though, as she'd remembered the three Garibaldis stored in her sock drawer.

Blotto stretched and waddled from beneath the table. She patted him on the head and he began to lick her hand, pushing his long tongue between each of her fingers.

After a while, her mother shouted, 'You should come out here, Flossy. It's divine.'

Geenie wiped the dog's saliva down the back door and continued to watch through the crack.

34

George emerged from the studio. He stood on the step, shielding his eyes from the sun. He was wearing his writing cardigan, which Ellen said he should never wear out of the house. It was pale blue with a cream collar and big cream buttons, and was so long it almost reached his knees.

He didn't say anything for a long time.

'There you are. How's Karl, darling? Getting to the good bits yet?' Ellen hitched herself up on one elbow and smiled in George's direction. 'Surely it's too hot to be indoors, even for Marx?'

George stepped onto the lawn and frowned. He stared at Ellen for a long time, his eyes going up and down her body but never resting on her face.

'Ellen. What on earth are you doing?'

'I should've thought that was obvious.'

He ran a hand over his mouth. 'Where's your bathing suit?'

'I don't know, darling. I'm not going bathing.'

George's frown deepened. 'It's still only April . . .'

'Almost May. You should get some sun on those marvellous legs of yours,' said Ellen. 'It does the skin tone no end of good.'

He looked about. 'Won't the neighbours—'

'There are no neighbours. We're miles from anyone. We're practically in the wilderness. And you're still wearing that infernal cardigan.'

'I'd hardly call Harting a wilderness.'

They stared at each other for a moment. Then Ellen sat up and thrust her arms out towards him. 'Nudity,' she said in a loud voice, 'is the magician of the genders.'

George let out a laugh.

'It's not funny, darling. It's poetic. James told

35

me.'

'What does it mean, I wonder?' asked George, walking towards her.

'It means,' said Ellen, settling back down on her towel, 'that you should get undressed immediately.'

George looked about again.

'It is rather hot, isn't it?'

'Blistering.'

He started to remove his cardigan. 'And no one's about.'

'Not a soul.'

From behind the back door, Geenie watched as George slipped his braces from his shoulders and began to unbutton his shirt.

'I suppose it wouldn't hurt.'

'How could your magnificent body possibly inflict pain on anyone or anything?'

George's chest was speckled with patches of black curly hair. He folded his shirt carefully and placed it on the grass. Then he removed his shoes and socks, unbuttoned his trousers and bent over to step out of them.

Geenie made her decision. With Blotto trotting behind, she strolled into the garden and stood before them with her hands on her naked hips. 'Is there room for me?'

'Good grief—'

Ellen sat up. 'Flossy! How wonderful! Now we can all be magicians together.'

George hopped about on one leg, trying to get his braces in place and his socks on at the same time.

'Don't be shy, darling. Lie down next to me. George is sunbathing, too.' Ellen held out a hand

and her daughter took it. The sun was fierce on Geenie's shoulders, and her neck was hot beneath her pile of heavy hair. But Ellen was right: it was wonderful, the sun on every part of you: back, bottom, legs, belly.

'I've got rather a mound of work to get through, actually,' said George, still hopping. His sock seemed to have jammed on his toes. 'I think I'd better get back to it.'

'What's the hurry, darling?'

He gave up on the socks and finally snapped his braces into place. 'I've got to finish something. Lots to do before Diana arrives.'

'But you said—'

'Second thoughts. You girls carry on.'

'Please stay,' said Geenie.

But he wouldn't look at her. He'd fixed his gaze over their heads, on the door of his studio. Plucking his shirt from the grass, he walked back inside and closed the door firmly behind him.

Geenie looked at her mother. Ellen's cheeks had swelled with laughter, which she managed to hold for half a minute before letting it out in a long, loud rush. Geenie flung herself down on the towel and laughed too. Their bodies shook together, Geenie curling her legs to her chest and rolling from side to side, Ellen clutching her own elbows and rocking back and forth. They laughed and laughed until they ran out of air and had to calm down. Then they laughed again. When they were exhausted, Geenie slotted into Ellen's side, her small hipbone curving into her mother's waist, and Ellen put an arm around her shoulders. Geenie closed her eyes and stayed still for as long as she could, savouring the warmth of her mother's flesh.

Eventually, Ellen sat up. 'Poor Crane,' she said, laughing again.

'Who's Diana?' asked Geenie.

'She's George's daughter, darling. She's coming to live here for a bit. Didn't I mention it?'

'When?'

'Soon.'

Geenie tried to nudge herself back into her mother's side, but Ellen gave a shiver and stood up, looking at the sky. The clouds were thickening.

'What's she like?'

'I don't know, darling. A bit like George, probably. But a girl, and eleven years old.'

'Will she like me?' asked Geenie.

'What a ridiculous question.' Ellen frowned, still gazing upwards. 'Maybe I was a bit optimistic. We'd better go in.'

Geenie watched her mother's naked bottom wobble towards the house and wondered if Diana knocked holes in walls, too.

FIVE

It was her second go at rolling out. Mrs Steinberg had asked for a savoury tart, 'a quiche—like the French eat, you know the sort of thing.'

Kitty did not know the sort of thing. She'd spent most of the morning looking for something like it in *Silvester's Sensible Cookery*. Egg and bacon pie sounded nearly right, an open flan with a cheesy filling, although Mrs Steinberg had mentioned artichokes, not knowing, probably, that the season hadn't yet begun. There were certainly no artichokes at the greengrocers' in Petersfield, and if she'd have telephoned to ask if she could add them to the order, Mr Bailey would have laughed. Cabbages aplenty, Kitty, he would have said, but whoever heard of artichokes in April? What's the matter with that American woman? Doesn't she even know the seasons?

Kitty wondered if she did. She had yet to see her in stockings, even though it had been a cold spring until now, the air licking around your calves and shrinking your feet inside your shoes. And there had been only one occasion on which she'd seen her in a hat, a terrible woollen beret that covered half her face, when it had suddenly hailed a week ago. You could just see that great nose sticking out, like a fat coat hook.

The marble rolling pin was heavy and Kitty was careful to place it behind the sugar jar so it wouldn't roll off the table and onto her foot. It was an awful rolling pin—flour slipped from its shiny surface, and now the pastry was sticking and tearing as she rolled. Mrs Steinberg had told her it had been Dora's pride and joy, and was quite the best thing for pastry. Kitty wondered how Mrs Steinberg would know this. She'd never seen her so much as put the kettle on to boil, let alone roll out shortcrust.

She gathered up the pieces of dough and pressed them together. She'd roll out one more time, then she'd have to start again. The sun glared through the kitchen window and sweat was blooming along her top lip. It was typical that the first really warm day should come while she was making shortcrust. Everyone knew heat was bad for pastry, and Kitty's hands were, for once, very warm.

She raised the rolling pin and smashed it down on the lump of pastry to get it going. It was easy, now, to flatten the greying wodge. She managed to roll it out into a ragged circle, almost thin enough, then a corner stuck on the pin and a flap ripped up, like a hangnail. Bugger. It would have to be patched up in the dish. She could force a lump of pastry into the hole and press it with her thumb. With a bit of egg it might stick.

Looking out of the window, she saw Mr Crane sitting on the step of his studio, rubbing his eye. He was handsome, with his slick of dark hair and strong chin, and younger than Mrs Steinberg, Kitty guessed, by at least five years. When Lou had caught a glimpse of him in town, she'd said he looked *intense*. It was a shame about his eye.

'Can I have a biscuit?'

That child had a habit of sneaking up on you. You'd just be dusting the mantelpiece or scrubbing the rim of the lavatory, and there she'd be, asking for something. Now she was leaning on the stove, her chin tucked into her chest in the same way as her mother, sucking on a long strand of hair that looked like a wet worm hanging from her mouth.

'Go on, then,' said Kitty.

Here was the queer thing, though: Geenie took the Garibaldi from the barrel, but never seemed to eat it. Kitty knew this because she'd begun to find slightly chewed biscuits hidden behind cushions. Once she found three, all of them nibbled at the corners, stacked side by side in the sitting-room cupboard. It was a shocking waste, but Kitty told herself that she was not responsible for the child. It

40

was her mother's look-out.

'What are you doing?'

'Making a French tart for your lunch. Bacon and egg.'

'A quiche.'

'That's it.'

Geenie pretended to examine her biscuit for a few moments. Then she said, 'Can I help?'

This was another thing the child did: offer to help and then get in the way.

'No. Thank you, Miss.'

'Please.'

'There's nothing for you to do, Miss.'

'I'm bored.'

Kitty sighed. 'You can grate the cheese, if you like.'

Geenie screwed up her nose. 'I hate cheese.'

'You could measure out the milk, then.'

'Cheese smells like sick.'

Kitty floured the pastry dish. 'You're a rum sort of a girl, aren't you?'

'What are you doing that for?'

'So it won't stick, Miss.'

'It always sticks, doesn't it?'

She mustn't blush, not in front of the child.

Kitty gathered the pastry around the pin and prepared to lift. She'd have to be careful not to let anything brush the tassel of that greasy lantern. If she could just transport the thing without a rip . . .

'Can I have another biscuit?'

The pastry gave up; a large strip fell in folds on the table. 'Bother!'

Geenie stuck a finger into the crumpled mess. 'Can't you roll it out again?'

Kitty stared at the table. 'It's too far gone. It's

41

got too warm.'

'What difference does that make?'

Now Kitty felt the blood stinging her cheeks. 'I don't know, Miss; it's just ruined, is all. I'll have to start over.' It would be impossible with the child here, asking questions, and she only had—what? an hour left, at most.

'Here.' She held out the grey ball to Geenie. 'Have this to play with. It's yours.'

Geenie pressed a finger into it with such force that Kitty's hand dipped.

'You could make something with it, couldn't you, Miss?'

Geenie prodded the dough again, gently this time. 'I could try,' she said.

Kitty placed the tacky pastry firmly in the girl's hand. 'I'm sure you could make something out of that, with all your talents,' she said. Geenie was always drawing something, or drawing on something. Last week she'd done a scribble which she claimed was a map of the world on the kitchen table. Luckily it was only in pencil, and Kitty had been able to scrub the thing off. She thought Geenie's efforts a bit slow for a girl of eleven, but she said nothing.

'I could try,' Geenie said again, smiling.

'I'm sure you could, Miss. You could make something lovely. A real work of art.'

The child took the pastry and walked out of the kitchen, swinging her blonde hair.

'Or you could hide it somewhere,' Kitty muttered under her breath.

*   *   *

42

Arthur was batting at a wasp. With the patched-up egg and bacon pie in the oven at last, Kitty watched him from the sitting-room window. His arms windmilled around his head. The movement had caught her eye whilst she was dusting and she'd nearly dropped Mrs Steinberg's African mask, the one that looked a bit like Bob. Of all the things in the room, she sensed this would be the worst to drop. She held it tight in both arms now as she watched Arthur jogging on the spot, his limbs bouncing like those of a puppet jolted from above. He seemed to be moving to the rhythm of the thumping noise coming from the library: Mrs Steinberg's typewriter. The woman was always in there, banging out something or other on those keys. Arthur swatted the air again, his mouth opening in horror. But he made no sound. He simply danced on the grass, batting the air around him.

Later she could say to him, the still, controlled Arthur with the straight moustache: *I know your weakness*.

She wouldn't say that, of course. It was the sort of thing Mae West would say, with a hearty wink. Kitty would ask, instead, if he had room in his bag for the piece of egg and bacon pie she'd put by. She'd ask him if he could squeeze it in, this piece of pie so carefully cut, and wrapped in waxed paper, twice, so the grease wouldn't leak, because she knew Arthur worried about things being clean and neat: when she went to his shed to fetch vegetables, she'd seen the numbered rows of tools, the swept corners of his tool box. And she worried about the pie being crushed in his bag by his flask and his book as he cycled home.

43

Arthur always had a Western with him. At the kitchen table he held it with one hand and ate with the other, keeping the book at arm's length, as though frightened of smearing the pages. His eyes rarely strayed from the words, making her wonder how the bread arrived at his mouth, how he bit into his boiled egg without chomping his fingers. He'd a different book every week. Kitty guessed he got them from the twopenny library in town. Or perhaps he had someone who bought them for him? He'd yet to mention any girl. She'd seen him at the Savoy on his own last week, which must mean there was no girl. She'd been there with Lou, and had spotted Arthur leaning by the ticket booth, scrutinising the poster for next week's performance of *Come Out of the Pantry*. It was strange, seeing him away from Willow Cottage, in his smart clothes. She'd noticed how white his collar was. They stood under the lights of the foyer, and he'd looked at her and said, 'Lovely here, isn't it?'

Kitty gazed through the window again. Arthur had stopped windmilling his arms. The child was talking to him, holding the lump of dough in the air. Arthur crouched down and took the dough in his hands. He rolled the lump around his palm, weighing it as though it were something precious.

That was her dough and the child had given it away. And now Arthur would know that she, Kitty, had ruined the pastry and wasted a whole batch.

She opened the kitchen window. 'Miss Geenie!'

She hadn't meant to shout, but now they were both looking towards her. She'd have to follow through, as Lou would put it. *That's the trouble with you, Kitty*, her sister always said. *You never follow*

44

through.

'Lunch is almost ready, Miss. Come in and wash your hands.'

The girl stared at Kitty in silence, her mouth slightly open. Arthur straightened up and nodded to Kitty. 'You'd best go in, Miss.' He gestured towards the door.

'It's too early for lunch,' grumbled Geenie. 'Where's Ellen?'

Kitty couldn't lie. 'I'm not sure. But lunch is nearly ready.'

'Can't I come in when Ellen says?'

Kitty couldn't get used to Geenie calling Mrs Steinberg by her first name; it gave her a start every time she heard it. *Ellen.* It just wasn't who she was, just as *Mary* was not who her own mother had been.

'I—I think you should come in now, please, Miss.' Her voice wasn't as steady as she'd have liked.

Arthur was looking at the ground, the lump of dough still in his hand.

Geenie folded her arms. 'In a minute,' she said.

'I should get on,' said Arthur, with a half wave at Kitty. 'Lots to do.'

She tried a smile, but he was already walking back to his shed, gripping the dough in his fist.

SIX

It was red, with white handle grips and chipped lettering on the crossbar. George wheeled it through the back garden, whistling.

Geenie had never heard him whistle before. It reminded her of Dora, who'd whistled though it was unladylike. When she was washing up, or ironing, Dora had whistled, and Geenie had tried to whistle, too, but her lips were too soft to get the shape, somehow.

They watched him from the library window, mother and daughter leaning together on Ellen's desk, stretching their necks. George's shirt sleeves were folded up close to his armpits, the way Arthur's often were.

'It's broken,' said Ellen. 'He's brought a broken bicycle home.'

The brake cables clattered against the spokes, raining ticks across the garden.

Ellen marched out of the house, and, after giving it a second or two, Geenie followed behind, quietly. She knew that if she stayed in the shadow of her mother's skirt, she wouldn't get in much trouble. There was a certain position she could take behind her mother which usually meant that people didn't seem to notice her.

'What are you doing with that?'

George had leant the bike against the wall of his studio and stepped back to admire it. He didn't look at Ellen. Instead, he ran a hand over the saddle.

'Lovely, isn't she?'

'Broken, Crane. *It* is broken.'

Geenie noticed that her mother was pronouncing all her words very clearly.

He shrugged. 'Not for long.'

Geenie grabbed one of the trailing cables in her fist and gave it a tug. 'What's this, George?'

'That's a broken bit,' muttered her mother,

prising the cable from her.

George took the cable from Ellen. 'It's fixable, though.' He crouched down and held the end of the cable before Geenie's face. 'Perfectly fixable.'

'Really, Crane, you look quite proletarian.'

George bit his lip. 'Ellen—'

'I'm joking. You couldn't look proletarian if you tried.'

He bit his lip again. Then he said, 'I happen to like bikes.'

'How many do you need? You already have one, which you never use, and I've offered you a car of your own. Besides which, there's the Lanchester, which you're free to use any time.'

George smiled at Geenie. 'But I like bikes,' he said again, sending a pedal spinning with one hand. 'And anyway. It's not for me.'

He looked up at Ellen, who was standing with her hands on her hips. 'Can Geenie ride?' he asked. 'Diana can. And since she'll be here soon, I thought it only fair that Geenie has her own bicycle. Then they can ride together.'

'Why would Geenie want to ride a bike? She doesn't need to. She can ride a horse. What good's a bike on the Downs? A bike's only any good on a road, where a car's much better.'

George straightened up and folded his arms. He looked into Ellen's face and she looked back at him.

'And that thing is far too big for her. Really, Crane. For an intellectual you're awfully slow sometimes.'

'Why are you so set against this?'

Ellen shifted her gaze to the willows at the bottom of the garden. She tapped her foot. For a

47

few moments, all three of them listened to the leaves swishing in the breeze, and waited.

'Ellen?'

'I'm not against it.'

'Oh?' George laughed. 'It sounded like you were. But if you're not . . .'

'Not entirely.' She traced a semicircle in the wet grass with her shoe.

'I could give you a backie.'

'What on earth is that?' Ellen smiled a little. 'It sounds slightly obscene. I might like it.'

'It means I cycle and you sit.'

'I'd much rather have a horse between my thighs.'

'Have you ever tried?'

'A horse?'

'A bicycle.'

Geenie stepped out from behind her mother. This was her chance. 'Ellen can't ride a bicycle.'

Ellen's hand landed on her daughter's shoulder and pressed down, hard. There was a long silence.

Geenie persisted. 'She's never learned to ride a bicycle. Have you, Ellen?'

George's eyes flickered towards Ellen. 'Really?'

'You can give *me* a backie, George,' said Geenie.

'Shut up, Geenie. That's enough.' Through her thin cardigan, Geenie could feel her mother's nails.

George drew a hand slowly across his mouth. 'You can't ride a bike?'

Ellen let go of her daughter and threw her hands in the air. 'Not really.'

'Not really? Can you, or not?'

'No! All right? No! I cannot ride a bicycle. Who cares about riding a damn bicycle? There's more to life than pedalling along roads. More to my life, anyway.'

'I'm just a bit surprised. I thought everyone—'

'Everyone what?'

'Could cycle.'

'Well, I can't. It's just one of those useless things I never learned, like ancient Greek and cricket.'

'But, riding a bike. It's, ah, well . . .'

'It may have escaped your notice, Crane, but I was brought up by a family of New York millionaires. No one in my family rides a bicycle. NO ONE. It's just not something you do if you're a Steinberg.'

'All right, all right.' He reached out to touch her hand, but she pulled away. Geenie wondered if she should step into that place behind her mother which would make her invisible again.

'James never rode a bicycle.'

George didn't reply. Geenie tried to remember if she'd ever seen Jimmy on a bicycle. Cars were more his thing. She remembered him letting her rest her head on his thighs during long journeys, when she would gaze at his hands on the steering wheel, marvelling at how he could touch the sides quite lightly, it seemed, and the car would move this way or that.

'He never rode a bicycle. Ever.' Ellen's eyes were very wide, and her chin was jutting forward.

'No,' said George. 'Of course not.'

There was another long silence.

After a while, George said, 'Look. None of that means that Geenie shouldn't learn, does it?'

'It's not up for discussion.' Ellen turned and began to walk back to the house.

Geenie decided not to step into that place

behind her mother. Instead, she stood beside George and watched Ellen stride away. George sighed and patted the saddle again, as if it were a faithful dog. Geenie gazed at his lopsided face, and saw that his cheeks had hollowed.

'But I'm not a Steinberg.'

Ellen stopped. Very slowly, she turned around. 'What did you say?'

George covered his eyes. Geenie looked at her mother. Ellen's chin was tucked tightly into her chest, and she knew she may as well carry on. It would be as bad either way. 'My name's Floyd,' she said. 'Regina Eleanor Floyd and I want to ride a bike with Diana.'

Ellen charged towards her daughter and grabbed her by the upper arm. 'And where's Charles Floyd now? Do you see him?'

Geenie did what she always did when her mother got mad: she went silent.

'Do you see him?'

Geenie looked down at the grass and shook her head.

'No. That's because he's not here. He left. Charles Floyd, your illustrious father, abandoned us before you were two years old. But I am here, Ellen Steinberg, your mother, is here. And that makes you a Steinberg too, do you hear me?'

Geenie looked at George.

'I said, do you hear me?'

Geenie swallowed hard. If she kept her head completely still, if she concentrated on the individual blades of grass and the way some of them were curved and some of them were straight, the tears might not start.

George cleared his throat. 'Now then. Ah. Look.

Might it not be a good thing if Geenie here were to have a little go? What harm can it do?'

Ellen let go of Geenie's arm.

Geenie held her breath. Some of the blades were twisted right round, so they looked like tiny tubes of grass.

'Come on, Ellen. It's just a bicycle. Geenie didn't mean what she said, did you, Geenie?'

Like hollow green tubes. A few of the tubes had water in them.

'She's sorry. She'll always be a Steinberg, won't you, Geenie?'

Geenie looked up at George. His eyes were brown and soft, and she knew she could say yes and not mean it, and it would still be all right.

She nodded.

After a minute, her mother said, 'She could fall off.'

'Ellen.'

'She could fall off and break a leg. Or an ankle. And whose fault would it be? Who'd be responsible?'

'I would,' said George. He put a hand on Geenie's hair, and breathed out. 'I'd be responsible.'

*　　　*　　　*

The first time was terrible. The saddle was much harder than it looked, with lumps in the wrong places, and, just when she thought she'd got a good grip on them, the pedals kept whipping round and banging Geenie's ankles. Her socks would be stained with black, her shins stained with bruise. The handle grips were hard, too; they were cold beneath her fingers, and slippery to touch. Like the pedals they could escape without warning, causing the whole thing to swerve and topple beneath her.

Her mother watched silently from the window as Geenie grappled with the bike and George tried to steady her. Geenie could see Ellen's pale face beyond the glass. Her nose looked particularly large and pink that day. She said it reacted to the weather: any dampness caused a swell. The cottage was always damp, and the grass outside was wet after a thunderstorm in the night.

The wheel slipped again, and Geenie's feet skidded on the grass, but she managed to keep the thing upright by gripping the crossbar between her knees. She looked up at the window and caught her mother's eye, but Ellen did not move from her ringside position. She just stared out, nose glowing slightly, mouth drawn in a tight line.

Geenie realised her legs were shaking, and her fingers ached from gripping the handlebars. She stood still for a moment, allowing herself to breathe.

'I don't think I can,' she said, looking at George, who was holding the back of the saddle.

'You'll get it. Right foot on pedal and push off. I've got you, so you won't fall.'

'I can't.'

'No such word as can't. Only won't.'

He wasn't usually like this, his words coming fast and sounding like the truth. Normally he left gaps, sighed and hummed. But now he was telling her what to do, very clearly, and she found that she wanted to follow his instructions.

'Both hands on the handlebars?'

She took hold of the tough white rubber again

and squeezed.

'Yes.'

'All right.' He paused. 'Remember what I told you?'

'Keep looking ahead.'

'Good. And?'

'Don't look down.'

'Good girl. And?'

'Keep pedalling.'

'Exactly.'

There was sweat on his forehead, and he had his sleeves rolled up again. His hair, usually greased back in place in a short wave, was sticking up in a peak above his forehead.

'All right?'

'Yes.'

She glanced at the library window, but her mother was gone.

'Off we go, then. And push!'

At his command, she pressed her right foot on the pedal and lifted her left from the floor. This was the worst moment: one foot in the air, the other groping for the flat surface of the pedal, the bicycle's balance depending on finding it. Everything wobbled as her foot floundered madly.

'Steady.'

She found it. Pushed down. And the bicycle moved forward.

'I've got you. Keep pedalling.'

She pushed down again and the spokes rattled. The grass sighed. The breeze was suddenly loud in her ears.

'Very good. Keep going.'

His footsteps were behind her as she pedalled. She pedalled right across the grass and along the

53

side of the house, past the garage and to the front gate.

'Feel good?'

He sounded breathless, but she kept pedalling. If she kept pedalling, she could be on the road and away from the house and no one could stop her. She could pedal across the village and up the Downs, and over the top to the sea. She could keep going, her feet pushing down, pushing down, pushing down, her hands light on the handlebars, the saddle warm between her thighs. All she had to do was keep looking ahead.

She was out in the lane now. The may bushes were frothy with white and smelled of clean laundry. Cow parsley brushed her arms.

She pushed down. She looked ahead.

It wasn't far to the end of the lane, where the road began. Geenie sat up straight and pedalled, letting her legs go light as the wheels gathered momentum and the pedals seemed to push themselves around. It was like swimming, only better: she was dry and warm, and she could go faster, right to the end. But there was that same feeling of weightlessness, of being borne up, held above the path by rubber and air.

The end of the path was near now, and she looked back. Just to check if he was still there, because she'd have to turn the bicycle, or stop, and she wasn't sure how you did either of those things.

He was not holding on to the bike. He was not running behind her. Instead, he was standing at the beginning of the lane, and he was starting to clap. He was applauding her as if she had achieved this thing.

Then the bike swerved and there was cow

parsley in her face and a branch scratching her arm in a long sharp line, but she kept pushing her feet down and looking ahead and somehow the bike straightened again and she was back on the path.

'Brake!' George was shouting. 'Brake, Geenie! Pull the brakes!'

She squeezed the brakes and crashed her feet to the floor at the same time, so her shoes dragged along the stones and her bottom came right off the seat. She kept braking and dragging until the bicycle came to a stop, and only then was she able to unlock her fingers from the handlebars. The whole frame crashed to the side, and so did she.

There were small stones in her cheek and the back wheel was on her leg.

'Good girl,' she heard him shout. 'What a journey!'

Geenie sat up. Brushing herself off, she gazed at the puffed clouds bubbling overhead, and she did not cry. When she got back to the cottage, she'd say nothing about this to her mother, she decided; she'd keep it all to herself.

SEVEN

All week, Kitty longed for her bath. At Lou's, she'd become used to taking a bath on whatever evening she liked, but here she had to take it on a Friday, between eight and ten o'clock. When the time finally came, she waited until nine, when Geenie was usually in bed, and Mrs Steinberg and Mr Crane were in the sitting room together. Venturing out of her room at any other time was just too risky: Mrs Steinberg might be wandering the house, looking for Mr Crane, and Geenie might be anywhere at all.

She gathered up her dressing gown, towel, and the copy of *Garden and Home* Lou had given her, and listened at the door. Kitty's room was only reachable through the kitchen, and it was unlikely anyone would be in there at this time. Occasionally she heard Mr Crane's steady footsteps on the flags at night; in the morning there would be crumbs on the table and butter left out by the sink.

She opened her door, walked across the kitchen floor, and then listened again to check no one was in the corridor.

In the kitchen, she could hear music coming from the sitting room: a man's deep voice, but not Bing Crosby or even Al Bowlly. Lou loved Bing, but Kitty found his songs too sleepy. This voice was much raspier, younger. *The things I do are never forgiven* it sang. Then there was a bang, and Mr Crane's laugh.

Kitty imagined that Mrs Steinberg was dancing around that huge room. Now that the wall had come down, there was certainly plenty of space for it. Mr Crane would be sitting in his armchair, watching, perhaps with a book on his lap. The woman would be flinging her arms about, just like her daughter when she was dressed up and acting out those solo plays of hers on the lawn. And wearing no stockings.

It was probably safe to make a dash for it.

She opened the door. The hallway looked clear. It was impossible to see around that blasted corner, though, and she almost shrieked when she came across Blotto, sitting on the hall floorboards, waiting for some action. The dog looked up hopefully, then got down on his belly and shuffled along the floor like a huge hairy insect towards Kitty's feet. Deciding it wasn't safe to stop and pat, Kitty stepped past the creature and pressed along the hall, her stockinged feet rasping on the bare wood.

There was Mr Crane's laugh again: sudden and surprisingly loud.

She didn't run along the corridor, not exactly. But she must have taken the two steps up to the bathroom too fast, because now she was holding out her hands and the gown and towel were wrapping themselves around her legs as she went down. Her shin bone cracked against the step, but she didn't yelp; she went down silently, still clutching the magazine in one hand, then sprang up again, grabbing the gown and the towel with the other hand as she leapt inside.

Once in the bathroom, she leant against the door and tried to breathe normally. She couldn't hear any footsteps. Perhaps no one had heard her fall. If Mr Crane had heard, would he have come to see what was wrong? Or would he have shrugged and continued to watch Mrs Steinberg dance without stockings?

The bath was huge, with gnarled claw feet and brass taps which squealed as she twisted them. The geyser choked. It would take at least ten minutes to even half-fill the tub; sometimes she thought it would actually be simpler to use the public baths in Petersfield, as she'd done before Mother died. Whilst waiting, Kitty sat on the bath's edge and opened her magazine.

Are You the STAR in Your Husband's Life? she

read. *Or have you allowed yourself to slide into a minor, supporting role?* Wasn't that what wives were supposed to do? Slide into supporting roles? Not that her own mother had done any of that. She was always the one who went to the pub whilst her father waited in. 'Once he looked at the clock when I came home,' she'd told her daughters. It was one of her many stories, meant to prove that they were all better off without him. 'I told him, don't you dare look at that clock.' She'd gripped the arms of her chair as she spoke. 'And he never did again.'

> *Remember your husband is human. What he really expects of you is that you should continue to be the leading lady in his life, the heroine of the domestic drama, and that every now and then you should spring on him a new act. In that light, look at the woman you see in the mirror and ask yourself today: 'Is she slipping or is she still a star?'*

Had Mrs Steinberg read this? Kitty had never seen the woman with a magazine. She was always carting big books by authors with foreign names about. Not that Kitty had ever seen her actually reading. It would be easy, Kitty thought, for Mrs Steinberg to become a leading lady, if she put a bit of effort in; that was what money was for, wasn't it? Money could put a shine on the ugliest of women, as Lou often pointed out, particularly when she saw a photograph of Mrs Sweeny in the *Daily Mail*.

She dipped her fingers in the bath. Still warm enough, although the water had started to run cold.

Unbuttoning her frock, she glimpsed her reflection in the full-length mirror which stood in the corner of the room, and she turned away to unhook her stays and roll down her stockings. Then she stepped in the bath quickly, so as not to catch sight of herself again. Kitty had yet to look at the whole of herself in that glass; it was the first full-length mirror she'd been confronted by. She'd seen parts of her body at Lou's house, of course, in the dressing-table glass: her shoulders, small and yet fleshy; her belly-button, like a comma in her rounded stomach; her breasts, which seemed alarmingly blue. Once, she'd even peered at the dark nest between her legs with a compact, but had been unable to see much with just the bedside lamp, which had been a bit of a relief. But never the whole thing together.

She slid into the water, turned over on her stomach, and rested her cheek on the enamel. It wasn't very comfortable this way but if she balanced right, she could pretend she was floating in the sea. She could still hear music coming from the sitting room, and she began to rock back and forth, the water rippling over her hands and thighs and backside as she pushed herself along the bottom of the bath. It was like the time she'd gone to Bognor Regis on the Sunday School outing and had spent hours letting the tide wash her up and down the sand, the whole length of her brushing the beach as the sea moved beneath. She closed her eyes and listened to the raspy young voice coming from downstairs. *I hear music, then I'm through!* It was full of—what? Something like movement. Sweetness, too.

There was no more laughter now, just the low

gurgle of water in the pipes, and the ticking of the recovering geyser. Were they dancing together? Kitty herself had danced with a man only once. Her sister had set the whole thing up, introducing her to Frank, who'd worked at the bakery with Lou, at the Drill Hall dance. Kitty remembered the way he'd let his fingers wander from her shoulder to her neck, feeling the hairs that lay there like weeds—that's how she'd always thought of her hair, like a clump of weeds on a riverbank, thick and straight, fanning out in broken ends, no particular colour. She rinsed it in vinegar every week but it was still the brown-yellow shade of Oxo cubes. All night she'd felt that she was pushing against his steps, because he kept getting them wrong; she hadn't meant to do that, and told herself to stop, but he would keep standing on her feet when she'd polished her shoes specially, and he wasn't the lightest of men, so she'd had to try to take his hot hand and correct it. Eventually he'd barked, 'You're leading!' and she'd apologised over and over again but his hand was crushing hers by then; the bones in her fingers crunched together as he said, 'For Christ's sake, what's the matter with you?' She'd thought of her father looking at the clock and what her mother would have said to him to stop him dead, but she'd carried on dancing until the music stopped. Then she ran from the dance floor and out of the Drill Hall without her coat or hat, and Frank hadn't come after her.

But not all men would be like that, she thought. Dancing with Arthur, for example, would be different: Arthur left his boots at the door before walking on her kitchen floor; he rinsed out his own cup after tea; his fingers were nimble when they loaded his pipe with tobacco.

But dancing with Arthur would be nothing like dancing with Mr Crane.

She opened her eyes, rolled on to her back and took up the soap. After she'd scrubbed herself everywhere she could—soaping between each toe, along each leg, swishing the water about between her thighs without touching anything for too long, then sliding the bar up her stomach and across her breasts, round the back of her neck and down her arms—she heaved herself out of the bath.

Now was the time to look, before she could think about it too much, before she was cold and shivering and needed to put the dressing gown on.

She stood before the full-length mirror. At first, she looked only at her own face. She was not, she'd decided long ago, pretty: her nose was too wide, her chin too prominent. But if she turned and looked back over her shoulder—like those photos in *Film Pictorial*—she wasn't too bad. It was always better to look at her face when it was rosy from the heat, and viewed like this, all cheek and naked shoulder, her hair wet and dark and even a bit wavy, she looked not quite herself. It was strange how like another person she seemed, as she gazed at the length of her body in the mirror; strange how it all connected up, all the parts of herself she'd often thought separate: thighs to bottom, stomach to chest to neck and arms, and her head on top. She tried to take it all in, putting a hand on her hip and smiling. She blushed at herself in the pose, then giggled, leaning forward and putting her hand to her mouth so the tips of her breasts shook; she felt them beneath her arm, swaying. Taking her hand away, she watched her own fingers connect with her breast, and saw her nipple turn brown and wrinkled like a walnut. Was it normal for flesh to move of its own accord like that?

There was a noise from the sitting room: a shrieking laugh. It wouldn't be long, then, before the other noises began. She turned away from the mirror, pulled her dressing gown tightly around her, and sat on the rim of the bath to watch the water run away.

EIGHT

The sunlight, striking through the large French windows, flooded the dining room with warmth. Ellen and Geenie were at George's sister Laura's house in the nearby village of Heyshott, waiting for the new girl. They sat together at the wide table, watching petals fall from the vase of bluebells at its centre. Ellen was wearing her best red jacket, the one she'd had made in Paris with the white collar and cuffs, and her red heels. The jacket made her neck itch and she thought about removing it, but she wanted to look respectable for this meeting. She should have put more powder on, too. She could feel that her cheeks were flushed and damp, like Kitty's always were at mealtimes.

Geenie kept rubbing at a knot in the wood, and Ellen clamped a hand on her daughter's arm to still her. Diana's mother, Lillian, was supposed to have dropped Diana in time for lunch. Now it was half past two, and there was no sign of Lillian, or of the girl. Ellen was, she told herself, ready to face the other woman in Crane's life. She did pride herself on her tolerance of ex-wives. It was, she felt, a necessary part of being a bohemian. After all, Rachel had actually married James while he was living with Ellen, and she'd never run on at him for that. Rachel had been a pathetic creature: lumpy ankles and nails bitten down to the flesh. She'd begged James to marry her, saying all she wanted was the title—*Mrs Holt*; she'd promised never to bother him again if he granted her this one last chance of respectability. Ellen felt it was the least she could do not to carp about it, seeing as she'd stolen James from under Rachel's (small) nose in the first place. And, in fact, Rachel had gone quiet after that. Whenever Ellen had thought of this other woman who was out there, legally bound to her lover, she'd always reminded herself that she was the one who had him in the flesh.

But Lillian was different. And not ex, even, not yet. What made it worse was that Crane wouldn't say a word about her. She'd asked him again, last night, after the usual. Running a finger down his stomach, she'd enquired how he and Lillian had got on in bed. He'd looked at the ceiling and considered. He always considered his replies. Then he'd said, 'Well enough.' She'd tried another tack. How had they met? This time she'd propped herself up on one elbow and smiled, pulling the sheets up over her breasts to help him concentrate. 'Through a friend,' was the considered reply. Why had they separated, then? At this, he'd winced. 'It just died,' he'd said, very quietly, and he turned onto his side and said he'd like to go to sleep.

'She's late,' said Ellen, squinting up at Laura. 'Just like her husband. Like her *estranged* husband, I should say.'

Laura was leaning back on the French windows, smoking. In shiny black riding boots and a man's green cotton over-shirt, dramatically back-lit by the sun, she looked like a film star in a girl's horse-riding adventure. Her legs, hugged tightly by tan jodhpurs, were long and thin, like Ellen's own, but, Ellen noted, Laura's thighs were rounded like risen loaves, and her knees had no hint of knobble. Her black hair, cut in a bob with a severe fringe, was as glossy as her boots. When they'd first met, Ellen had thought Laura exactly the kind of woman she herself would love to be: sophisticated, daring, unpredictable. Glamorous. Gradually, though, it had dawned on her that Laura could only live the life she did because her solid, intellectual and thoroughly tedious husband, Humphrey, was always waiting in their well-appointed parlour for his wife's return.

Laura narrowed her eyes, slid them sidelong, and drew on her cigarette.

'I suppose ballet dancers are always late,' Ellen continued. 'Artistic temperament and all that. I don't know why I don't start being late. It might help my bohemian credentials. What do you think, darling? Would your brother love me more if I were late?'

'*Is* she late?' Laura asked, exhaling a curl of smoke.

'Over two hours, darling.'

Laura nodded and slowly slid one hand over her rounded belly, first along the top of the little bump, then along the bottom. 'I don't have a watch.'

Ellen snorted. 'How romantic!'

'Not romantic. Practical. If you don't have a

watch, you're never late, and you never expect anyone. Stands to reason.'

Ellen let out a hoot. 'Laura, you are a strange creature.'

Laura brought her cigarette to her mouth in a long sweep and sucked on it.

'Talking of expecting—when's this damn baby due, darling?' asked Ellen.

Unpeeling herself from the French windows, Laura walked over to the table. She walked slowly, her boots clacking on the polished floor like a swashbuckler's, the sun flashing behind her. She leant over Geenie so the tip of her bob pricked the girl's ear, and ground out her cigarette in the ashtray.

'Autumn, I think.'

'You're not sure? Not even of the month?'

'I told you, Ellen. I don't have a watch.' She leant her elbows on the table and blinked at Geenie. 'Don't go dragging on that cig end,' she said, fixing the girl with her bright green eyes. 'How old are you, anyway?'

'She's eleven,' said Ellen. 'Twelve in August.'

'Is that all?' Laura shook her head. 'Never mind. A couple of years and it will all be happening for you, with hair like that.'

'Won't it just?' Ellen agreed. 'She's like something from a fairy tale, isn't she, Laura? Men can't resist helpless blondes.'

Laura smiled. 'Neither can women.'

Bobbie, Laura's help, poked her head round the door. 'Mrs Crane and her daughter are arriving.'

'Christ, I'm off,' said Laura. 'Tell Lillian I'll see her some other time. I can't face her prissiness just now. And I promised to meet Humphrey in

Petersfield at three. Got to keep the husband happy.'

She scooped up her riding hat and jacket from the top of the dresser. 'Don't go snaring any helpless men while I'm gone,' she said to Geenie.

Ellen watched her stride through the French windows and out into the garden, and—for just a second—wished she could straddle the back of Laura's horse and ride off over the Downs with her.

Bobbie cleared her throat. 'She'll be here most *imminently*, Mrs Steinberg—'

'All right, all right.' Ellen touched her hair, scraped back her chair and straightened her jacket. 'You stay put, Flossy.'

'Why can't I come?'

'I think I'll deal with this myself, darling.'

'I want to come.'

Ellen sighed. She bent down to look her daughter in the face. 'I'll bring her through in a minute, then we can all go home together. It'll only be a minute.'

*　　　*　　　*

'This is—' Ellen stopped and stared.

She'd opened the door to the dining room with Diana in tow, only to find her daughter standing against the French windows, holding Laura's cig end. Geenie was leaning her head back on the glass and trailing the fingers of one hand across her stomach.

The new girl stepped from behind Ellen. 'Hello,' she said. 'I'm Diana.'

'I am a helpless blonde, darling,' declared

Geenie, and she lifted the cig to her mouth and sucked, closing her eyes.

Ellen looked from one girl to the other, then burst out laughing. Diana smiled, showing a gap between her front teeth, and Geenie blew out a big breath.

*   *   *

On the way home, Diana was quiet. She was even prettier than Ellen had expected. Her black hair shone like wet stone, and her eyelashes were as thick as a doll's. Ellen chattered as much as she could, occasionally looking over her shoulder for a response, but the girl just stared out of the car window.

'You'll love our cottage, Diana, I'm sure of it. It was a damp heap of ugliness when we first came, wasn't it, Geenie? Now it's quite the palace. Albeit a small one. And very modern, too.'

They'd been in the cottage for less than a year, and already Crane and Arthur had dug new flower beds in the garden, knocked kitchen and scullery into one room, installed the chugging electricity generator and built the writing studio. Sometimes she felt all Crane wanted was to demolish the entire cottage and start again. But, she reasoned, it was better to let him get on with it. Let him knock down all the old stuff, if that's what he wanted. Much better to forget the past. Hadn't that been what she'd wished for, when they'd moved to Harting after James's death? She hadn't let Crane loose on the library, though. That was her place. It was where she worked every day, typing up James's letters. She'd collected enough now for a whole book. It was important work, and she wanted it finished by the end of the summer.

Ellen glanced over her shoulder again. Diana hooked her dark hair behind one ear and carried on staring out of the window.

Geenie was just as bad. After her little cigarette show, she was now sitting on the other side of the back seat, gazing at her knees.

'Your daddy's done wonders,' Ellen continued. 'He's really transformed the place. It's our country idyll, isn't it, Geenie? He's very clever with his hands.'

'I know,' Diana said, but still she didn't look round. For some reason, she reminded Ellen of Josephine Baker: perhaps it was those smooth cheeks and lively eyes. She could see Diana easily controlling a pair of cheetahs whilst dancing an exotic number.

'My mother says houses are his forte,' added Diana.

'And writing, darling, your daddy's a very clever writer, isn't he?'

'But houses are his forte,' Diana insisted.

'What's forte?' asked Geenie.

'It's like a special talent, darling, like you and dressing up.'

'Or drawing,' said Geenie. 'That's my forte, isn't it, Ellen?'

She looked up then, hopefully, and Ellen conceded, 'That too.'

'My mother's forte is dancing,' said Diana. 'What's yours?'

'Mine?' Ellen asked. The may blossom flashed past as she bit her lip. She couldn't very well say sex. *My forte is fucking your daddy*.

68

'I should say it's helping people. Making them happy and comfortable.'

Diana looked confused. 'Isn't that what servants are for?'

Ellen turned into a slip road rather too fast and a man on a tractor shook his fist at her. 'Ellen's concentrating, darling.'

Of course, Diana's mother probably had lots of fortes. It had been a short meeting, for which Ellen was glad. Lillian had worn a mint green hat like a miniature meringue, and a green short jacket with mother-of-pearl buttons. Her eyebrows were heavily plucked. But, Ellen had noticed, she looked old for her twenty-eight years. Perhaps all that dancing took it out of you. And Lillian's legs— the part Ellen had glimpsed beneath her fish-tail calf-length skirt—looked no better than her own. She'd greeted her brightly enough, but had looked at her watch when Ellen suggested tea at Willow Cottage, which she'd done on a whim, really, suddenly interested to see how Crane would react to seeing the two women together.

And now here was this girl, thankfully much more like her father than her mother—big brown eyes, a straight, strong nose, prominent cheekbones—but when she closed her mouth, her lips were Lillian's: large and slightly bunched together, as if she had plenty to say, but couldn't quite bring herself to the bother of letting it out.

'What do you like?' Geenie asked Diana.

Ellen had almost forgotten Geenie was in the car. It was strange how her daughter did that, seemed to disappear under her cloud of blonde hair. She'd done it since she was small, her chin receding first, her eyes dropping to the ground, then her shoulders sagging forward, until her face was almost entirely covered by hair. It was what had made James call her 'Flossy'. When she decided to make her presence felt with a scream or a tantrum, it was all the more shocking. Ellen remembered the time she and James had been fighting, and neither of them had known that Geenie was under the table until James threw a dish of hot beans at Ellen, and they'd splashed Geenie's toes, making her yelp. They'd stopped, then, and spent the afternoon bathing the girl's feet in a jug of iced water in the garden. That was in the early days, when such an event was still enough to stop them rowing.

She turned into the drive of Willow Cottage.

'Do you like dancing?' Geenie asked the other girl.

Diana shifted in her seat. 'I'm still thinking,' she said.

'Thinking?'

'About what I like.'

Ellen stopped the car.

'What do you like?' Geenie asked again.

'Come on, then, time to get out.'

'What do you like?'

'Reading,' said Diana.

'Oh,' said Geenie.

Ellen got out of the car and opened the door for the girls.

'And dressing up,' said Diana. 'I like dressing up and being in plays.'

*   *   *

Diana forked up her luncheon-meat salad with one

70

hand. Unlike Geenie, who scattered crumbs and left mounds of lettuce untouched, Diana ate everything and left the plate clean. Then she went on to tackle Kitty's apple pie, using her spoon like a knife to cut the pudding into even chunks before slowly chewing each piece.

'Look at that, Flossy,' said Ellen. 'A good appetite, even for Kitty's food.'

Diana did not return Ellen's beam, but Ellen pressed on regardless. 'Good girl, Diana. Geenie picks at her food like I don't know what. You'd think she ate between meals, but she doesn't, do you, Flossy? No interest in food, is what I sometimes think. Like her father. Too wrapped up in her own thoughts to notice.'

'I liked Dora's pies,' said Geenie.

Ellen ignored this.

'I like food,' announced Diana. 'Pies included.'

'I dare say your mother's taught you that.'

Diana looked steadily at Ellen. 'No,' she said. 'My mother eats like a bird. She's a ballet dancer and they can't eat much or they get fat and lose their grace.'

'How miserable for her!'

Diana scooped another piece of pie.

'George eats a lot, doesn't he, Ellen?' Geenie pushed her own plate away and leant towards her mother. 'He eats like a horse, doesn't he? That means you've got a bird and a horse for parents, Diana.' She giggled.

'Maybe,' said Diana, clicking her nails together.

'George—your father—is totally indiscriminate when it comes to food. He'll consume anything that's edible. Or even inedible.' Ellen looked down at the remains of Geenie's luncheon meat. 'I think

71

I'm going to have to get someone in to teach Kitty a thing or two about cuisine. How to use salt and pepper, that sort of thing.'

'Can we play now?' asked Geenie.

Ellen threw up her hands. 'Why not?' she asked. 'Games are so much more interesting than food.'

The girls scraped back their chairs and Ellen watched the two of them disappear.

NINE

Lou looked like an oversized mermaid in the new dress. The shiny green fabric was clamped to her thighs. Her breasts were squashed into a loaf shape, and her waist had become a series of rolls. It was Macclesfield silk, crème de menthe green, she said, with three-quarter-length sleeves and a cowl neckline. The hem didn't quite touch the floor.

'It's bloody well shrunk.'

Lou had inherited their grandmother's ginger curls, which meant green was her colour.

'I'll murder that laundry woman.'

It was Saturday night, and Mrs Steinberg, Geenie, Mr Crane and the new girl had gone to his sister's for dinner, telling Kitty she may as well take the evening off. So here she was, in Lou and Bob's bedroom, kneeling on the Axminster, her fingertips beginning to sweat as she held the hem of the dress and looked up at her sister.

'Can you do anything at all?' asked Lou.

Kitty pulled the hem taut and examined it.

'You must be able to do something, Kit.'

She stood and took her sister by the shoulders, turning her round so she could see the back of the dress. 'Hmm.' She whipped the inch tape from around her neck and drew it across Lou's back. She wasn't sure why she did it, but it was what her sister would expect. Some sort of measuring and working out in order to reshape the garment to her size. Kitty knew she could do nothing to this dress to make it any better. But when she had a tape around her neck and pins in her mouth, her sister seemed to move easily in her hands.

She pinched a piece of fabric at Lou's waist.

'Ouch! That's me you're squeezing!'

'I might be able to let it out here . . .' She spoke from the corner of her mouth so as not to drop the pins. Turning her sister around again, she ran a hand over the neckline, trying to smooth it down over Lou's chest.

'How are things at the cottage? You haven't said much about it.'

'I could let it out at the back, maybe . . .'

'Could you?'

Kitty stabbed a pin into the shoulder of the dress.

'What's she like then, the American?'

'She's—unusual.'

'I knew that much. What does she do all day?'

'She types.'

'Types what?'

'I don't know. She wants me to call her Mrs Steinberg.'

Lou raised an eyebrow.

'The girl calls her Ellen.'

'She doesn't call her Mother?'

'Not as far as I've heard.'

73

'How peculiar.'

'Perhaps it's an American thing.'

'Don't be idiotic.'

'They've lived all over, Lou, in France and everything.'

'She *is* her mother, isn't she?'

Kitty hesitated. In a way, Mrs Steinberg didn't seem much like Geenie's mother. She let the child play outside as she pleased, even when it was wet and cold. She didn't bother about her dirty knees. She'd paid no attention when Geenie had painted her eyes with kohl on Kitty's first day. She hadn't even insisted that the girl go to school, saying she wanted to find the right one in the autumn and let Geenie be a 'free spirit' all summer.

But they did have exactly the same chin, and, whenever the two of them were together, the girl was always looking at her.

'Of course she is.' Kitty pinned the dress from the shoulders so the whole thing shifted up and away from Lou's thighs. The waist was now under the bust, and the hem hung in the middle of Lou's shins.

'We might be able to add a waistband . . .'

'A waistband?'

'Give you some more room around the middle.'

'But that would completely ruin the look, Kit. It's supposed to be high-waisted, and fitted on the hips. It's long-line, see?'

'Hmm.'

'What about him, the poet?'

Kitty unpinned the shoulders and stood back from the dress. 'He doesn't seem like a poet.'

'What does he seem like, then?'

'I don't know. A teacher, or something.'

74

'Like Bob?'

Lou had met Bob when she'd worked in the bakery. Bob loved macaroons and, after his first wife died, always went to Warbington's for them. Lou told Kitty that he'd held her fingers, once, when she'd handed him his change; she'd known then that she would be his wife. On Lou's request, Bob had got Kitty the cleaning job at the school. He was a senior master there; he'd joined after Lou had left, but he'd taught Kitty. A huge picture of Queen Elizabeth was tacked on the wall of his classroom, and when he told the pupils about her *parsimony* he'd thumped the desk and his shirt had come free of his trousers.

Their mother had said it was a miracle, her daughter having the good fortune to marry a school teacher, even though Bob was forty-five and Lou only nineteen when they'd wed.

Kitty had trouble thinking of Bob as anything but Mr Purser. Living in his house, she'd been careful to keep her voice low and look just below his eye-line when he spoke to her.

'Not like Bob. Turn around.'

Lou did as she was asked.

'You're settling in, though?'

Kitty glanced at her sister's reflection. Lou was wearing a small smile, but her eyes were watching her sister's face.

Kitty held her gaze. 'Yes, I suppose.'

'That's good, isn't it? You're making yourself at home.'

'Hmm. Can you put your arms above your head?'

Rolling her eyes, Lou flung one arm in the air. There was a sharp crack as a seam snapped. She glared at Kitty in the dressing-table mirror. 'I told you. The bloody thing's shrunk.'

Kitty gathered up a handful of fabric from the back of the dress and examined it.

'I'm going to have to buy new, aren't I?' said Lou.

'I might be able to unpick it and make a skirt—a different shape, perhaps, but . . .'

'Don't be an idiot. I can't wear a skirt to the school-masters' summer dance.'

'But we should try to make something, Lou. It's such pretty stuff.'

Lou shrugged off Kitty's hands. She reached behind and tried to unzip herself. There was the sound of another seam breaking.

'Help me, then!'

Kitty pulled the puckering zip slowly, being careful not to catch her sister's skin in its teeth. Lou stepped from the pile of silk. Beneath her white French knickers, her thighs were flecked pink, like coconut ice.

'You might as well have it.'

'Lou, I couldn't.'

'Just take it, will you?'

Kitty gazed at her sister's face in the mirror. Lou set her mouth in a line. 'I'll get Bob to buy me another. God knows he owes me.'

*   *   *

Lou had folded the dress in brown paper for Kitty to take home. In the car with Bob, Kitty kept the package flat on her lap, resting both hands on it, partly to steady the parcel as Bob took the winding lane back to Harting, and partly so she could move her fingers over it and hear the rustle of paper on silk. She could already picture the dress next to her own skin. The colour, perhaps, wasn't as suited to her, with her dull brown hair, as it was to Lou, but that didn't matter. That dress reflected all the light in a room. Even if she never wore it (and where would she?), even if no one ever saw her in it, it would still be hers; she could look at it hanging in her wardrobe that smelled of cinnamon, and she could touch it whenever she liked.

There was no car in the drive when Bob dropped her at the cottage. That was good. She might have time to put the dress on and creep to the bathroom to look at herself in the full-length mirror before they came back.

She was just about to let herself in the back door when the tiny window of Arthur's shed caught her eye. It was glowing in the darkness. She returned her key to her bag and, still holding the dress, squinted into the night. There was no breeze, and hardly any moon. Surely he couldn't still be in there, at this time on a Saturday evening?

If he'd left the paraffin lamp on by mistake, she'd have to go and put it out. It wouldn't be meddling, it would be what Mr Purser, Bob, used to say at school: safety first, children. Safety first. He'd said it at home once, when Lou had handed him a pair of scissors with the blades pointing in his direction, and Lou had told him not to speak to her like one of his pupils. He'd looked at the floor and received the scissors in silence. Kitty held that picture of Bob's downcast eyes in her mind whenever he rustled his newspaper in her direction.

As she walked to the shed, she became aware of

the smell of the grass. It had been a warm day, and the earth seemed to have loosened in the sun. She'd left her coat unbuttoned all the way home. The brown paper crackled beneath her hands. The only other sound was the generator in the garage, which had slowed to a low chug.

She knew she should call his name, in case he was in there, to warn him, but something stopped her from speaking aloud as she reached out to pull the shed door open.

There were the rows of nails, numbered, each with the correct tool hanging from it. There was the shelf full of labelled tins, and the stack of terracotta pots in one corner. And there was Arthur, sitting in his deckchair, asleep.

In the low light of the lamp, Arthur's face seemed to flicker. His head had dropped forward and his mouth was slightly open. He was still holding his pipe and a book was open on his lap. An empty tin mug and a flask stood on top of an upturned flowerpot beside him.

He opened his eyes and looked directly at her. 'You're back,' he said.

Her mouth jumped into a smile. 'I saw the light—from your lamp—I was worried, in case you weren't here and you'd forgotten . . .'

'Why wouldn't I be here?'

She clasped the package to her chest.

He fixed his gaze somewhere above her right shoulder and stretched out his arms. 'Got a parcel?'

She smoothed the paper. 'A dress.'

He nodded.

On the wall next to him was a calendar with the days crossed off, each 'x' the same size and shape.

'A dress for dancing,' she said, and felt herself blush.

Then something beneath Arthur's deckchair caught her eye. On its side, with mud on the heel, was a round-toed shoe of brilliant green.

She almost pointed at the shoe, wanting to tell him that she had the other in her wardrobe. But when she looked at him, he kept his eyes on his book, and began to flick through its pages.

Kitty turned to go, wishing she'd ignored the glow from the window and got on with trying the dress. Mr Crane and Mrs Steinberg would be back soon, and then it would be too late for the bathroom mirror.

'I suppose you dance quite a bit, then?'

She stopped.

'Young girl like you. Should be dancing. Like Ginger Rogers, eh? I expect you've been dancing all night.'

She looked into the blackness of the garden and said, 'Yes. Yes, I have.'

'Drill Hall?'

'Yes. I danced all night. It was lovely.'

There was a silence. Then she heard him rise from the deckchair and walk towards her. The lamp's glow died, and she waited there, holding the dress to her chest and with her coat unbuttoned, until he'd closed the shed door and was standing next to her in the darkness. There was the smell of his pipe, and the flash of his large hands as he lit it. He sucked in, blew out, gave a series of small coughs, then said, 'Perhaps we'll go together one day. Dancing.'

All Kitty's nerves seemed to up-end themselves. 'Dancing?' Her voice came out shrill.

'I can dance, you know.' He gave a little laugh. 'You might not think it to look at me.'

Kitty put a hand to her hair. 'I didn't mean—'

'I daresay you're tired. I'm dead on my feet myself.' He cleared his throat. 'It was good of you to look in.'

She nodded.

'I'll say goodnight, then.'

'Goodnight.'

Arthur stayed where he was, feet evenly planted in front of his shed, smoking his pipe.

As she moved quickly towards the house, Kitty had a sudden thought: did he sometimes stand there all night and keep watch over the cottage? She was sure she could still hear him chewing on his pipe when she opened the back door and stepped inside. And it wasn't until she was in her room and had hung the emerald dress in the wardrobe that she heard the crunch of Arthur's bicycle wheels on the gravel.

TEN

When they reached the landing, Geenie said, 'This is my room. And that's Ellen's. Your father sleeps in there, but he has his own room, too. And that one will be yours.'

'Aren't there any other rooms?' asked Diana.

'Only downstairs.'

'Hasn't your mother got an awful lot of money?'

'I think so, yes.'

'Then why hasn't she got a bigger house?'

The question had never occurred to Geenie,

who'd lived in all sorts of houses, big and small, all over Europe. She'd presumed that most houses in the English countryside were cottages, which meant they were small.

'I don't know.'

'Does she like it here?'

'Not much.'

'Do you like it?'

Geenie didn't know the answer until the word came out of her mouth. 'Yes,' she said. 'I like it.'

*　　*　　*

George had chosen the glazed chintz curtains with the peacock pattern and the eiderdown in matching greens and blues for her bedroom. Ellen had brought her old French furniture from their house in Paris. But Geenie herself had chosen the picture on the wall above her bed. It was an illustration from one of Jimmy's favourite books: *Jack the Giant Killer*. It showed the moment when Jack came upon the three princesses imprisoned by the giant, each one hanging from the ceiling by her own hair. Jimmy had always taken great pleasure in reading this scene aloud to Geenie, particularly the part about the ladies being kept for many days without food in order to encourage them to *feed upon the flesh of their murdered husbands*.

The two girls looked at the picture. The princesses looked quite happy to be hung up by their hair. Great swirls of it twirled and curled around metal hooks, as though the princesses' bondage were merely a matter of hair-styling. Their dainty shoes pointed downwards, like ballerinas' feet. George had some postcards on the wall of his writer's studio of the *Soviet People Enjoying a Healthy Lifestyle*, which he'd brought back from Russia. They all wore gym knickers and little cotton vests with belts and pointed their feet downwards in a manner similar to these princesses.

'That one looks like you,' said Diana, pointing to the fair-haired princess at the front of the picture. 'A helpless blonde.'

Geenie didn't say anything, but she'd always thought the blonde princess *was* a bit like her. Her face was round and her lips made a little red cross. Her nose was a mere line down the centre of her face—quite unlike Ellen's *dog-nose*, as Jimmy had once called it. She swung from her hook with grace and charm, unruffled by her fate. She was the only princess who looked the least bit impressed by Jack's appearance. A handbag dangled from her fingertips. Geenie made a silent vow to get one like it, with a jewelled clasp and the thinnest of straps.

'Do you think Jack marries one of them?' asked Diana.

'No,' said Geenie. 'It says in the story that he gives them their liberty then continues on his journey into Wales.'

'Perhaps they didn't want to marry him.'

'Why not?' said Geenie. 'He rescued them, didn't he?'

'They could have got off those hooks easily enough by themselves. All they had to do was untangle their hair. Or cut it off.'

'Maybe they didn't want to cut their hair. When my mother cut her hair off Jimmy cried.'

Diana shrugged. 'Let's dress up,' she said.

Geenie pulled the dressing-up things from the

bottom of her wardrobe, where she kept them in a tangled heap. Plunging her wrists into the twists of fabric on the floor, she wrenched each item from the muddle. There was a long sable coat with gathered cuffs (once Jimmy's); a brocade waistcoat with tortoiseshell buttons; a blue French sailor's jacket; a slightly squashed hat made entirely of kittiwake feathers; and a long white nightie trimmed with pink lace. There was a short silk dress with a dropped waist, turquoise blue in the bodice, green in the skirt; a huge corset, camomile-lotion pink, which had once belonged to Geenie's grandmother; a pair of silk stockings, laddered; a fez; and an ivory fan showing scenes from Venice. There was a white Egyptian robe with gold trim and boxy neck, in the Tutankhamen style, which Ellen had bought on her honeymoon. There was a red and white checked Arab headdress; an electric blue feather boa; and a huge hooped petticoat, which had been Ellen's when she was a little girl in New York. And there was a pair of jade Turkish slippers, studded with glass and turned up at the end like gondolas (which Geenie was forbidden to wear, in case she tripped over them on the stairs), and a matching long jade necklace.

Diana picked the necklace from the top of the pile. 'I'll have this,' she said. She ran the beads across her face, rubbing each one on her cheek.

'Then you'll have to wear the slippers.'

'Why?'

'Because they match.'

Diana frowned. 'I want to wear the white thing, though.'

'But that's Egyptian. It's what I wear when I'm being Cleopatra. And the beads aren't Egyptian.'

Geenie twisted the feather boa around her neck. It was hot and scratchy against her skin.

'Show me, then,' said Diana. 'Show me your favourite outfit.'

Geenie thought for a moment. The corset was one of her favourites, but she didn't think that she should tell Diana that.

Just as she was reaching into the pile of clothes to find something more suitable, Diana caught her elbow. 'Tell you what!' she said, 'Let me guess what it is.'

'You won't guess.'

'I will.' Her eyes flashed and she clasped her hands together. 'I will guess.'

'Go on, then,' said Geenie, straightening up.

Diana's hand hovered over the bundle of silk and cotton, feathers and lace. 'Let's see. It's a process of deduction, like in a detective story.'

'I don't like those.'

'Nor do I. But my mother loves them. Dorothy Sayers.'

'My mother loves Dostoyevsky.'

Diana pulled out the ripped silk stockings. Pulling one taut over her face, she breathed heavily and leant close to Geenie. 'Now I'm a robber.'

'That's not my favourite.'

'I know that.'

Diana dropped the stocking and picked up the brocade waistcoat. 'It's not this.'

'No.'

Diana held out the white nightie with the pink lace. 'Or this.'

'Of course not.'

Diana heaved the sable coat from the heap and

hung it from her head, like a hooded cape. 'This smells,' she said, 'like a dead animal.'

'That's because it is a dead animal,' said Geenie, throwing herself back on her bed and stretching her arms above her head. 'It was Jimmy's.'

'Who's Jimmy?'

'He lived with us for ages after my father left. I don't remember my father, but I remember everything about Jimmy. He was a true bohemian.'

Diana peered out from her dark cave of fur. 'My Aunt Laura's one of them. But my father's a Communist.'

The girls looked at one another.

'What does that mean?' asked Geenie.

'He thinks the working classes should be—equal with us. Or like us. Something like that. He went to Russia a couple of years ago.'

'What for?'

'To see how they do communism there. He said the ballet was very good, and everything was clean and the people were happy.'

'Did *you* go with him?'

'No.'

Diana sat on the bed beside Geenie and let the coat drop to her shoulders. 'Did Jimmy really wear this?'

'He wore it on car journeys. He drove from our house in Paris to Nice in one go.'

'Did you go with him?'

Geenie shook her head.

'Where is he now?'

Geenie sat up. 'He's dead.'

Diana pulled the fur coat tighter around her and said nothing.

After a while, Geenie said, 'Can I wear it now?'

and Diana shrugged the coat from her own shoulders and placed it around Geenie's. Then she stood back and frowned, as if concentrating very hard. 'It suits you,' she said, nodding.

Geenie wrapped the coat tightly around herself and smiled.

ELEVEN

Although Willow was a large cottage, the corridors were narrow. In the downstairs hallway, Kitty had to turn sideways to get along from the kitchen to the sitting room with the tray, due to a narrow bend that could catch elbows and was already covered in ancient dents and nicks where other trays and limbs had made their mark. It wasn't much better upstairs; by far the easiest way to fold sheets, as Kitty was doing now, was to hang them over the banister like sails and gather the corners together, tucking the sheet under her chin and widening her arms to their furthest stretch as she did so. You had to be a bit careful with this method, because Mrs Steinberg's sheets were surprisingly old. The cotton was thick and smooth, like the icing on Lou's Christmas cakes (her sister was marvellous at baking, and even understood the intricacies of icing), but there was the odd rip here and there which someone, probably Dora, had darned. The stitches were uneven, and they formed bumps on the sheets, like scar tissue. Kitty worried that these vulnerable points might catch on a picture hook or a sharp corner of banister as she flapped, and then the sheet would tear and she'd have to explain; she might even have to mention that Dora's darning really wasn't up to much in the first place, which would be awkward.

As she drew up the corners of the sheet, the scent of Lysol caught in her nostrils. Mrs Steinberg insisted a few drops were included with all the bedding when it was laundered by the woman in Petersfield. She came once a week to collect all their linen, and always rolled her eyes at the sight of the bottle of bleach.

Kitty had just got the last sheet tucked into a decent shape and was about to transport the whole pile into the airing cupboard when Mrs Steinberg called her name. She hadn't realised anyone else was upstairs. At this time in the afternoon, Mrs Steinberg was usually typing in the library, or sleeping. Once Kitty had walked into the sitting room at half past three and found her mistress splayed over the cushions, mouth open, eyes half closed. A long snort like a glugging sink came from her nose, and the whites of her eyes flickered.

'Kitty. I'm in the bedroom. Can you come in?'

What was she doing in there at this time of day? A cold queasiness crawled through Kitty's stomach. She had a sudden vision of Mrs Steinberg in bed with Mr Crane, both of them sitting up, naked to the waist. There could be no other explanation for the woman being in her bedroom in the middle of the afternoon.

'Kitty? That is you out there?'

Mrs Steinberg's breasts would probably be quite flat and long, what with childbearing, and three husbands, if you counted Mr Crane and the last man, who no one ever talked about, except the girl; Jimmy, that was his name—

'Kitty?'

And Mr Crane was very keen on tea in the afternoon; in fact, that was the next task on her list. Surely they wouldn't dare to ask for a tray to be brought up after *that*?

Kitty straightened her apron and faced the bedroom door, which was slightly ajar. A slit of light was all that was visible of the room beyond. 'Yes, Mrs Steinberg?'

'Come in here, please.'

Kitty's mouth jolted into a smile. 'What is it, Mrs Steinberg?'

'Come in here.'

That woman's voice had metal in it.

'I'm just folding the sheets—'

'Damn it, why won't you come in here?'

Kitty pushed open the door a little, being careful to keep her eyes focused on the doorframe. 'What is it, Mrs Steinberg?'

The curtains—green silk, decorated with Chinese boatmen in large hats with long poles, which Kitty had often admired—were open, she could tell that much by the light. Mr Crane's shoes weren't anywhere near the door. But perhaps he'd removed them and left them in his room before going to her. He had a room at the other end of the corridor, complete with a wardrobe full of clothes and a bed covered in a sea-blue eiderdown. But Kitty knew he never slept in there. His cream cotton pyjamas (she'd expected a poet to have silk, and was surprised by the practical choice of fabric) were never dirty. They were bundled under his pillow each morning. Kitty sent them off with the rest of the laundry, but she knew they hadn't been worn. They smelled too fresh.

'Come and sit down, Kitty.'

She didn't sound as if she'd just had relations, which was what Lou called it. 'You'll learn, Kitty, when you're married,' she'd said to her one day as they were sitting by Lou's fiery orange azaleas. 'Relations aren't always what you think. And a woman has to be flexible.' A little smile on her face and a flush on her cheek. The words rushing out in the warm spring afternoon.

'Kitty!'

She'd have to go in.

She took a step forward and let her eyes settle on the edge of the bed where Mrs Steinberg was sitting, fully clothed, holding a handkerchief in one hand. Her face *was* a little flushed. But her eyes were slightly pink, and there was no smile. And no Mr Crane.

'What is it, Mrs Steinberg?'

The woman seemed to be breathing oddly, unevenly, taking a little breath in and letting a big one out.

'Sit with me, Kitty.'

There was a notebook and a cardboard folder on the bed, full of what appeared to be letters.

'I was just doing the sheets—'

'They can wait.'

Kitty sat on the bed, being careful not to touch the folder or any of the papers. It was a wide bed— the widest she'd seen—with large acorn-shaped brass knobs on each corner of the frame. Sleeping alone in such a bed would be like having a whole house to yourself.

Mrs Steinberg placed her long fingers on Kitty's shoulder. 'I'd like to ask your advice.'

'My advice?'

Kitty couldn't remember anyone asking her for advice before. Certainly not Lou or her mother. Looking at Mrs Steinberg, she saw that the other woman's hair was even coarser than her own. It never stayed where it was put, and she always had her hands in it, pushing it this way and that. She ran her fingers through her fringe now, rubbing at it as vigorously as Blotto scratched his ear. Blotches of freckle the colour of toffee covered her large nose and her orange lipstick had dried out around the edges of her mouth.

'I hope you don't mind me speaking frankly to you, Kitty.'

Kitty shook her head.

'As you've no doubt gathered by now, I've lived a rather strange life. I've had so much fun, and I've seen lots of things. And I've tried to learn.'

In order to avoid the other woman's eyes, Kitty gazed at the silver ring which flashed on Mrs Steinberg's finger as she spoke. The woman had a habit of staring at you very intently whenever she said anything, as if she wanted to hold you in place with her cool eyes. Kitty wished this conversation were taking place somewhere else, somewhere away from the bed where Mrs Steinberg had relations with Mr Crane, and with something in the room to distract her, like Blotto, or even Geenie.

'And I've always chosen men who might teach me something. If you know what I mean. I've always thought that any fun must also be about learning something . . . James, my second and dearest husband—which he was in all but name— used to say that a life without learning was a wasted existence. I hope I've honoured that sentiment.' She stretched her legs in front of her.

90

No stockings again, and sandals with the thinnest ankle straps. Her toenails were painted green, but, Kitty noticed, the colour didn't quite reach the ends of each nail. 'And I so want to learn. But I've never been very good on the domestic side of things.'

There was a pause. Kitty filled it by nodding.

Mrs Steinberg laughed. 'So you agree.'

'Agree with what, Mrs Steinberg?'

'Never mind.' She pressed her fingers into Kitty's shoulder. 'What I want to ask you, Kitty is . . . I want to ask for your help.'

Kitty couldn't think of any correct response to this statement.

'I'd like you to help me become a domesticated woman.'

'Domesticated?'

Kitty hadn't thought herself particularly domesticated. She wasn't like Lou, who their mother called a *tidy little homemaker*. At home Kitty had thrown her dirty clothes in a pile, never baked a cake and left the washing up to her mother. Domesticated was just her job. Before she came to Willow, she'd never made even rough-puff pastry.

'You see, the thing with Mr Crane is that he's really rather old fashioned, despite all his communist sympathies. And I think that's what he'd really like me to do, in his heart of hearts. Become a housewife. A really good one. His own mother's an absolute angel. And he adores you, of course, Kitty.'

Kitty felt a heat rise up her throat and spread across her cheeks. She looked down at Mrs Steinberg's ankles.

'You must have noticed it. I have. He really admires the work you do, for us and the girls. You've taken it all on, the cooking, the cleaning—the *domestic science*—with such aplomb.'

The metal had returned to her voice.

'Thank you, Mrs Steinberg.'

'So all I'm asking is that you show me, Kitty. Show me how to keep house.'

Kitty nodded, still staring at the brittle ankles.

'When you're ready, you could give me a few lessons in cookery. We could go through a book together.' She paused. 'And, from now on, I am going to take full responsibility for *both* girls. Diana will be a daughter to me.' Mrs Steinberg gripped her handkerchief and smiled. 'This is the beginning of my life as a true wife and mother.'

Kitty smiled back, wondering what the woman had thought herself to be up to this moment.

TWELVE

By day, Diana was calm. Her lips did not jabber; her nose did not twitch; her voice was level; her eyes were straight. She moved carefully around the house, sitting in chairs to read books rather than lying on rugs, joining her father to listen to the wireless in his studio rather than sprawling in the garden to sunbathe. And when her fingertips touched Geenie's hand at dinnertime, while passing the salt or the water jug, they were cool and dry. Wherever she went, Diana seldom left a mark.

But one night Geenie heard a groaning quite

different from her mother's usual nocturnal noises, and she knew it must be coming from Diana's room.

The noise sounded like a 'whoa', as if Diana were riding an out-of-control horse. Geenie imagined the creature bucking in Diana's bed, trampling the mattress so the girl flew in the air, rolling the sheets to rags at her feet.

When Geenie found her, Diana's room was lit a blue-grey by the moon, and she could see the sheet was stuck to the girl's stomach like a wet curtain. Diana's nightgown was wrapped around her thighs. A strip of dark hair clung to her forehead, and she made the noise again, a long and wavering *whoooah*.

Geenie stood in the doorway, watching the other girl's nightmare. Her own nightgown was dry and heavy, the lace prickly at her neck. Diana thrashed again. She was trying, Geenie realised, to speak: her mouth was working frantically, the muscles around her eyes quivering, but no sound— other than the *whoa* noise, which happened once more—would come out.

She'd have to go in and rescue her friend from this damp hell.

She stole into Diana's bedroom. Sitting on the edge of the bed, she put a hand on Diana's ankle. It was very hot, but not wet. The sweat had yet to reach all the way down there. Slowly, Geenie applied a gentle pressure to the ankle. She wasn't sure if this was the right thing to do, but she'd heard Jimmy say that waking sleepwalkers was dangerous, so she thought this careful, doctorly approach was best. Doctors always sat on the edge of a bed and applied gentle pressure. That's what they did when Jimmy broke his ankle falling from his horse, before his operation, and that's what they did when she herself had caught pneumonia after he'd died.

She decided she should work her way up: a touch on the ankle, the knee, the side, the wrist. There would be no sudden moves or noises.

Very slowly, she began to increase the pressure on Diana's ankle, staring at her damp face all the while. The girl's nose twitched and her arm swung out and above her head so suddenly that Geenie ducked. But there was no *whoa*. Geenie put a hand on Diana's other ankle and gently squeezed there, too. As she increased the pressure, the girl stopped thrashing and her face fell still. Diana's eyes half opened, showing flickering whites, which made Geenie start back and release her grip. She wondered how she could explain her presence on the edge of the other girl's bed. But then Diana turned, gave a long sigh, and began to breathe easily.

Geenie sat on the bed, looking at the side of Diana's calm face in the moonlight, until her toes felt frozen together and her back was stiff.

*   *   *

Every night after that, Geenie lay awake in her own double bed waiting for the *whoa*. She'd never slept in a small bed (her mother didn't believe in them) and for as long as she could remember she'd spent hours trying out different positions on the wide mattress before sleep. There was room for four Geenies in that bed. The headboard was a complicated grid of iron, twisted and hammered

94

into swirls, from which her mother had hung a few pairs of old earrings which rattled each time Geenie moved. The hoops clanked, the drops clacked. Her eiderdown was lilac silk and stained in one corner with a banana-shaped blob of ink. Geenie didn't remember where that had come from.

She thought of the mattress as something like the huge map of the world which Jimmy had kept on his study wall. Each of its corners, its dips and lumps, were countries in which she could try to sleep. The far left was rocky terrain, with good breezes: ideal for hot nights. The mid-right was flat and firm, comfortless but solid; it offered a long night if you managed to drift off there. And the very centre, where the mattress gave out and yielded to her every move, was deep water where dreams were guaranteed. Lying there was like rocking in a ship at sea; waves of sleep came up to meet you, then pitched you back into wakefulness.

When waiting for Diana's nightmares, Geenie favoured the flat, unsurprising middle-right plane. Sleep was least likely to grasp her there.

She waited, thinking of how Jimmy had once come into her bedroom at night and looked over her. She was six years old, and had listened to another long row for what seemed like hours. She could never quite make out the thread of the argument, only occasional words, such as *your money* (Jimmy) or *not fair* (her mother), or, once, *better writer than you* (her mother again). It had been quiet for a while when the door handle shook and turned. She could smell him immediately: whisky, tobacco, glue, sandalwood talcum powder.

As Jimmy opened the door, and the light from

the landing brightened her room, Geenie lifted her eyelids a fraction of an inch so she could spy on him. She wished she looked deeply, sweetly asleep, with her blonde waves chasing across the pillow, so Jimmy could stand and admire her and think about how much he'd lose if he left her mother. But instead she was curled in this tight ball, her fist clenching the sheet, her hair caught behind her neck, both feet tucked up below her bottom, and her eyelids fluttering with the effort of remaining slightly lifted.

She didn't move. She listened to Jimmy's breathing, which was slightly laboured, as if he'd run up the stairs. His hand would be on his hip, as it always was when he was watching something— her mother dancing on a tabletop, or Geenie riding her horse. He might be smiling his bright, sudden smile that made his cheeks wrinkle, the way he had when she'd shown him the drawings she'd done on the paving stones outside their London house. 'Ellen will never forgive you,' he'd said, smiling.

She waited for him to retreat. She thought perhaps he'd come to calm himself. She hoped the sight of his sleeping Flossy—even in this strangled position—did that.

But instead he sat on the chair by her bed. She closed her eyes in case he saw her lids flickering. The smell of whisky grew warmer. His breathing was steadier now. Perhaps he would sleep there tonight. Perhaps Ellen had locked him out of their bedroom and he had nowhere else to go. Geenie's bedroom was the only place he could rest. That wasn't true of course. There were plenty of guest rooms and a huge chaise longue downstairs in his study.

Her limbs were stiff from staying in one position for so long, curled in this tight ball. Her toes started to itch with heat. How long would he sit there? She opened her eyes a crack. Jimmy had his face in his hands and was rubbing at his cheeks. Then he looked at her and she clamped her eyes shut again. Perhaps she should do heavy breathing to make her sleep more convincing.

'Geenie,' he said, in a soft voice. 'Are you awake?'

Her legs not moving, her arms not moving. Just the air in her lungs, out of her lungs, in her lungs, out of her lungs.

It was silent for a long moment before the sob. And even then, she couldn't be sure it was a sob, because she couldn't open her eyes again. Was that thin rasp of air the sound of Jimmy crying? That sudden rush of breath, was that the sound of Jimmy's sadness? She couldn't be sure. There was no way to be sure of that.

THIRTEEN

On Sunday afternoon, when she was free until Monday morning, Kitty prepared herself for tea with Lou. She put on her blue frock with the lily print, which was nipped in at the waist in just the right way, and took the bus from the village to Petersfield.

On the journey, she peered at the Downs through the dirty glass of the bus window. She'd overheard Mr Crane telling Arthur that this landscape was inspirational, and wondered what he'd meant, exactly. Did the mere sight of grass get him going on a poem? How did those ordinary hills, so bare and bald, inspire anyone? They made Kitty think of chapped hands and eyes streaming in the wind. The picture in Mr Crane's unused bedroom of rugged mountain tops and vast lakes— that was more the sort of thing, surely. Something you could really call a view.

Perhaps she should go up on the Downs again sometime, and look at them in more detail. Close-up things revealed a lot. She was working on an embroidery design she'd bought from Wells & Rush of Victorian girls rock-pooling on a beach, and that was all tiny details: the shine on the pebbles, the black beads of the crabs' eyes, the way the children's lines caught in the water. It was going to be lovely when it was finished. The Downs weren't like that. They were blankly green, empty of trees, and they seemed to hold the village captive, keeping the air from the streets.

Often she visited her parents' grave on the way to Lou's, pulled whatever weeds had sprung up around the base of the stone with her hands, and knelt before it to try to say a prayer. She knew it wasn't what Mother would have wanted: prayers weren't her thing. But what else were you supposed to do at gravesides?

Today, though, Kitty went straight to Lou's. Reaching Woodbury Avenue, she opened Lou's gate, which had *60* worked into the wood, and walked up the box-lined front path.

'It's you.' Lou opened the door and peered over Kitty's shoulder. 'I thought it might be Bob, coming back for his extra set of irons. He's always on that bloody golf course lately. Come in, then.'

Lou led Kitty through the house, with its familiar scent of Nettine and new paint, to the back garden: a square of lawn framed by forget-me-nots, delphiniums and white moon daisies. In the centre of the lawn was a deep red rose bush. Red, white and blue: they'd planted the garden for the Jubilee last year, not long after they'd first moved in. Lou said it was Bob's pride. But Kitty knew it was Lou who did the work: she'd seen the dirt beneath her fingernails, the calloused forefinger of her right hand, like Arthur's.

They sat on Lou's wicker garden chairs.

'What do you think of my new skirt, then?' Lou smoothed it over her thighs and twisted to the side, jutting out her chin and widening her eyes. It was calf-length, bright orange with two pleats at the knees, and tight enough to show the curve of her bottom. 'It's rayon. Dries like a dream but a bit scratchy. Bob says this is his favourite colour on me, but I'm not sure. Is it a bit much, do you think?'

Today Lou was wearing her red curls straightened and rolled at the ends so they rested on her shoulders and glinted as she moved. They reminded Kitty of the fox stole Mrs Steinberg kept hanging in her wardrobe but never wore.

'It's lovely.'

'I expect your American woman has dozens.'

'Not as many as you'd think,' Kitty began, reaching for an egg and cress sandwich from the little camp table Lou had placed on the lawn. 'I've seen her in the same outfit lots of times. She likes quite, well, boyish things. Buttons and military whatnot.'

'I thought that bohemian lot were all scarves

and no underwear.'

Kitty giggled. 'Lou!'

'Well. That's what I've heard. And she is on her third husband.'

'He's not her husband.'

'Exactly.'

Kitty bit into her sandwich. The bread was a strange mixture of soggy and slightly crispy. Lou must have made them this morning. She'd always been very organised.

'It must be nice, to have anything you want,' Lou continued. 'If it was me, I'd have a new cashmere coat, plenty of Swiss lace petticoats and dozens of silk stockings. And a georgette swagger suit. I've seen just the one in Norman Burton's.'

'She doesn't wear stockings.'

Lou raised her eyebrows. 'What does she wear then?'

'Socks, sometimes.'

'Like a schoolgirl?'

'Short ones. I think it must be an American thing.'

Kitty looked at the back of her sister's house. The sparkling kitchen window reflected the scene back to her: two sisters sitting on a lawn, one in a rayon skirt and the other in an old frock. New garden furniture with blue cretonne cushions. The Jubilee garden. It was fortunate that the King had died in the winter, because a red, white and blue garden would have seemed inappropriate when the nation was supposed to be in mourning.

'What does *he* think of that?'

Kitty reached for another sandwich, then changed her mind. 'Is there cake, Lou?'

'Later. Marble. What does he think of that, the

no-stockings thing?'

'Who?'

'The poet, you ninny. Handsome Henry. Crake.'

'Crane.' Kitty twisted her hands in her lap. 'I don't know what he thinks.'

'Are you blushing?'

Kitty took a sandwich and bit into it. 'No.' The yolks were powdery, too.

'He is handsome, though, isn't he?'

'Is he?'

Lou tutted. 'She's a lucky so-and-so. Fancy having all that and not even being married to it. I suppose she can afford it.'

Now Kitty did blush.

'And having you to cook and clean for him, too.' Lou stretched her neck to one side and closed her eyes. 'Sometimes I wish I had a char. Then I could go and do something else occasionally.'

Kitty said nothing.

'Not that Bob's very demanding. But it's a big house to clean all on your own.'

'Easy, though. What with it being so square—modern, I mean.'

Lou shot her sister a sideways look. 'I suppose.' She sighed. 'I'm a lucky bugger, when you think of it.'

'Mother would have loved it.'

Lou picked up a sandwich, prised it open with one finger and studied the contents. 'It's you she would have been proud of, though.'

'Get off. What about you marrying a schoolmaster? She never stopped on about that.'

'But I don't actually *do* anything, though, do I? Not any more.'

When she was fourteen, Lou had begged their

101

mother to let her stay at school so she could become a teacher, but their mother had said there was no way she could afford to support her until she was qualified. And, anyway, Lou was sure to meet some young man and change her mind before that, and then it would all be a waste. Kitty remembered the long nights of her sister's sobbing in their bed. She'd always tried to comfort Lou, if only in an attempt to get some sleep herself, and Lou had always resisted, turning away and crying all the harder at the slightest touch.

Lou dumped the sandwich back on the plate. 'The bakery wasn't much but it was something. Now I don't do anything that's of use to anyone. It's not as if I've even got any children to look after.'

'You will have, though, Lou.'

Lou shook her head and smiled. 'How do you know that? It's been two years already.'

'You keep house for Bob, and cook—'

'But like you said, that's easy.'

Kitty touched the ends of her hair and looked at her sister. 'Not for Mrs Steinberg, it isn't. She's asked me to show her how to do it.'

Lou widened her eyes.

'She said she wanted to become *domesticated*. She's asked me to help her learn how to be a housewife. I don't know what to do about it.'

'*I* know what to do about it,' said Lou. 'I know exactly what you should do. You should show her how to scrub the floor and heave the bloody mangle round. You should get her on her hands and knees cleaning the lav. See how she likes it.'

'I don't think she wants to learn that bit.'

'I'm sure she doesn't.'

'I think it's more the cooking and things. And the children . . .'

'But you're not the nanny, Kitty, you've always said that. You're the cook. She should be looking after them already, shouldn't she?'

'Yes, but—'

'If a woman has children she should look after them herself. What's the point in it, otherwise?' Lou bit her bottom lip and stared at the rose bed.

'Thing is,' said Kitty, 'I was wondering, Lou, if you could help me.'

Lou's gaze snapped back to her sister.

'You're good at that sort of thing,' Kitty continued. 'You were always better than me.'

Lou waved a hand in the air. 'It's just getting a recipe from a book. Anyone can do it.'

'She can't.'

'But what does she want? I can't do anything fancy.'

'I don't know. The basics, I suppose . . .'

'You can do that. I've never heard anything like it, a lady asking the staff for recipes. What's wrong with her?'

'Please, Lou. All you have to do is show me a few things. And then I can show her. What about that lovely omelette you made the other week, with the bacon in?'

'Savoyarde.'

'That would be the sort of thing. She likes French things.'

Lou ran a finger along her neckline. 'I suppose I could show you a couple of things. I did make a nice kedgeree last night. Bob was amazed that rice could be so edible.'

On the way back to the cottage, Kitty decided to get off the bus a stop early. It was a lovely evening; the sky was streaked all kinds of pink. She was free until the morning, so why not walk back? Lou had Bob to drive her in their Ford. She, Kitty, would walk. She'd seen young couples on the hills by the cottage, both wearing shorts and carrying packs on their backs. Rambling, they called it. She wondered what it would be like to walk in shorts, baring your legs to the cows. Cold, probably. And what did they carry on their backs? Maps, compasses, treacle biscuits? Notebooks, perhaps, for moments of inspiration. That was probably what Mr Crane did, although she'd never seen him in shorts.

Smiling at the thought, she stood on the verge of the main road to Harting and looked about. There was a cut-through across the fields back to the cottage somewhere. Arthur had mentioned he walked home this way sometimes in the summer, 'to make the most of it'.

She couldn't find a gate, so she squeezed through a gap in the hedgerow, scratching her arm on a branch. A thin line of blood rose to the surface of her skin. She rubbed at it for a moment before making her way around the edge of the field. The wheat was almost to her waist, bristling green. Kitty couldn't remember ever walking in the fields like this before. When they were younger, she and Lou sometimes cycled from their house in Petersfield to Harting; they'd shared a bicycle between them, and would take it in turns to sit on the saddle whilst the other stood and pedalled.

The picnic was always the bit Kitty liked the best—
a piece of cheese and bread, perhaps a slice of
apple cake if their mother had felt like baking.
They always ate in the village churchyard, then
cycled home along the road again. Kitty
remembered feeling that the devil must be in that
churchyard. The pointed wooden doors and mossy
arches of the church were, she thought, where the
devil was likely to lurk. If it was God's house,
wouldn't the devil want to hang about outside?
That way, he had more chance of getting in and
causing havoc.

She reached a patch of trees which she thought
she recognised, but she couldn't see the cottage
from here. Leaves flicked in the wind. Her shoes
were beginning to feel damp. The only way, she
decided, was to go through the wood.

Although it had been a warm week, the ground
was boggy, and mud crept over the edges of her
shoes. As she went deeper into the wood, it was so
quiet that she became aware of her own breath.
She wished, now, that she'd accepted the piece of
marble cake Lou had offered her to take home.
She could have stopped for a bite then.

Did Arthur come this way? She couldn't see any
track through the trees, which were getting denser.
She'd have to go back. What had she been
thinking? Even if she had reached the back of the
garden, there was the stream to cross. She'd have
to go back to the road and walk all the way round
and through the village.

The sun was getting lower in the sky. If she still
had a bicycle, she could get away from Willow on
her free evenings without having to pay for the bus.
Perhaps she could cycle up to the church and sit in

105

the graveyard again, to see if the devil had made an appearance yet. When they were younger, Lou liked to stretch out on the graves and sunbathe, hitching her skirt above her knees and closing her eyes. Kitty herself kept upright. When Lou had asked her why she didn't lie down, Kitty told her, *you never know who'll come along.* 'Exactly,' Lou said, and smiled.

They'd waited long hours like that, some Sunday afternoons, Lou's legs going goose-pimply as shadows dragged across the graves, and Kitty's bottom turning to stone. The yew trees smelled of mould, and the grave they most often chose was dedicated to Mary Belcher, she remembered that. Mary Belcher had a headstone, which had fallen over and now lay flat in the grass, all to herself. Was it better to have room in the grave, or to have company? Would it be good to have someone else in there, waiting for you? Or better to be left in peace? She thought that her own mother would have preferred to have been left in peace, but she was in with their father, even though the two of them had hardly spoken when he was alive, so Lou said. What Kitty remembered most about him was the ripe smell of tea on his breath every evening when he kissed her goodnight. And how he used to go up the side passage of the house to fart, putting a finger to his lips. 'Don't tell, Kitty-Cat,' he'd say. Their mother said he'd been a fool to go to war when he was already too old, and even more of a fool to die of the flu when he got back.

She was at the road again now and her toes were rubbing together. Starlings clattered in the trees. She thought again of the marble cake she could have brought back in her bag. The hills were taking on their hunched appearance as the sun went down. All chalk and dust and wind.

She was almost at the edge of the village when a car drove up behind her. It was Mrs Steinberg's new vehicle: a yellow MG sports car with headlamps like moons.

'Can I offer you a lift?'

Mr Crane was squinting against the low sun, one arm reaching across to open the passenger door for her.

She hid her handbag behind her back and looked down at her damp shoes.

'I'd be pleased to drive you back, Kitty, if you'd like.'

He didn't smile, exactly, but he'd opened the door now and was holding out a hand. 'Do climb in.'

'Thank you, Mr Crane, sir, but I'm fine, really I am.'

He was wearing a dark green corduroy jacket and no driving gloves or hat. His hair had gone awry and was hanging down over his forehead, which seemed to make his lopsided eye squint all the more.

'I was hoping to put this blessed car to some sort of use.'

'Thank you so much, really, Mr Crane, but I was walking, you see—'

At this, he turned off the engine.

'Do you often walk?'

'Yes—no, I mean, I'd like to, but . . .' She twisted the strap of the handbag behind her back. 'I was thinking of getting a bicycle.'

She hadn't meant to say that.

He nodded. 'Cycling is enormous fun, isn't it?

For me, though, walking is absolutely the best way to travel. But—well, Mrs Steinberg has bought me this car, so one really ought to use it.'

'Yes.'

'Lovely here, isn't it? For walking.'

'Yes. It is. Lovely.' She shifted from foot to foot.

'With the Downs just there.'

'Yes.'

That leather seat *would* be comfortable.

'You can cut through to the cottage across that field, you know.'

'Oh?'

'Quite wonderful now, with the wheat at full height.'

Kitty touched her hair.

'Of course, you have to cross the stream, but there's a narrow bit, where it's quite safe to jump.'

'I see.'

'Anyhow.' He started the engine again and reached across to close the door. 'I mustn't hold you up—'

'You weren't.'

He looked at her then, and she thought that he smiled.

'Glorious evening. Enjoy it.'

As he drove off, he lifted one hand and waved and said something that she didn't quite catch, but she nodded anyway, then stood looking after the disappearing car.

Lou would have got in with him, skirt hitched up to show her good knees, rounded and pale like curls of butter. *You never knew who might come along*, and here she was, still walking in her stiffening shoes, with no cake in her bag and at least another mile to go.

FOURTEEN

Ellen had always been the one who washed her daughter's hair, and now she washed Diana's too. Both girls had beautiful hair, and plenty of it: she hadn't cut Geenie's since the girl was four, and every year its cloud of blonde not only grew longer, but seemed to expand widthways, becoming thicker and fluffier. Diana was dark, like her father, and her hair slipped over her shoulders like a living thing, a muscled eel or a stretching cat, but she showed no sign, yet, of being aware of her own prettiness. She simply hooked the glossy eel behind one ear and carried on reading.

As a treat, Ellen was using her own shampoo for the girls, Rubenstein's *Ecstase*, jasmine scented, ordered from London. Its golden bottle glinted on the window ledge. She hated lilies, roses, violets and any other scent that reminded her of her own mother, who, she reasoned, probably never once washed her own hair, let alone anyone else's. Sandalwood, jasmine, bergamot, ylang-ylang—these were the perfumes worth wearing. Their muskiness was more honest, closer to the earth. She loved the smell of Crane's fingers when he'd been helping Arthur to cut the rosemary or when he brought her a sprig of thyme, saying she should make Kitty put it in with the bird.

The girls bathed together. Their long legs jostled for space in the tub, and they pretended to fight over the soap. Today Ellen made them sit back to back for the hair washing—that way she could kneel on a towel and scrub from head to head without too much stretching. She was still tired after last night's drinking, which had gone on till two in the morning (although she'd noticed that Crane himself had stopped at midnight), and knew that she should save any elasticity left in her body for Crane.

Scooping up a huge handful of blonde and black hair, she soaped both manes together, winding them in a kind of maypole until Geenie stopped giggling and protested at her scalp being pulled. 'Ellen! Stop it!'

Ellen dropped the hair and reached for the jug in silence.

She found her hands running through the black streaks down Diana's back for longer than was necessary, and became aware of her daughter's big blue eyes on her.

'It's my turn now. And I'm getting cold.'

'Diana's not complaining.'

Geenie swivelled round and pressed her big toe into Diana's thigh. 'Diana never complains, Ellen, you've said so yourself.'

Diana smiled. 'Don't I?'

'And don't start complaining, Diana, that's my advice. Men don't like it.' Ellen squeezed the moisture from the girl's hair, and then thought to add, 'And neither do other women.'

'I think she should complain more. I think it's unnatural not to complain.'

Ellen filled the jug with clean water from the tap.

'Who told you that? Put your head back.'

She poured water over her daughter's hair, digging her fingers into her scalp, chasing out the

110

suds, until Geenie cried out again.

'Don't make a fuss.'

'George says that complaining can change things.'

'George says a lot of silly things.'

'Can I get out?' asked Diana, standing up suddenly and dripping water onto Ellen's shoulders. Unlike Geenie, whose hips had recently begun to fan out, Diana was thin as a stripling.

'There's a towel over there,' said Ellen.

Whilst Diana stood with the towel held up to her nose, Ellen filled the jug again. 'Head back, Flossy.'

She began to pour, but as she did so, Geenie went limp and slid herself into the bath until she was fully submerged in the water.

Ellen put the jug down and sat back on her heels. It was just a matter of waiting. She knew Geenie couldn't hold her breath for long. Behind her, Diana sighed, then came to kneel by the tub. Together they watched Geenie as she lay beneath the water. Ellen noticed the small swellings around the girl's nipples, magnified by the bathwater, but—she looked down—no real pubic hair yet. Her amphibian daughter. Any chance she got, she went under.

*   *   *

'Why aren't you writing?'

Ellen had had a drink—just one, just a gin and it—and wandered outside into the warm evening. Only half an hour until supper. Soon she'd be preparing it herself, of course, something light and fresh and French; but for now, Kitty was perspiring

111

over another roasted piece of pig.

She hovered in the doorway of Crane's studio, smiling. She knew she shouldn't be here when he was trying to work. Crane never disturbed her when she was typing, although she often wished he would. If only he would ask about the letters, just once; then she might let it all come out. But he hadn't shown the slightest interest in what she did in the library.

He did have the most charming taste, despite the messiness of his studio. On his desk was a beautiful red porcelain vase with orange dots painted up one side; it reminded Ellen of a woman's thigh, it was so rounded and yet so long and elegant, with a fluted, open neck. Beside it were the usual piles of poetry books, newspapers, dirty cups and sheaves of paper. James had always said that what Crane needed was a good editor, rather than a willing publisher. Someone to take a scalpel to all that self-indulgence. James could've done it himself, of course, if he'd have thought it worth his while. Not that she'd encouraged him, she remembered now. Something had made her want to limit any contact the two men had, and she'd always been rather glad when James had dismissed Crane in that icy way of his.

'You're not writing?'

Without looking at her, Crane stretched back in his chair and sighed. 'Reading.'

He said it as if it were just as good.

'Reading what?'

She was through the door now, putting her hands on the desk beside him.

Crane rose from his chair. 'Marx.'

'Of course.'

When he was this close, she could smell him. At first she'd loved the smell, that warm, leathery scent; but now that the hot weather seemed set in, his sweat was beginning to turn a little sharp. She'd have to say something soon.

'Do you object?' he asked.

'I never object to reading, you know that. But sometimes there are better things to do.'

'Like what, Ellen?'

'Like . . . writing.'

He moved closer to her. She closed her eyes.

'Crane,' she said, 'you've never kissed me here—'

Reaching past her, he ripped the sheet of paper from his typewriter. He paused to plant a light kiss on her cheek, then he folded the paper and put it in his pocket.

'What was that?'

'Writing,' he said. 'Or as close to writing as I've got today.'

'Is it your novel?'

He dropped into his armchair. 'I don't have a novel, Ellen.'

'Yes you do. You told me. You're writing a novel. It's inspired by the Sussex Downs.'

He'd said to her, when they first came here: 'You make me want to write stories again.' He'd said that. And she'd imagined herself in the pages of his book: the exciting foreign vamp, raising the English gent from his metaphorical grave. *Am I the woman in your book?* she'd ask, knowingly. How could she not appear in his book, after all she'd given him?

'What was the point in coming here, in giving up your job at the publishing house, if you're not writing?' She gave him a few moments, leaning on his desk and staring down at him, waiting for his reply.

Eventually, he dropped his eyes and said in a quiet voice, 'It was for you.'

She wished she had a cigarette, so she could exhale scornfully, like Laura.

'I gave it up for you,' he continued, swallowing. 'Had you forgotten?'

She tried to remember. True, she'd been the first to suggest that he didn't have to go to work. A gentleman shouldn't have to hold down a day job. Messing about in the offices of a publishing house wasn't what he should be doing with his life. Besides, London was such a long way away, and it was where Lillian was, with her kick-pleat skirts and her neat nose.

'I've bought you something,' she said.

She hadn't, but it was good to change the subject. She'd been thinking about buying him another typewriter, a newer one—it didn't feel right that hers was a more modern model than his—but she hadn't quite got around to it yet.

'I wish you'd stop.' His voice was still quiet, but steady.

'Stop what?'

'Buying things. For me.'

'Don't you like things?'

'Well. I—'

'You used to like things. New books. Pens. That cashmere coat. You liked them.'

'Of course I liked them, I loved them. It's just . . .'

She'd bought him a silk tie, that was the first thing; he'd looked pleased but had never worn it.

Bottles of whisky didn't go down well, either. And there was the MG, of course; she'd had to nag him to take it out of the drive the other day. Blotto had been the best present, probably the only one he'd really liked: they'd bought him from a breeder in Midhurst, and in the car on the way home the dog had panted so heavily that Crane insisted they stop to give him a drink from a puddle. He was ten weeks old, small enough to fit in Crane's jacket, which was where he'd hidden for hours when they were back at the cottage. Finally they'd prised him out, and he'd trembled in the corner of the kitchen until Crane scooped him up and took him to the studio. Now the dog slept beneath Crane's desk every night.

'Look. I don't want to fight,' he said, his mouth working in a way she recognised: he was trying to make himself smile. It was how he always avoided a row. Side-stepping her just when she was working up to it.

He rubbed at his chin. 'Isn't it almost time for supper?'

'Another piece of pig.' She pulled a face.

He grinned a little then, his lopsided eyes creasing. 'What's wrong with that?'

'Nothing. It's going to change soon, though.' She hadn't meant to tell him, but he would push her to these things. These declarations. Sometimes they were the only way to get a real reaction from him.

'Things are going to change.' She spoke rapidly. 'I'm going to be cooking. And looking after the girls. I need *something* to do out here, don't I?' She felt the blood rising to her face. 'You're keen on the importance of work, and workers, darling, aren't you? Earning your place in the world and all

115

that. I'm going to earn mine.'

He leant forward in his chair and opened his mouth to speak, but she cut him off.

'It's going to be wonderful, George. I'm going to be a domesticated woman. Can you imagine? Kitty's going to help me.'

She should have had another gin and it before she started this, but it was too late to stop now.

'That sounds—ah—intriguing—'

'All I need is another baby, and then I will be quite the little housewife.'

Now he was staring at her, his mouth open.

'Don't worry, darling. It won't hurt. Well. It won't hurt *you*, anyway.'

'Ellen.' His voice had lowered. It was the tone she'd heard him use when Diana said something out of place. 'Are you—ah. Are you serious?'

She knelt by the side of his armchair and looked up at him. She waited for a while, hoping he would meet her gaze. But his eyes seemed fixed on his own knees. So she said, 'Yes, I am,' and took his hand in hers. It was a knobbly hand and a skinny wrist. But his skin was smooth. In her experience, most English gentlemen had skin like this: boyish, pale, easily marked. 'Don't you want us to have a child, George?' she asked, softly.

He gripped her fingers. 'Well—I suppose we've always said, haven't we, that we came here to be a family together . . .'

'That's what we said.'

'The thing is, though, I *am* still married to Lillian, officially, and—'

Ellen jumped up. 'What difference does that make? You live here with me. We're already a family, you and Diana, me and Geenie . . .'

He closed his eyes. He seemed to be counting breaths.

She really should have had another gin. She pushed her hair away from her forehead and held it for a few moments, pressing down on her own scalp while she tried not to shout. 'It's just—I want to be—you know, *proper* for you.'

'You *are* proper, Ellen.' He caught her fingers and brought them to his lips. 'You've always been that.'

She knelt by him again. It was a great effort, but she managed to keep her voice steady. 'You'll think about it, darling?'

With his eyes closed, he nodded, and, after a moment, he took her head in his hands and kissed her so hard it was all she could do not to flinch.

FIFTEEN

Sweat pooled in the crease at Kitty's waist as she scrubbed the kitchen flags. The soapy water in her bucket was almost scalding, and her hands and face felt as red as the tiles. It was better, though, to do the floor in the morning, while the kitchen was still shady, and before Arthur's tea at eleven. She could sit down, then, and watch him eat one of the walnut pyramids she'd made yesterday; he might even say something more about dancing. Every time they had tea together she expected him to bring it up again, but he hadn't said another word on the subject.

'What are you doing?'

Kitty knew, now, that it wasn't always necessary

to answer Geenie's questions. If you waited long enough, pretending not to hear, or could look as though you were very, very busy, the girl might move on.

'Why are you doing that?'

Perhaps not today, though. 'It's my work, Miss.'

'It will only get dirty again, won't it?'

Kitty dropped her brush into the bucket and pulled it out again, slopping soap suds over her apron. 'Yes, Miss.'

'So wouldn't it be better to leave it?'

Kitty pushed her brush very close to Geenie's bare toes and wondered how she could get the girl to go outside.

'Why do things have to be clean, anyway?'

'I think I heard Miss Diana calling for you earlier.'

Kitty had hardly heard the new girl speak since she'd arrived in the house a week ago. She was usually just behind Geenie, looking at you with her dark eyes, then looking away when you spoke, listening to Geenie's questions without asking any of her own.

Geenie cocked her head to one side. 'I didn't hear anything.'

Kitty tried another tack. Nodding towards the back door, she said, 'Don't step over there, Miss, will you? It's soaking—'

Before she could finish, Geenie was running towards the door. 'I won't slip,' she called over her shoulder. 'Look.'

Kitty sat back on her heels and watched the girl disappear into the garden.

Half an hour until Arthur's tea break. She began scrubbing again, concentrating on the sound of the bristles on the flags. A ragged rasp, rasp, rasp. It reminded Kitty of her mother's breath when she'd taken to her bed after Lou was married. At first, Kitty had thought it was just one of Mother's phases; a day or so in bed hadn't been uncommon after their father died. The two girls would make cups of beef tea and take them upstairs, then fetch them down again an hour later, cold and untouched. They played together then, Kitty remembered; she and her sister actually played together, quietly, on the kitchen rug, while they waited for their mother to appear. At any other time they squabbled and kept their games separate, but when Mother was in bed, Lou would show an interest in Kitty's tea-set, and Kitty would sit still as Lou read aloud from *The Girl's Book of Adventure Stories*.

But years later, when Lou had left for married life with Bob, Mother had taken to her bed for a week. After work Kitty sat on the counterpane and pretended to embroider whilst listening to her mother's thickening breath. The room began to smell of glue, no matter how long she left the window open. When Lou came she looked at Kitty, her face creased into odd angles, and said, 'Why haven't you fetched the doctor?' Kitty didn't like to say *it's just one of her phases, you remember them*, because now Lou was here that suddenly didn't seem true. Mother said all she wanted was a little Petroleum Compound and some rest, but when she saw Bob she'd murmured, 'The teacher'll see me right,' and Bob had rocked back and forth on his heels and declared he would telephone for the doctor from his house because this was *a most serious situation*.

There was a stubborn mark just here, beneath the table, where Geenie had spilled her paints. Kitty scrubbed and scrubbed until her eyes blurred.

'Diana's stuck.'

She hadn't heard the girl come in, but here she was again, her bare feet leaving prints on the wet flags, panting like Blotto.

'She's stuck!'

'Stuck?'

'In the tree!'

Kitty stopped scrubbing and took several breaths. 'Have you told Mr Crane, Miss?'

Geenie tucked her chin into her chest. 'He's not here. They've gone into town.'

'Your mother, too?'

'Yes. I told you.'

'What about Arthur?'

'What about him?'

Kitty threw her brush into the bucket. 'How long has she been stuck, Miss?'

'I don't know. Quarter of an hour. We were climbing and now she says she can't get down.'

Kitty stood and wiped her hands on her apron. 'You'd better show me.'

Outside, the sculpture of the naked bottom glared in the sunshine as Kitty followed Geenie to the end of the garden. Where was Arthur? Wasn't it a man's job to get children out of trees? If he really wanted her to go dancing with him, shouldn't he be coming to the rescue?

Geenie pointed to the sprawling willow by the stream. Blotto was racing around the base, barking.

'She's stuck,' the girl said again.

Shooing the dog away, Kitty stood looking up at

a pair of bare feet. Inside the cavern of the tree's branches, the sunlight was fractured with green. Everything seemed to flicker as Diana's feet swayed high above.

'Are you all right, Miss?'

'She should jump, shouldn't she?' said Geenie.

'No!' Kitty covered her mouth with a hand. 'I mean, I don't think so, Miss.'

Geenie sauntered around the trunk, digging her toes into the soft dirt of the bank. 'She might fall in the stream.'

Kitty suddenly thought of the woman in the awful painting above her bed, summoning up the courage to plunge into the waterfall. The water would be deliciously cold on such a sunny day. It was really too hot for a vest. She should've gone without.

'Should I go up and fetch her?'

'I don't think so, Miss.'

'What shall we do then?'

Kitty looked around the garden, hoping to see the red streak of Arthur's moustache. 'When will your mother be back?'

'How should I know?' Geenie was hanging on a low branch, her feet skimming the dirt below.

'It'd probably be better if you didn't do that, Miss. It's making the branches move.'

Kitty looked up into the tree. Surely if the girl got up there she could get down again.

'Do you think you could come down, Miss Diana?'

There was no reply.

Kitty glanced at Geenie, who was still hanging on the branch. 'How did she get up there?'

Geenie rolled her eyes. 'I told you. She climbed.

121

She's like a cat. Her mother's a ballerina.'

Kitty touched her hair. So he'd been married to a dancer. She hadn't imagined that.

She cleared her throat and called again. 'Won't you try to come down, Miss? Please?'

There was a long silence. They watched the girl's feet swaying above.

Then there was a voice, surprisingly flat and calm. 'I don't think I can.'

Geenie grinned. 'What shall we do?' She skipped around the base of the tree, and began to chant. 'What shall we do? What shall we do? What shall we do?'

Kitty's hands were greasy with sweat as she ran them down the front of her apron. Where the devil was Arthur? Reading in his shed, probably. She knew that's what he did when Mr Crane and Mrs Steinberg weren't about. He stood his spade in the earth and disappeared, emerging only when a long farting sound announced the arrival of Mrs Steinberg's car.

Kitty took off her apron, folded it, and placed it on the ground. As a girl, she'd never climbed trees. Lou had been the one who came home with holes in her stockings and grit in her knees. Once Kitty had managed to scale a slippery log in the school yard, but towards the end she'd fallen and twisted her wrist, and that was the end of that.

'What shall we do? What shall we do?' Geenie chanted.

Taking hold of the nearest branch with both hands, Kitty pulled herself upwards. The whole tree seemed to shake. She attempted to grip the trunk with her feet, but the soles of her shoes were slippery and she was soon back on the ground.

She unlaced her shoes and kicked them to one side. Reaching up beneath her skirt, she unhooked her stockings, rolled them down and folded them on top of her apron. Then she started again.

Geenie stopped chanting, sat on the bank, and watched.

Every time she reached for another branch, bark grazed Kitty's skin, but she was off the ground now and Diana's feet were dangling above, pale and arched. Is that what her mother's, what a ballerina's, feet looked like? She heaved herself up to another branch, clinging to a spindly twig that was piercing her side. Kitty knew she must not, at any point, look down.

Probably Mr Crane would return to find two females stuck in a tree, instead of one. She hadn't thought that poets would like dancers. It didn't seem very likely, somehow, that people who spent all day with words would like people who spent all day jigging about. She tried to grasp the trunk with her bare knees and hauled herself up another level. A piece of bark broke off under the pressure of her foot and fell to the ground. She mustn't think about the slipperiness of her hands in this heat. It was good, at any rate, to have her shoes and stockings off, even if it was up a willow tree in search of a silly girl.

Then she thought: what am I to do when I reach her? A child of eleven would be too heavy to carry even on the flat, and Kitty herself was small and slight. Diana was almost at her height already.

She reached for Diana's foot, but her fingers came just short. 'Do you think you can come down with me, Miss Diana?' She couldn't yet see the girl's face, only the long stretch of her legs and the mushroom-shape of her gathered skirt. 'Can you just get to where I am?' Kitty could feel the warm air on the backs of her knees. She must be at least twelve feet above the ground now. She peered through the branches over the garden. The cottage seemed a long way off.

'Is my father back yet?' asked Diana.

'No, Miss.' Kitty tried to grasp the girl's foot again, and wobbled so severely that her stomach leapt towards her lungs.

'He's not back?'

Kitty took a breath. 'Not yet, Miss.'

'I think I might stay here. Until he comes.'

Diana swung her foot away from Kitty's reaching hand.

'Is she coming down?' called Geenie.

Kitty tried to steady herself. Her fingers were beginning to feel numb from gripping the branch so hard. 'I think you should come down now, Miss Diana, please.'

'But my father might be here in a minute.'

The leaves flickered in the breeze.

'Please, Miss. He might be hours, mightn't he?'

'How do you know?'

Kitty closed her eyes. She must not look down. 'It will be all right, Miss.' Her voice was shaking. 'I'll help you.'

The branches shuddered again as Diana kicked out her foot. 'But he might come! Don't you understand? My daddy might come!'

Kitty was sure she could hear her own knees creaking in time with the branches. She licked a bead of sweat from her lip. Then she reached for Diana's ankle again, caught it, and held fast. The girl let out a little yelp.

'You've got to come down.'

To her surprise, the girl gave a loud sob.

'Come on now,' said Kitty, softening her voice.

'You won't tell him I got stuck, will you?'

'Of course not.'

Diana sniffed. 'You're hurting my ankle.'

As Kitty let go of Diana's foot, the girl slipped from her branch and hung before Kitty for a moment, her plump lips open, her eyes wide and slightly red, her limbs stretched at impossible angles; then, before Kitty could say anything, Diana swung herself to a low branch, then a lower one, and finally launched to the ground, where she landed with a *whump*.

'Is she hurt?' Kitty called.

There was no reply, just the sound of running, and Blotto's high-pitched bark.

Kitty looked down. It didn't seem so far, after all. The dog was still standing there, yapping at her. For a moment she considered what would happen if she stayed in the tree. How long would it be before anyone noticed? Then she thought: Arthur *would* come. In the end. But she couldn't wait for that.

Her fingers seemed jammed with heat and her knees were shaking, but somehow her feet found their hold. Slowly, she lowered herself through the branches and to the ground. The girls had disappeared and there was still no sign of Arthur. The bloody floor could wait. Who would notice, anyway? Leaving her apron, stockings and shoes on the dirt, Kitty sat on the bank, dipped her bare toes into the stream and wondered if her cooling feet were anything like a ballerina's.

SIXTEEN

After Diana slid from the tree so gracefully—
Geenie didn't hear a sound until the other girl's
feet were on the ground—the two girls ran into the
cottage together, stifling giggles. Geenie wasn't
entirely sure what they were laughing about, but
the sight of Diana's puffed-up cheeks and bunched
lips was enough to build a laugh in her own belly.
Once they reached the kitchen, they looked at one
another and let go; Diana opened her mouth and
howled, grabbing the handle of the stove to steady
herself. Geenie collapsed on the damp tiles and,
catching sight of Kitty's abandoned bucket,
laughed harder. It wasn't until her ribs were aching
and her cheeks felt as if they'd been stretched
behind her ears that she noticed Diana had
stopped laughing and was sitting at the table,
staring at her own hands.

Geenie swallowed another giggle and got up
from the floor. 'Are you all right?'

Diana's dark hair fell over her eyes as her head
drooped forward.

'How did you manage it?' asked Geenie. 'You
slipped right past her.' She stepped closer to her
friend. 'Diana?'

'He didn't come.'

'Who didn't?'

Diana didn't reply, but Geenie knew the answer.

Then there was a rattle and a cough, and Arthur
appeared. He stooped in the doorway, removing
his boots. 'Hello there,' he said, heading for the tea
kettle, not looking at the girls. 'Where's Kitty?'

126

'Let's go upstairs,' said Geenie.

*   *   *

The box of watercolours was still open on the floor, the brushes stuffed in the jam jar of water. Geenie ignored the splodge of cobalt blue that had now dried on her bedroom rug.

Geenie's room felt damp with heat and was always gloomy, even in summer. Diana lay back on the bed, holding a copy of *The Arabian Nights* above her head.

Geenie frowned at the other girl's foot. 'Flowers?'

'We had flowers this morning,' said Diana, without looking up.

'How about swirls?'

'Whatever you like.'

Geenie licked her thumb and rubbed it along Diana's sole before beginning. It was good to have a slightly damp surface. Then she sucked on the end of her paintbrush. The wood was beginning to flake and tiny strips of it caught between her teeth.

'Burnt sienna?'

Diana shifted on the bed but said nothing.

'Or vermilion?'

'Either.'

'Vermilion, then.' Geenie wetted her brush and loaded it with so much paint that it dripped down the sides and trailed across her fingers.

'Hold still.' She clasped Diana's foot and brought the brush to her skin.

'That tickles.'

Geenie flicked the brush between Diana's toes.

'Stop it!' Diana threw her book to the floor.

127

Red paint had speckled the bedclothes. Both girls looked at the drops in silence.

'I'm sure George would have come, eventually,' said Geenie. 'And the way you leapt from your branch was absolutely amazing. Like a gazelle, or something.'

Diana laid her head on the pillow and sighed. Geenie waited, brush in hand. Should she begin again? A pattern of swirls was all worked out in her head. They would start small, right in the centre of Diana's foot, then get larger, spreading out to lasso each of her toes.

After a while, Diana said, 'Did I tell you about my mother's feet?'

Geenie had already heard all about Diana's mother's toes, and how Mrs Crane had found it hard to walk on normal shoes since she'd become a ballerina, but she said, 'Tell me.'

'Her toes are like claws. She has special muscles in them. She can stand on pointe for ages. When my father saw her in *Pulcinella* he was *intoxicated*.'

Geenie decided her swirls would have to wait for another day. She held out her brush. 'Do you want to do me instead? You can do whatever you like.'

'All right.' Diana sat up. 'Take off your blouse.'

Geenie did as she was asked, glad to be rid of the blue, heavily embroidered garment, which was slightly too small for her and was clinging to her armpits in the heat. Her nipples prickled in the air. She stood before Diana, who looked her up and down without smiling.

'Turn around.'

Geenie faced the door, scooping her hair away from her back with one hand. She could hear Diana rubbing the brush in the paint. Then she was jabbed, hard, between the shoulders, and Diana splurged paint right across her cooling skin.

'Don't get it everywhere. Ellen won't like it.'

'It's a bit late for that.'

The brush was prickly, and Diana pressed so hard that Geenie almost lost her balance. But she said nothing. She heard the other girl's breathing become heavier, and felt the outward rush of warm air on her left shoulder as Diana concentrated on covering her back with paint.

'You'll be like a Red Indian.'

Geenie's arm started to ache from holding her hair, and her skin felt tight where the paint was beginning to dry.

Diana's brush reached the bottom of her back. 'I'm going right down,' she said.

'*That* tickles.'

'Keep still.'

Geenie closed her eyes to keep from squirming. Cold paint was dribbling into her knickers.

Diana sat back on the bed. 'It's perfect. Look.'

Looking over her shoulder, Geenie saw her own reflection in the hand mirror Diana was holding up. The paint was already cracking as she moved. There were streaks of orange in the hair at the back of her neck, and the strokes on her lower back were sketchier than those on her shoulders, but the effect was dramatic.

'You look wild,' said Diana. 'We could do all of you. Like in a show. My mother wore an all-over sheath once. The newspapers said it was shocking and degenerate.'

Geenie studied her red back, thinking she looked like she had some kind of disease. Then she said, 'I don't think we've got enough paint.'

'Suit yourself.' Diana dropped her brush into the jam jar and went back to her book.

*   *   *

That night, after listening to the soft *whoas* for a while, Geenie let herself into Diana's bedroom, closed the door, and tried to still her breathing. The other girl wasn't rolling around, but a low whimper came from her lips, as if she were trying to speak.

Geenie sat on the end of the bed and watched. She thought of Diana sliding through the willow, of how the branches would have caught her arms and legs, grazed her knees and elbows. When she'd landed on the ground, had she turned an ankle, or bashed her toes? Was she hurting? Were there bruises she hadn't shown to anyone? All through dinner, she'd been silent. Geenie had known she shouldn't mention the tree incident, no matter how much she longed to blurt out the details to Ellen, especially the bit about Kitty taking off her stockings and climbing into the branches. So she'd been quiet too, occasionally scratching at the flaking paint on her back until her mother had snapped, 'Have you caught fleas from that dog?'

She moved up the bed, flicked on the bedside lamp, and looked into Diana's face. It was glowing, despite the crease between her eyebrows; her cheeks were plump and flushed, and saliva glistened on her open bottom lip. Geenie put a hand to Diana's forehead and held it there for a moment. Then, when she'd found the courage, she moved her fingers gently back and forth across Diana's brow. Her own feet were heavy with cold

130

and her legs were beginning to go to sleep, but she kept stroking the other girl's skin.

Suddenly Diana took a big breath and opened her eyes wide. She stared at Geenie for a second, her pupils huge and black. 'I thought you were my mother.'

Geenie said nothing.

'I thought I was at home.' Groaning, Diana turned over in the bed.

The blankets muffled her movement, but Geenie could see Diana's shoulders heaving.

'Do you miss her?' Geenie whispered.

The blankets heaved again.

Standing up, Geenie pulled Diana's sheets back and climbed into bed beside her.

It was awkward at first: Diana's bed wasn't as large as Geenie's, and it was a squash just getting all her limbs onto the mattress. Their knees clashed, and she didn't know where to put her hands. 'I'm cold,' she said, moving closer, trying to burrow into Diana's warm fug.

When Diana opened her arms, Geenie was surprised by how small she was, despite her height; up close like this, the other girl's body seemed wispy, full of angles and protruding bones; even her chin was tiny and hard as she dug her face into Geenie's chest and wept. But eventually the two of them closed their eyes and found sleep.

SEVENTEEN

There was the snap of cotton being shaken out before she saw anything. The snap of cotton,

131

followed by Geenie's voice: 'You be Clark Gable. I'm being Claudette Colbert.'

Kitty was on her way downstairs to clear away the breakfast things, having finished sweeping the landing, when she heard the sound, and noticed Mrs Steinberg's bedroom door was ajar.

'Draw a moustache on me, then.' Diana's voice came from Geenie's bedroom, and Kitty stopped, her soft broom in her hand, and glanced through the crack from where the snapping sound had come.

The blood seemed to thicken and slow in her veins as she stood in the gloom of the landing, holding her broom and watching Mr Crane dressing.

He was standing with his back to her, looking at himself in the mirror, his green shirt in his hand. He was naked to the waist. His shoulders were wider than they appeared when clothed, his waist slim, his spine straight, and at the very bottom of his back there was what looked like a large dimple, an indent of pale flesh just above where his braces hung down to his thighs. A soft place.

As he moved to slip an arm into a sleeve, the muscle on his shoulder jumped and stretched. He swung the shirt across his back, the fabric billowing out, and pushed the other arm in. With several shrugs, he eased himself into the shirt, smoothing it over his chest and belly with one hand, tucking it into his trousers with the other.

The girls laughed together and Kitty gave a start. But a quick glance over her shoulder confirmed that Geenie's door was still closed.

She was about to move away and get on, ready to pretend she hadn't been peeking; ready to pretend she hadn't seen Mr Crane's naked back and shoulders, hadn't felt any tingle along her neck and down her spine; ready to pretend she didn't now know that he chose not to wear a vest beneath his shirt. It was just a matter of getting her legs going and her heartbeat back to normal. But then he began the business of buttoning, and she knew she couldn't move. She would have to stay and watch.

He started at the bottom and worked his way up towards his throat, teasing each button into its hole with a little twist of his fingers whilst staring at his own hands in the mirror.

'*I* have to tell *you* what to do!' shrieked Diana. 'I'm Clark Gable!'

Kitty realised she was holding her breath.

Tugging his cuffs into place, he turned to the side, frowned at himself, then cupped his hands and wiped them over his hair, pressing it into shape. When he was satisfied, he pulled his braces up.

His eyes shifted then, and Kitty was sure he'd noticed her reflection in the mirror—the shadow of a girl in an apron, her hair unwashed since Friday, spying on him. She found, though, that she could not avert her gaze, and for a second it seemed as though they were staring directly at each other in the mirror. Blood was loud in her ears and a heat forced its way from her stomach to her chest to her head as his eyes remained, fixed and unblinking, seemingly on hers.

That's that then, she thought. It's back to Lou's.

But he looked towards the window, and a broad smile crept across his face as he reached across for something out of Kitty's view.

133

At last she managed to move. She walked downstairs as quickly and quietly as she could, clutching the soft broom to her chest, a pulse still pumping in her ears and belly.

*   *   *

'What's this, then?'

'It's a French bun.'

'Is it now?' Arthur turned his plate around, watching the cake as if it might make a sudden move. 'Fancy.'

She'd made them yesterday, for Mr Crane's tea, using a recipe from Lou. Arthur had the one that was left over; the icing was a little cracked around the edges, but it didn't matter. Arthur ate everything quickly and neatly and always said, afterwards, 'That was good.'

Kitty sat and picked up her tea.

Arthur took a bite, then went back to reading his Western, glancing towards her just once to nod his approval.

'Did—did Geenie say anything to you, yesterday?'

He seemed to finish reading his sentence before answering. 'What about?'

Kitty swilled her tea round her cup. The back door was open and a warm breeze blew at her ankles. It was going to be another hot day. 'About the willow tree.'

He swallowed the last of the bun, licked his fingers and shook his head. 'What would she say about it?'

'Nothing.' Kitty stood and began to clear the crockery.

'That was good,' said Arthur, still gripping the plate as she lifted it from the table. Their eyes met and she held his gaze until he looked down at his own fingers on the china. When he'd let go, he wiped his moustache with his hand. 'What about the willow, then?'

'Diana got stuck there yesterday morning.'

'Stuck in the tree?'

'She was up quite high.'

'I never heard nothing.'

That's because you'd disappeared, thought Kitty, crashing the crocks into the sink. You'd probably dozed off over one of your silly books.

'What happened?'

She wasn't sure, now, why she'd begun to tell Arthur this story. She kept thinking of Mr Crane's fingers on his shirt buttons, how he'd taken such care over each one, how he'd watched himself whilst he dressed. The flick of his muscle as the cotton sailed behind him.

She turned the hot tap. There was a belch and a spurt of water flew out.

'What happened, Kitty?'

'Diana was climbing the tree and she couldn't get down.' She looked out of the window towards the studio. The door was closed, but the windows were flung wide open and the curtains were shuddering back and forth.

'I had to go and get her.'

'Why didn't you ask me?'

Submerging her hands in the warm water, she began to scrub at the teacups. 'Because you weren't here.'

There was a pause. 'Can't think where I was.'

'Doesn't matter now.' She'd never understand

135

why Mrs Steinberg didn't buy a new, matching set of good white crockery. All her cups were different shapes and colours.

'Just a minute, though. You went up that tree?'

She turned to face him, her fingers dripping. 'Yes. I climbed the tree and I got the girl down.'

That hadn't been quite what had happened, but how could she explain to Arthur how Diana had slipped before her, springing to the ground like a damn monkey?

His moustache was twitching, as if he were holding in a laugh. 'You climbed the willow tree?'

'Yes. I said, didn't I?' With a damp hand, she wiped the hair away from her forehead.

His eyes were narrowed but bright. She noticed they had specks of yellow in them. As he continued to look at her, his moustache twisted in an odd shape, the yellow in his eyes sparking, she found herself shifting on the spot.

'Well!' he said. 'Well I never!' He let out a sudden laugh, so loud that Kitty jumped. It was more of a shout—or a kind of bark—than a laugh: gruff and low, as if it escaped him without his knowledge.

She tried not to smile.

'However did you manage it?'

'I don't know, I . . .'

'I don't think I could do it,' said Arthur, slapping the table. 'Get up that tree. There's not much to hold on to, is there? Spindly as hell.'

Kitty shook her head and laughed. 'It wasn't easy.'

'I bet it wasn't!'

'I didn't want to look down.'

'I'm certain of it!'

136

'I had to take my shoes and stockings off,' she said. 'I felt five years old again.'

At this, Arthur ducked his head and was silent. Kitty covered her mouth with a hand.

'Well,' he said, quietly. 'To think of it. Kitty up a tree. I wish to heaven I'd seen it.' When he pushed back his chair, she saw his cheeks had coloured. He didn't look at her as he walked to the door and began putting on his boots.

She turned to the sink, rinsed out the last cup and placed it on the drainer. When she looked towards the door again, he was still standing there, and he was staring straight at her. Her eyes remained steady, and a moment of silence passed before he said, 'What I mentioned the other night—'

'Yes?'

'About dancing—'

'Yes?'

'Well. I just want you to know. If you think you'd like to, the offer still stands.' His forehead was shining with perspiration.

She found herself smiling. 'All right, then.'

He let out a breath. 'Friday?'

She nodded, once, quickly.

Beaming, Arthur walked through the door and out into the sunshine. Kitty could hear him whistling all the way back to his shed.

EIGHTEEN

It was going to be a perfect evening. She'd asked
Kitty for coq au vin, and the results hadn't been
bad—the bird was a little stringy, and why did
British mushrooms taste of nothing?—overall
though, it was much more satisfactory than the
usual boiled beef or rabbit pie, and had
complemented the Beaujolais well. She'd changed,
too, into her long cream silk with the drape
sleeves; she didn't usually bother dressing for
dinner, unless they had guests (and who came now
they lived in the wilderness? Even Laura's visits
were becoming rare), but after she'd blurted out
the thing about the baby, she felt she should make
an effort for Crane.

As if to avoid any mention of the subject over
dinner, he'd lectured them on the three million
unemployed, telling the girls how lucky they were
to be living here, rather than in one of the
'distressed areas' of the country, where the miners
couldn't feed their families. Diana had pointed out
that it wouldn't matter if *she* lived in a distressed
area; she'd still have a gentleman poet and a
ballerina for parents, which Ellen had thought a
fair assessment, but Crane had put down his knife
and fork very definitely and said, 'Never, ever take
your wealth for granted,' which had put Diana into
a sulk.

Now the girls were in bed, and Ellen and Crane
had retired to the sofa with a new bottle, she
hoped to get him off politics. It wasn't that she
found it boring, precisely; she was always willing to

learn. It was just that she'd heard it all before: the misery of the unemployed, the suppression of the masses, how only revolution could bring true equality and an end to the class system that was tearing the country apart. And she agreed that it would be better if things were a bit more evenly spread, but wouldn't it be more pleasant—and perhaps, in the end, of greater importance—to discuss art and literature, as she had with James? Of course, when she'd made this point, Crane had insisted that art and literature should be the spouse, that's how he'd put it, the *spouse* of politics: the two could not be separated. Though she'd said nothing at the time, Ellen didn't quite see it. Wasn't the joy of great art the offer of escape, the opportunity to submerge oneself in personal, particular passions? Politics seemed slightly grubby, not much to do with her, and not nearly as much fun. And Crane always became so deadly serious whenever he started on about Marx and how *the world's future lay in the hands of the workers*.

'You really should join the party, Ellen, if you're—ah—serious about things, you know.'

He rolled his empty wine glass between his palms and looked at her squarely. Not a good opening. It wasn't the first time he'd said this, and she'd never liked being told what she *should* do. She thought perhaps this stemmed from her father, who'd done nothing he should, apart from make money. He'd spent most of his time travelling around Europe with his mistress, a woman named Valentina. Ellen had caught sight of her once over the glove display in McCreary's. Her nanny had nodded, and she'd known that the woman with the dark eyebrows and the chiselled nose was her father's lover.

'But I'm not a worker or an intellectual, darling. They wouldn't have me.' She held out the bottle to him, but he shook his head and placed his glass on the floor.

'I thought you were going to be a housewife.'

After topping up her own glass, she sat on the sofa beside him and swung one leg over the other, flashing her bare feet. Her toenail polish needed re-applying, she noted, but her ankle was as slim as ever.

'What of it?'

'That's work, isn't it?' He clasped one of her gold-beaded cushions before him, as if holding on to a lectern. 'You could tell them you have full-time employment, looking after two children and the cottage.'

'Oh, Crane,' she sighed. 'You really are a unique man.'

He smiled. 'So you'll do it, then?'

Laughing, she snatched the cushion from his hands and swiped him over the head, splashing his trousers with Beaujolais. 'If I do, what will you do for me?'

He wiped himself down, gave a theatrical sigh, and looked towards the ceiling. 'Well. Let me see. We could see what I could—ah—come up with . . .'

She grabbed his hand and pulled him to the door.

*　　　*　　　*

She had a moment to prepare before he came upstairs: Crane always insisted on going outside to

140

'feel the air' before coming to bed. He was absolutely mad on fresh air. All the men she'd ever slept with were, even though they declared themselves intellectuals. She suddenly wondered what it would be like to sleep with a man who hated the outdoors. Or a man for whom the outdoors was a place of work, rather than worship.

Selecting a red silk negligee, she reflected that the sex had always been pretty good, just as she'd known it would be from the day they'd first met. James had invited Crane to the house in Paris. Dora was sick, she remembered, and Ellen had been standing in the kitchen, flicking the broom about, when Crane had taken over. Holding her elbow, he'd unpeeled her fingers from the broom handle and begun. It was like he was dancing with the broom, his long legs carrying him swiftly to each corner of the kitchen, his arms twirling the bristles round to reach the furthest, most dust-filled, locations. Bringing the dirt together in a hairy mound in the centre of the tiled floor, he'd negotiated the pile of wine bottles stacked by the stove without knocking a single one over. As he'd pushed the broom past her lace-up shoes, she wished she'd gone barefoot, so a bristle might have touched her toes.

When he'd finished, he turned to her, his cheeks slightly pink from the effort, his dark eyes shining. She'd noticed the squint, of course. Not an athlete, she'd thought, not like James; but there was something angular about him that she liked. He was straight-backed and long-limbed, but he did not look too strong for her.

Then he'd shown her how to sweep the dust onto opened sheets of newsprint, gathering each corner together and depositing the whole package in the waste basket without spilling anything. It was like a magician's trick, this disappearance of dirt in newspaper; she'd watched him as if he were producing a dove from his sleeve or a flower from behind her ear. She hadn't dared ask where he'd learned such a thing.

Back in London only a couple of weeks later (was it actually on the day James had told her he'd need the operation?—she shuddered to think), she'd met Crane in that pub in Fitzrovia. Was it the Wheatsheaf? Or the Bricklayer's Arms? He'd taken her to both, eventually, but before Crane she'd never been in a pub. Plenty of cafés and French bars, of course, but never an English pub like this, with men in caps, for God's sake, and stained raincoats, and a woman serving who had at least three teeth missing and hair the colour of Ellen's brightest Moroccan rug. The stools were incredibly small, the floor covered in cigarette stubs and spilled beer, but it was warm in there; everyone was very close together; it seemed there was hardly light or air: just smoke, and beer, and men. Someone was playing 'Hands Across the Sea' on the concertina. She'd loved it immediately.

He hadn't said much at all that time. He'd just kept kissing her, his lips tasting bitter-rich, like the beer he'd bought for them both. It was lunchtime and she'd been hungry—she would have suggested Taglioni's, if there'd been time—but she'd forgotten about that, because his hand touched her side, sliding in between her coat and her blouse and finding her waist, and they'd gone to Laura's place in town, a flat with dust an inch thick everywhere. And, she remembered, he'd been so

142

fluent. He'd warmed his hands by the gas fire before he touched her, then undid the clasp of her coat, slipping it from her shoulders; he'd known how to free stockings from suspenders and roll them down without fuss. As he unbuttoned her blouse his fingers trembled and there was a very serious look in his eyes, and even when he was inside her he'd looked at her the whole time; he didn't close his eyes until his moment, when his neck arched and seemed impossibly long, and his throat contracted, just as it did when he was formulating a thought.

On her way home to Woburn Square, watching the glow in her cheeks fading in the glass of the cab window, Ellen had allowed herself to imagine— just for half a minute—how convenient it would be for James to die, suddenly and painlessly, so she would be free again, and blameless.

Now she surveyed the results of the scarlet negligee in the glass, and decided it was far too obvious; she'd do away with clothes altogether and go naked. She'd never had the knack for clothes, anyway, particularly anything frilly or chiffon. James had never minded, saying he preferred her straightforward approach, but she wondered if Crane, for all his Bolshevism, wouldn't rather see her in feathers and furs, like Lillian.

'It's a beautiful night.' Crane came into the room, smiling. 'The moon's beaming.'

Then she knew what she should do. Right now. Jumping out of bed, she cried, 'Outside!'

Crane looked her up and down.

'Let's. Please, let's go outside. Under the moon. We've never—have we?' She pulled her dressing gown around her. 'Come on!'

143

'I—'

'Back to nature, darling, close to the earth, isn't that how the proletariat procreate?'

He smiled. 'Ellen—'

But she was already on the landing, sprinting towards the stairs.

Strange, how they'd never performed outside before. James had been very keen on it, especially in the summers, by the lake at Heathstead Hall. In fact, she'd grown a little tired of grazing her shoulder blades on stony ground and inspecting her elbows for bruises in the morning. But Crane, despite his worship of the outdoors, had never suggested it, and for a while she'd been glad of a mattress beneath her back and a cover on top.

It was past midnight and there was, of course, no one about. Crane was right about the moon: it left a silver stain on the garden and, she was delighted to see, lit up the beautiful sculpture of female buttocks that she'd always loved. That had to be a good omen.

The gravel path crackled beneath her feet as she trotted along, giggling to herself. Kitty's window looked onto the garden, but she was no doubt fast asleep after grappling with that bird. The girl had looked quite worn out when she'd brought the plates through; Crane had advised her to get an early night, at which she'd blushed furiously, as if he'd suggested tucking her in bed himself.

Ellen looked over her shoulder. He was following her, albeit slowly and still in his trousers. 'Come on!' she hissed.

By the stream, beneath one of the willows, would be the best spot. Even though it was a warm night, the soil on the bank was sticky beneath her

144

toes. It was all right for Crane—he still had his shoes and socks on. Unlike James, he wasn't a sandals man, and she was glad of it. She could never stand the sight of men's toes. They always seemed to be gripping something, usually the soles of their damned sandals; there was something simian about it.

'Here?' He looked around.

Leaning back on the gnarled trunk, she untied her dressing gown. There was the sour smell of stream water, and the click-click-click of leaves in the breeze. Here was as good a place as any, although her feet were tingling with cold and Crane's eyebrows seemed to have been raised since she'd made her suggestion in the bedroom.

Ellen closed her eyes and waited.

To her relief, he stepped forward and kissed her. It was a dry, rather precise kiss, and she pulled him closer, trying to soften his lips with hers. When his mouth had warmed, she tugged down his braces and, twisting her arm between their two bodies, began to unbutton him. Her fingers knew exactly where to go, and she could feel the tautness in his stomach as she slid her hand into place.

Immediately his lips went to her neck, but, as she took him in her hand, she found he was still small and soft.

'George?'

He was sucking at her neck as though it were a segment of orange. Trying to squeeze out all the juice.

'George.'

He lifted his head but did not look at her. They were both breathing hard.

She mustn't say anything, she suddenly realised.

145

If she wanted this baby she'd have to pretend it was her fault.

Giving a little shiver, she offered, 'Sorry, darling, it's just I'm feeling a bit cold all of a sudden. Shall we go inside, after all?'

She was about to step away from him, but he said her name, caught her by the shoulders and shoved her against the tree. His eyes were fierce, and when he began kissing her again, his lips and tongue were so forceful that her head was driven back into the trunk and the bark dug into her scalp. He pressed his whole body against hers, and for a moment she panicked, thinking he was going to push the breath right out of her, flatten her into nothing against the willow. But then she reached up and felt the dampness of the night in his hair, and she remembered who they were: Ellen Steinberg and her lover, outside, not caring who knew or who disapproved, and she let herself go with it.

Crane gathered her thighs in his hands and lifted her until she was in the right position. Ellen closed her eyes and told herself to hold on, to hold on and feel nothing but the pressure of her lover's body.

NINETEEN

After some confusion over which button fastened to which strap, Mrs Steinberg had finally got her apron on the right way round. The sight of the woman clad in starched white cotton made Kitty take a step back. She looked strangely like the angel in the painting above the altar of her old Sunday School church in Petersfield: shining, determined, and stiff as a ship's sail.

'What are we starting with, Kitty? I'm terribly excited about this, aren't you?'

Kitty hadn't slept all night. On Sunday she'd asked Lou's advice about what to cook for the first 'lesson' with her mistress, and Lou had been very clear: 'Mutton cutlets. You can't go wrong. It's all in the presentation.' She'd presented Kitty with a set of cutlet frills—little paper collars for the bones—which would make the dish look 'just like it does in the White Hart Hotel'. The meat should be breadcrumbed, deep-fried, and served standing upright around a mound of peas, on top of a layer of piped mashed potato. Last night, every time she'd closed her eyes, Kitty had seen sheep wearing frilly white cuffs.

'Cutlets, Mrs Steinberg.'

It was eleven o'clock and they were standing on opposite sides of the kitchen table, a pile of meat and the basin of breadcrumbs, which Kitty had risen at half past six this morning to make, between them. Kitty had been careful to place them away from the reach of the lantern's greasy tassel.

Mrs Steinberg put her hands on her hips. 'Cutlets?'

'Mutton cutlets, Mrs Steinberg. Mr Gander's boy brought them this morning. Best end of neck.' Kitty gestured towards the package on the table.

Mrs Steinberg peeled back the paper wrapper and peered at the red flesh. With her forefinger, she prodded each piece in the meatiest part. 'Just cutlets?'

'Oh no. There's a special way of serving them,

you see, on a layer of mashed potato . . .'

'Don't take this the wrong way, Kitty dear,' Mrs Steinberg flashed a half smile, 'but don't you think we could attempt something a little more, well, adventurous?'

Kitty felt her lips tighten. She glanced towards the window. Outside, Mr Crane was doing his exercises, swaying his arms back and forth, his elegant hands white in the sun.

'What about something French, for example?'

Kitty made herself look back at her mistress. The woman's cheeks had a greyish tinge, and her eyes were a little bloodshot. But despite appearing tired, she was still constantly moving: touching her hair, tapping her foot, licking her bottom lip, which she did now, as if in a hurry to get somewhere.

'I've got a book,' Kitty ventured, knowing she could always cook the cutlets by herself, without Mrs Steinberg interfering. And if the woman chose the recipe, well, then it would be her responsibility.

She fetched *Silvester's Sensible Cookery* from the shelf by the sink, noticing that he was still striding about outside, his arms waving. Remembering the jump of his muscle as he'd pulled on his shirt, she held the book tightly to her chest.

'Let me see,' Mrs Steinberg snatched the book and thumbed through its pages, muttering under her breath. *'Oyster patties*—why mess with perfection?—*Beef à la Mode*—not more beef— *Kromesques of Veal*—have we any veal?'

Kitty shook her head.

'Omelette Soufflé. Well, that's French, I suppose. And I am very good at scrambled eggs, Kitty; did I ever tell you that? Now, let's see.' Mrs Steinberg tapped her foot and nodded to herself as she read

the recipe through. 'Sounds simple enough. Take six eggs—' She looked up.

'In the larder, Madam.'

'Naturally.' Mrs Steinberg closed the book.

Whilst her mistress was in the larder, Kitty sat at the table and waited. Outside, there was a clunk as the door to the writing studio closed. That meant he wouldn't come out again for a while.

A voice floated through the larder door. 'Where, exactly?'

'Second shelf. On the left.'

'Damn.' Mrs Steinberg came back into the kitchen and circled the table. 'There's only four. Why have we only four eggs, Kitty?'

'I've ordered more for tomorrow morning, Mrs Steinberg.'

Then Kitty heard a stifled sound, something like a chirp, or a giggle. Behind her mistress, she saw Geenie and Diana peering through the doorway, hands over their mouths.

'What was that?' asked Mrs Steinberg, turning.

The girls ran off.

'I—don't know, Madam.'

Mrs Steinberg was tapping her foot and holding her hair away from her face, stretching her forehead in the most peculiar way. 'Right. Well. It looks like it'll have to be cutlets, then.'

Kitty looked at the clock. Half past eleven already, and no sign of Arthur. It would probably be better if he didn't come in for his morning tea today, what with the lesson and the invitation to the dance still hanging in the air. She still wasn't sure why she'd said yes, and had been trying to think of ways to take her answer back. It had been such a relief to hear him ask again, that the 'yes' had just popped out. Now she'd have to face a whole evening with him, and she'd have to try her hardest not to lead, like she had with Frank. Unless she could think of some excuse not to go.

'Where shall we start?'

'First we have to do the potatoes.'

'What do we have to do with them?'

'Peel them, Mrs Steinberg.'

'Right. Yes.'

'I can do it, though.' Kitty began spreading an old copy of the *Herald* on the table. 'The potatoes are in the shed—'

'I'll get them.'

Before she could protest, the woman had disappeared again, leaving Kitty standing, chewing on her forefinger, staring at the newsprint. This was going to take even longer than she'd imagined.

'Look,' said Mrs Steinberg, 'I carried them in on my apron! Isn't that what you do?' She tipped four small potatoes onto the newspaper, scattering the table, and Kitty's shoes, with dirt.

'Yes. That's what you do. Only—'

'What?'

'We might need a few more, eventually, for all of you . . .'

Mrs Steinberg looked at the vegetables. 'Oh. I hadn't thought.' The woman's hands dropped by her sides and she looked so downcast that, for a moment, Kitty considered consoling her. But then her mistress clapped her hands together. 'I know what we need! Music! Let's have some music!' And once more she disappeared.

Whilst the woman was out of the room, Kitty carried the potatoes to the sink and began to scrub them clean, staring through the window at the writing studio as she rubbed at the dirt. He'd opened and propped the door ajar, which was unusual. It must get warm in there, though, in this sunshine. He'd have to take his jacket off, and perhaps roll up his shirt sleeves. His bare wrists would be resting against the desk, rubbing against white paper.

'I thought you might need these.'

Kitty dropped her potato. She hadn't heard Arthur come in.

'I tried to tell her she'd need more but it was too late,' he said, standing close behind her and emptying a basin of potatoes into the sink. Muddy water splashed up her arms. 'Fetched you some peas, too.' There was the smell of aniseed and his breath warmed her ear as he whispered, 'You will come, won't you? On Friday.'

She squeezed a clump of mud between her fingers. 'I—I've got to see about the time off. Wednesdays and Sundays are my usual evenings.'

'Ask her today, then. Now's a good time.'

'Oh! Arthur! Duke Ellington or Glen Gray?' Mrs Steinberg was leaning on the doorframe.

'Duke Ellington, definitely, Mrs Steinberg.'

There were those yellow sparks in his eyes again, and he stroked at his moustache.

'I knew you'd be a fan of the Duke, Arthur, I just knew it!'

Arthur rolled his sweet around his mouth and grinned.

'Didn't you think so, Kitty? That Arthur would be a Duke man?'

Kitty said nothing.

'Best get on,' said Arthur, opening the back door.

'Don't you want your tea?' Kitty wiped her hair away from her brow.

Mrs Steinberg looked from Arthur to Kitty and back again.

'Later, maybe.'

'Music!' said Mrs Steinberg, heading back to the living room.

Kitty turned to the sink and watched Arthur walk to his shed.

'Don't you love this one, Kitty?' Mrs Steinberg was clicking her fingers in time with the beat. She twirled, her apron drawing a tight circle in the air. 'Divine. Hot and sweet.'

Kitty began to peel the potatoes while her mistress spun around the kitchen. 'Ah do-wap, do-wap, do-wap, do-wap—dah!' Her body, usually twitching and pulling this way and that, seemed loosened. There was no pattern to her movements—you couldn't say she'd mastered any particular dance—but Kitty couldn't stop watching her. The woman seemed changed by the music into a dipping, gliding thing.

'Hot and *sweet*.'

Kitty piled the potatoes into the pan and went to the sink to cover them with water, narrowly avoiding a collision with Mrs Steinberg.

'I danced on the tabletops in the Dôme, you know, Kitty. That's in Paris. Quite regularly. My first husband had to pull me to the floor to stop me.' She spun around, flinging her arms above her head and letting out a long hoot like an owl.

Kitty put the pan on the stove and started to smile.

'How can you stand there when there's music, Kitty? Dance with me.'

152

'I couldn't—'

'Come on.' Mrs Steinberg grabbed Kitty's wrists and pulled her away from the stove.

'The potatoes—'

Although she was smiling, the woman had a determined look on her face, and Kitty thought again of the angel in the church, its wings stretching and carrying it into the sky, and she started to move. She was suddenly sharply aware of her own body, of how the limbs joined together and creaked into life. If she wanted it to, would her left leg kick as high as Mrs Steinberg's? Would her bottom sway back and forth in that way?

'From the hips, Kitty dear, from the hips.' Mrs Steinberg grasped Kitty's waist and swung her from side to side. Laughing, Kitty allowed herself to move with her mistress. Mrs Steinberg pressed her thighs into the backs of Kitty's own and leaned back, taking Kitty with her.

'Now forward.'

With the other woman's arm around her waist, Kitty bent forward.

'Now hop.' They hopped on the spot. 'Now back. Now hop. You've got it!'

'Haven't you made lunch yet?' Geenie was standing in the doorway, her arms folded. 'It's almost twelve o'clock. Diana and I are hungry.'

The two women were panting; Kitty could feel Mrs Steinberg's chest rising and falling at her own back. Once her mistress had let her go, Kitty wiped her moist neck with her hankie, turned, and immediately fired the stove so she wouldn't have to look at Geenie while she was so flushed. Her fingers slipped on the pan, causing it to crash onto the burner.

153

Mrs Steinberg laughed. 'Oh, Regina, you look so cross. How can you be cross when there's such music, darling?' She spun over to her daughter. The woman's face, Kitty noticed, was shining with perspiration, and her nose looked bigger than ever.

Geenie folded her arms across her chest. 'Where's lunch?'

'Honestly, darling, sometimes you're so conventional. Will the world end if we don't sit down for lunch at half past twelve on the dot?'

The record had finished, but Mrs Steinberg was still dancing, swaying back and forth before her daughter, bobbing at the knee and reaching up into the air.

'The potatoes aren't even boiling, are they?' Geenie tapped her foot.

Her mother stopped dancing. 'And what do you know about potatoes?'

The girl looked directly at Kitty. 'I watch Kitty. When you're not here. She lets me watch.'

Mrs Steinberg took Geenie by the shoulders. 'You can watch me now, then. You can watch your mother do it.' Her high voice was dangerously even and clear. Marching the girl to the stove, she pushed Kitty aside. 'I'll show you how to get them boiling.' With a flick of her wrist, she turned the gas as high as it would go. The flame sprung around the pan.

'What are we having with it?'

'Cutlets.'

Geenie pulled a face.

Kitty tried to make herself as invisible as possible by sliding past mother and daughter, sitting at the table and beginning to shell the peas.

'Look, Geenie, I'm doing it. Your mother's

154

doing it.' Mrs Steinberg reached across Kitty, picked up a cutlet by the bone, and held it in front of her daughter's face. A drip of moisture fell through the air, landing on Geenie's bare toe.

'Ugh.'

'Don't be so silly. It's just meat. You want it juicy. Tell her, Kitty. You want meat juicy. It's got no flavour, no *life*, in it otherwise.'

'If it's dead, how can it have life?'

Eyes flashing, Mrs Steinberg held the meat out to her daughter. 'Why don't you touch it and see?'

Geenie stepped back.

Kitty had never liked touching meat herself, but she'd become used to it. Pulling the skin from anything was still a job she feared. She hated the way white fat would stick to the pink flesh beneath, trails of membrane stretching between the two parts of the animal like lengths of spittle.

'Go on. Touch it.'

With her eyes half closed, the girl held out her fingers.

'You'll have to come closer than that.'

But Geenie seemed to have frozen in position, her mouth skewed in disgust. Her bottom lip began to tremble.

Kitty stood up. 'I should get on—'

Mrs Steinberg was still staring at her daughter. 'Can't you even touch it?'

Kitty raised her voice. 'I should really get on with those now, Mrs Steinberg.'

The woman let out a long breath. Then she dropped the meat back onto the paper. 'You'll have to be more daring than that, Regina, if you're going to get on in life. If there's one thing I've learned, it's how to take a risk.' She turned on her heel and faced Kitty. 'We'll have lunch at half past one today.'

'Yes, Mrs Steinberg.'

'Our lesson has been ruined by my daughter, I'm afraid. We'll have to do it another time.' She unbuttoned her apron and hung it on the door.

'Mrs Steinberg?'

'Yes?'

Kitty hesitated. Her mistress's nose was inflamed, her mouth pulled tight, and Geenie was still standing by the stove, staring at the floor. But if she said it now, she might get the answer that would give her an excuse. 'Could I have my evening off on Friday this week?'

'Friday?' The woman sighed. 'I really need your help on Friday, dear. Mr Crane's sister is coming for dinner and I can't cope by myself.'

Kitty nodded.

'I hope it wasn't anything important?'

Kitty forced the last pea from its pod. 'Oh no. Nothing important.'

'Good. That's settled then.' Mrs Steinberg swept from the room with Geenie following close behind, her blonde head still drooping.

TWENTY

It was the middle of the afternoon and the girls were bored. Geenie lay on the grass in the sun and Diana sat behind her in the shade of a willow. Bees droned in the air around them. Diana didn't flinch, but, no matter how hard she tried to remain calm, Geenie had to squeal when a bee seemed close

156

enough to enter her ear. She was sure she could feel its prickly woolliness against her lobe.

Diana let out a loud tut. 'It won't hurt you unless you startle it.'

'Why not?'

'I don't know. It's what my father says.'

'Does he know about bees?'

'He's very knowledgeable on flora and fauna, as it happens.'

Geenie was silent. She wasn't entirely sure what *flora and fauna* meant. Another bee whirred past, and she flicked her fingers close to her ear again. A hot, rotten smell wafted over from Arthur's compost heap, and, in the distance, there was the regular thud of typewriter keys. Geenie knew this sound wasn't coming from George's writing studio. This sound was being made by her mother, who was typing in the library, as she did every afternoon until she went for her nap. Lately, Geenie had noticed that the door to George's writing studio remained closed during her mother's nap, and the only afternoon sounds that came from upstairs were Ellen's snores.

Both girls were wearing white cotton camisoles. After lunch they'd decided to dress up as Pierrot clowns, but, finding no pompoms, neck ruffs or pantaloons in Geenie's dressing-up pile, they'd had to settle for Ellen's old camisoles and lots of make-up. Diana had inherited some theatrical face paint from her Aunt Laura, who'd once been on the stage, and Geenie's face felt stiff beneath several layers of white pan-stick. She'd drawn a tear-drop on Diana's cheek, close to her eye—which had got smudged and now looked like a squashed currant—and a downward mouth around her own

157

lips, which didn't look as tragic as she'd first imagined, since it had turned out lopsided.

The thump of the typewriter stopped and Geenie sat up. 'Do you want to know what my mother is writing?'

It took Diana a few moments to respond. '*Is your mother writing?*'

'She's typing.'

'Yes. But that's different.'

Geenie decided that Diana's squashed currant now looked more like a flattened fly. 'Do you want to know or not?'

Diana sighed. 'All right.'

'She's typing Jimmy's letters.' Geenie left what she felt was a dramatic pause. 'For a book.'

Diana gave Geenie a sideways look. 'What evidence do you have?'

'I've seen it. The front page says: *Collected Letters of James Holt, edited by Ellen Steinberg.*'

'Why would anyone want to read that?'

Geenie leaned close to Diana so her blonde hair brushed the other girl's camisole. 'Because Jimmy was very clever, and people like reading about clever men.'

Diana rolled her black-rimmed eyes.

'And,' Geenie continued, 'and, there are probably lots of romantic letters in there. Love letters. You know. *My darling I cannot live without you, I am dying of this amorous affliction . . .*'

Diana began to smile. 'Shall we go and look, then?'

*   *   *

They crossed the crisp grass, padded through the

158

kitchen, where Kitty was huffing over the washing-up, and stood outside the library. Geenie listened at the door, pulling Diana in so close behind that she could smell the waxy scent of her make-up. Geenie was sure her mother would be upstairs by now, taking a nap. But, to be certain, she pressed her eye to the keyhole. It was dark in the library, even today, and she had to squint, but she could make out the outline of the empty chair by the desk, which was enough to convince her to turn the door handle.

The door creaked, just like it did in stories where children went places they shouldn't. Geenie put a finger to her lips and hunched herself up on tiptoes. Diana clutched the top of her friend's arm. Their camisoles rustled together as they crept across the rug.

'Where are the letters?' hissed Diana.

'Ssh!'

It was a tiny room, not a quarter of the size of Jimmy's library in their London house. There was no shining globe, no coloured maps on the walls. There were just shelves of books along every wall, the desk and chair, and, in the corner, the stuffed fox in a pair of spectacles and a hunting outfit which had been left in the cottage by the previous owners. Ellen had wanted to burn the fox on the fire, but George had said they should keep it, so it had ended up here, dust covering its red jacket, the bugle in its paw tarnished and bent.

Geenie stopped. Diana froze behind her. 'What?'

'I thought I heard something.' Geenie narrowed her eyes and looked about, but nothing was stirring in the hot afternoon. As her heart slowed, she pictured the scene of her mother bursting in, discovering the two sleuthing girls. She would swoop down on them, label them snoops, send them to their rooms. Then, later, she would feel sorry, call her daughter into the sitting room, sit her on her lap and read aloud from *The Last Days of Pompeii*, and Geenie would imagine the grey cloud hanging over the Romans' heads like a terrible speech bubble.

'That's horrible.' Diana was looking at the stuffed fox.

'It was here when we moved in. Your father wanted to keep it. He said it would remind us that someone lived here before.'

'Shall we take his glasses off? He'd be better without his glasses.'

'We're supposed to be reading the letters.'

Leaving Diana squinting at the fox, Geenie opened the cardboard folder marked 'personal' on the desk and took a letter from the top of the pile. The paper was thin and soft, the writing long and slanting. *Herbert*, she read. *Eliot's latest is, as you say, a masterpiece. What a pity he is such a dullard.* She let the letter fall on the desk and reached for another. *Emily, Come as soon as you can.* More interesting. *We are having a party on the fifteenth, and everyone will be here, waiting for you to perform . . .*

'Do you think they're in love?' With the fox's glasses balanced on the end of her nose, Diana was looking out of the window. Geenie peered over her shoulder. Outside, Arthur was saying something to Kitty. She was studying the ground, and he was looking at her hair. They didn't look to Geenie like two people in love. There wasn't any shine about

160

them. Kitty's cheeks *were* flushed, but in a blotchy way, like a rash, rather than a glow.

'Why?'

'Housemaids are always falling in love with gardeners and errand boys and whatnot, aren't they? My mother says they're all flighty, and you have to watch them.' Diana sat on the rug, pulled the glasses from her nose, and wiped her face, leaving a black streak across her cheek. 'And it's so hot.' She flopped on her back and stretched out her bare legs. 'Things like that always happen when it's hot.'

Geenie fished out another letter. After scanning the first few sentences, she began to read aloud. 'Here's a good bit. *How can I apologise enough for the other night, my darling bird? Sometimes Rachel's talk does make me light-headed—as you said—but she doesn't have the hold on me you imagine, my darling, please believe that—*'

'Who's Rachel?'

'She was Jimmy's fiancée before my mother came along. Jimmy married her, but he always loved my mother.'

'Why did he marry Rachel, then?'

'It was a formality.' This was the word Ellen had used when Geenie asked if it was true that Jimmy had married Rachel.

'What else does it say?'

Geenie skipped the next few lines, then resumed. '*When the operation is over and done, we'll make a new start—Paris, Geneva, Rome—wherever you want . . .*' She stopped.

Diana was looking out of the window again. 'Actually,' she said, 'I don't think they are in love, you know.'

161

Geenie sat at the desk and rested her cheek on the typewriter keys. The metal was cool against her skin. She closed her eyes and remembered it: how she'd come home from school and Dora had said, *Don't go up there*, and there were voices in the drawing-room, and she'd heard her mother's low wail. She'd started to shake, and had the sudden urge to go to the lavatory. Then, sitting on the icy seat, shivering, she'd waited for the sound of her mother's voice; and when it didn't come, she'd knelt outside the closed drawing-room door, and the doctor had appeared, saying, 'Little girls who listen at doors will hear things they don't like.' She'd never understood why *he* was the one who'd looked angry. For days after, Ellen had said that Jimmy was still in the hospital but was too ill for visitors, but Geenie knew he was dead; her mother's hands trembled and she hadn't changed from her blue knitted suit since that afternoon. Then Geenie caught pneumonia and everything was hot and still for a while, and there was only her headache, which seemed to thud in every part of her body, and Dora bringing up bowls of tapioca each evening. When she was better her mother said, 'We've got to be brave and get right away from here, it will be better that way, now Jimmy's gone.'

'Are you all right?'

Geenie lifted her head from the keys.

'Shall we look at some more letters?' Diana moved from the window and flicked through the pile. 'They were just starting to get interesting.'

Brushing the other girl's hand to one side, Geenie stuffed the papers back into the cardboard folder. 'No,' she said. 'I don't want to read any more.'

TWENTY-ONE

Ellen drove into Petersfield carefully. It was early morning, not past nine o'clock, and for most of the way she was stuck behind a cart spilling straw and mud over the road, for which she was glad. It gave her a chance to think, and she'd never enjoyed driving fast. James had thrown the Renault she'd bought him around like a chariot, thinking only of speed, of getting there in time for aperitifs, while she'd hung on to her seat, laughing nervously, her heartbeat shrill in her ears.

Crane had suggested the picnic, saying they should take Kitty and Arthur with them to the beach at Wittering. A summer treat for the whole family. He seemed to be referring to the staff more and more as *family* lately, but Ellen didn't much mind; at least it meant he was seeing her and Geenie as family, too, despite their not being married and there being no progress on the divorce from Lillian. But it was Ellen, of course, who had to oversee the whole outing, get Kitty going on the right foods (the girl had looked so crestfallen when Ellen had said no to Scotch eggs that she'd had to change her mind), and order suitable cold meat from Mr Gander; she'd even considered having some foie gras sent from Fortnum's, but had decided against it because of the expense.

Thinking about it now, this afternoon's outing would be the perfect time to make her announcement to the girls about her hopes for another child; if Kitty and Arthur heard it, all the better: everyone would know, then, of her seriousness about becoming domesticated. And it was absolutely right to have her hair styled before the event. No matter how it was set—pin curls, bias waves, brush curls—her hair always seemed to go its own way, but the new place in town looked surprisingly good—marble surfaces, a very clean front window, a list written in gold lettering which advertised MacDonald and Vapour Permanent Waving and promised *Life Experienced Operators Only*, whatever that meant. It was called Marie-Christine in the way of all such places in England; people seemed to think that some girl's name or other would stamp the place with a certain glamour.

She parked the Lanchester near the market place and walked along the High Street, passing a young man in chalk-stripe flannels and shiny shoes who smiled at her so widely that she almost stopped to ask his name. After he'd passed, she realised that she'd forgotten to wear a hat again. It was better just to put one on, although it was far too hot and she hated the sensation of the thing pressing down on her head, making her scalp sweat. Otherwise, the shop girls just didn't take you seriously, and you had no chance to convince them of your actual calibre after that first impression was gone.

The hairdressing salon was down a narrow cobbled lane next to a butcher's shop where whole rabbits and headless deer hung outside, giving the street a slightly ripe aroma which, in this rising heat, reminded her of Naples. She'd never quite become used to the particular scent of this town—it was unlike any other she'd experienced in

Europe. In the mornings, it smelled a bit like glue, but also, powerfully, of scorched clothes. Crane had told her it was the rubber factory. She found it vaguely unsettling: it was an intimate smell, a domestic sort of smell, that didn't seem right out of doors.

She pushed open the glass door of the salon. The floor was green tiles, the walls washed in pale pink, and it was already steamy inside. The girl sitting at the back of the shop was painting her nails; she nodded at Ellen and asked her to sit in a chair next to the window and wait for Robin, who would be out in a minute.

Ellen was surprised when a man of about twenty-five said good morning to her; she'd assumed Robin would be a young girl who would duck her head, laugh at all the wrong moments, and probably fix Ellen's hair into some tight and rather matronly shape which she'd have to comb out at home. The man was tall and wore a tunic that came high up his throat, like a dentist's. His own hair was slick and blond, and he wore it long at the front. His nose tapered to a blunt point, as if it had been chopped off at the end, and his cheeks were spattered with tiny scars which must have been caused by acne, but which now gave his face a weathered, worldly-wise look.

Touching the hand of the girl who was painting her nails, he twisted round to survey the appointment book. 'Mrs Steinberg?' he said, glancing across to where Ellen was sitting. The girl nodded.

'Get her washed, then. And don't take too long about it.'

The girl called Ellen to the back of the shop

and the usual business of the water too cold and then too hot began.

Once she was in the chair and the curtains—which were a hideous mustard yellow velveteen—were drawn around her cubicle, Robin pumped her into position. Then he stood behind her, examining her reflection.

'Can you make it shine?' she asked. 'And wave? I'd like it tidy, but not too tidy, if you see what I mean.'

He gathered bunches of her hair in his fists. 'Strong hair,' he said. 'Good condition. Never needs much.' His voice was hushed, important.

She'd never thought she had strong hair, but now he'd said it, it made perfect sense. 'That's probably why it'll never do a single thing it should,' she said.

'Is Madam from America, by any chance?'

'New York. But I haven't lived there for many years.'

'How glamorous! May I suggest a Hollywood wave? With some sculpture curls?'

What was his accent? He didn't sound like a local. More like one of those London actors who James had occasionally invited round for drinks. Slightly nasal, but with a lot of air in the voice.

'I don't want anything permanent.'

'Quite. A soft Hollywood wave will suit Madam very well. Such an elegant neck should be framed.'

She beamed at this, but he didn't return her smile. Instead, he reached for the glinting rack of scissors on the shelf below the mirror, and his hands began to fly with the blades, darting in and out, slicing through the air. Fronds of brown went this way and that as he cut Ellen into shape. As his

166

fingers worked, her face seemed to come into focus. A head-on view of herself was always the most flattering: seen from this angle, her nose looked almost a normal size.

He'd nearly finished cutting by the time he spoke again. 'Going somewhere special today, Madam?'

His hands were so quick and light.

'Just a picnic. Myself and my—husband. And our daughters.'

'Really, Madam? You don't look old enough, if I may say so.'

She laughed at this, but he was silent, easing his fingertips around the top of her scalp to tilt her head to one side.

'Your husband must be very proud.'

She caught his eye in the mirror. 'I'll let you into a secret, Robin.'

He'd begun working on the waves, dousing her head in setting lotion and easing ridges of hair around steel curlers.

'What's that, Madam?'

'He isn't my husband.'

A smile grew on Robin's lips. 'Shall we curl it here, so it's soft on the cheek?'

'Oh yes,' she said. 'Let's.'

*　　　*　　　*

After half an hour under the drier, Robin reappeared, whisked Ellen's chair round, and held a hand mirror to her face so she could inspect the back of her head. 'Better,' he said.

Her hair was indeed a sculpture of waves and light. Robin turned her this way and that, taking her in from all angles. As he swung the chair around, she noticed that his groin was level with her shoulder. When she looked in the mirror, her cheeks were flushed and her eyes were bright, and he was smiling at her, his tough cheeks wrinkling.

'Delicious,' she said. 'Absolutely delicious.'

'Would Madam like anything else?' He fingered the hair around her ears, allowing his thumb to touch her lobe for a second. 'We offer all sorts of services to help a lady relax. Facials, mud wraps, personal massage. It's very cool,' he added, 'in the back room.'

She could, of course, pretend not to know what he was suggesting; or she could pretend to be shocked, storm out of the place without paying and then collapse with laughter outside. But what would be the point, apart from saving herself a few shillings? She and James had gone to a brothel together in Paris once, and she'd watched as a tiny blonde rode him with an expression of utter boredom on her sour face. For James's sake, she'd allowed another girl, much larger, with dimpled cheeks and the shiniest teeth, to suck her own breasts while she looked on. Throughout, she'd had the sense of being somewhere else entirely, and had wanted to brush the plump girl from her chest, like an irritating child from her lap.

But there had been no men on offer there. No young men with tough cheeks, airy vowels, and smiles like satisfied iguanas.

'Maybe some other time,' she said, liking the way her voice suddenly sounded very New York.

'As Madam wishes.'

There was a pause.

'And might I suggest a longer visit—perhaps

168

even a permanent wave—next time?'

'What a good idea,' she said, admiring her own head of perfect curls in the mirror.

*   *   *

Something was happening in the town when she drove back along the High Street. People were standing in shop doorways and along the edge of the pavement, looking towards the market square. Up ahead, a truck was swinging across the road and there was an awful racket, like children screaming in a playground. Ellen stopped the car and got out. The truck was coming towards her, swerving, its engine crunching as the driver changed gears. The screaming noise became louder. Then she saw something beneath the vehicle, being dragged along the road. Whatever it was was bellowing and kicking. At first she thought it must be a horse: there was brown hair, and hooves; but as the lorry came nearer, she saw the fleshy open mouth, the flared nostrils and the wet, black eyes. It was a cow, caught somehow beneath the wheels of the truck and being hauled along the road, its spindly legs kicking frantically, its hide scraping the asphalt. It must have cut loose at the cattle market, she thought, only to meet the wheels of this truck. Everyone in the street was standing perfectly still, watching the scene with wide eyes, and the driver himself seemed intent only on getting away. She could see his red face behind the windscreen. His lips clenched as he scraped the gears again. There was a hot smell of cow and rubber in the street.

'Stop!' she yelled. 'You've got to stop!' Her arms

were up and waving, and she was stepping towards the truck. 'For God's sake! Stop!'

But he didn't stop. A hot blast of air hit her face as he drove past, finally getting the engine into gear. By now, the beast had stopped moaning. As the truck reached the end of the High Street, it spat the dead cow out behind, and roared away.

She ran towards the crumpled body of the thing. 'Bastard!' she cried. 'He must have seen it!'

All around her, a crowd of people were gathering in silence, staring at the mangled cow. Its hide was ripped down one side and its guts had left a steaming trail along the road. Its legs were impossibly skewed, as if it had skidded and fallen on a frozen lake.

'Bastard!' she shouted again.

A man took off his cap, stepped forward and held her elbow. 'No need for language, love. Are you all right?' He spoke gently.

She looked around her. A woman in a hat like a flattened fruit basket was whispering to a young boy whose hand was jammed in a paper bag of sweets. A girl with a freckled face was picking her nose and studying Ellen's hairstyle. No one seemed to be looking at the dead cow. Instead, everyone was staring at her. The man holding her arm cleared his throat and dropped his eyes to her stocking-less legs. 'Can't be helped, eh?'

'Can't be helped?'

'It's only an old cow. Nothing to fret yourself over.' He smiled.

'Why did no one stop that driver?' She shook the man's hand from her arm and turned to face him. 'Couldn't you see what was happening?'

The man looked at the ground. She noticed that

his hair was thinning and speckled with scurf.

'Why didn't someone stop him?' She realised she was shouting, but she didn't care. 'Someone should have stopped him!'

The woman with the fruit basket hat spoke up. 'Nothing to be done, now, is there, missus? Best to leave it.'

Ellen looked at the dead creature. Flies were already beginning to settle on its bloody head. It seemed to have sunk, somehow, into the road; its legs were limp, its neck lolled, its eye drooped. It was, she saw, utterly broken.

'Someone could have stopped it,' she said, but her voice was quiet now.

She was still trembling as she walked back to the Lanchester. Slumping into the car seat, she covered her face with her hands.

'Bloody Yanks,' she thought she heard someone say.

TWENTY-TWO

It didn't look nearly sturdy enough. 'Borrow it. You have just the figure for it, Kitty,' Mrs Steinberg had said yesterday. '*Petite*. Compact.' The top of the bathing suit was like a vest, but with thinner straps; the bottom had a tiny pleated skirt sewn onto a pair of shorts. It was pale blue cotton with white vertical stripes. Just the thing, her mistress had said, for a beach outing. Kitty stood in front of the small mirror propped up on her chest of drawers and held the garment to her body. Without even trying it, she could see it was far too

171

big for her. When they'd gone to the beach at Bognor as girls, she and Lou had swum wearing just their bloomers and knitted vests, but Miss Weston, their Sunday School teacher, had never got past the paddling stage. Kitty found it hard to imagine a grown woman throwing herself into the sea, in full view of the beach, wearing just a bathing costume. It was all right in the films, where they wore make-up and didn't have to actually get wet, but the reality was a different matter. She reached for her sewing bag and stuffed the bathing suit in with her embroidery. It was really the least of her worries, as she still hadn't quite managed to tell Arthur that she couldn't go dancing tomorrow night.

'All in, all in,' called Mrs Steinberg, waving to Kitty from the driveway. Her hair was, for once, settled in neat, shining waves around her head. In her halter-neck top and wide linen trousers, her shoulders broad and tanned, she actually looked quite handsome. Kitty smoothed her lily-print dress and climbed into the back of the car.

Mr Crane, who was sitting in the driver's seat, turned to face her. 'Glad you could come, Kitty. Glorious sunshine, isn't it? Perfect day for an outing.'

Kitty hadn't thought she'd any choice about coming, but she nodded and smiled, trying not to look at the exposed base of Mr Crane's neck. He'd unbuttoned his collar and was not wearing a tie. Unlike her mistress, he still looked pale, although his nose, Kitty noticed, had caught the sun and was rather pink.

'Here comes trouble,' he said, turning back to face the windscreen.

Geenie and Diana clambered in beside her, forcing her up against the car door. Geenie had on the long white robe she'd worn on Kitty's first day, and had drawn black lines around her eyes. Diana was wearing red shorts and a cream blouse, and was holding a book, but she also had lines drawn around her eyes. Both girls looked up at Kitty and blinked.

'What's in your bag?' Geenie asked.

'Embroidery, Miss.'

'You mean sewing?'

'Yes, Miss. Except you sort of make pictures with it.'

'Are you good at it?'

Kitty gripped the sewing bag tighter. She was about to say 'not bad', but she saw Mr Crane incline his head slightly towards her, as if waiting to hear the answer, and she changed her mind. 'Yes, Miss. I'm quite good. But mostly at dresses and that.'

Geenie kicked her foot into the back of the driver's seat but Mr Crane did not turn around.

'Does that mean you could make *outfits*?'

'Yes, I suppose so, Miss.'

The girl grasped both her knees and sat up very straight. 'Could you make me and Diana Pierrot outfits?'

'I—suppose I might . . .'

'Ellen!' shouted Geenie. 'Kitty's going to make us Pierrot outfits so we can do a proper show!'

'Where's Arthur got to?' Mrs Steinberg was standing outside the car on tiptoe, looking around.

'It isn't quite eleven yet,' said Mr Crane. 'Give the fellow a chance.'

Mrs Steinberg got into the passenger seat and

173

sighed.

'Can we ride donkeys?' asked Geenie.

'If there are donkeys, you can ride them,' said Mr Crane.

'There are always donkeys on English beaches, aren't there, Ellen? It's because the British don't know what to do with themselves by the sea.'

Mr Crane gave a short laugh.

'They're for poor people who can't afford horses,' corrected Diana. 'Aren't they, Daddy?'

Kitty remembered the donkeys at Bognor: stinking, insect-ridden animals that Miss Weston had warned all the children to stay well away from.

Mr Crane looked round then, frowning. 'They're for anyone who wants to ride them, darling.'

'There you are!' Mrs Steinberg trilled. 'Put the deck-chairs in the boot, would you, Arthur?'

Arthur did as he was told, then sat beside Diana. The girls moved along the seat so Kitty was now crushed against the car door, and Geenie was almost in her lap. He was wearing a pair of twill shorts, boots, a soft shirt and tie, and a knitted tank-top. His knees were red and knobbled. When he glanced in her direction, Kitty looked out of her window.

'We're so glad you could come.'

'My pleasure, Mrs Steinberg.'

'Kitty's going to make us Pierrot outfits,' Geenie said to Arthur.

'Is she now?'

'You did promise, didn't you, Kitty?'

She could feel all three of them staring at her. Looking round, she smiled at the girl's hopeful face. 'I did, Miss,' she said.

174

'Blotto! Come on!' The dog jumped onto Mrs Steinberg's lap. 'Let's go, then, Crane! To the beach!'

*   *   *

Mrs Steinberg strode ahead with Blotto; Mr Crane carried the picnic basket; the two girls dawdled behind him. At the back of the line, Arthur was puffing with two deckchairs and the rug, and Kitty followed, cradling her sewing bag.

A heat haze was distorting Wittering beach. A few families were sitting on the sand, legs bared, heads under newspapers or handkerchiefs, their bodies seeming to bend and buckle. A greasy shine had settled on the sea, which swelled lazily forward, then back. It wasn't at all like Bognor, where there was a narrow strip of gravelly sand, striped deckchairs for hire, Punch and Judy, fortune tellers and ice-cream parlours. Here it was all ridged sand and grassy dunes, no entertainment, and not a donkey in sight. And everything wobbling in the heat.

Arthur stopped to wipe his brow and Kitty had no choice but to catch up with him. They walked a little way together in silence, Kitty sneaking sideways glances at Arthur, whose face was now brick red and sweating. His arms were covered in pale ginger freckles that seemed to get bigger the further up they went.

'All set for Friday?' he said, looking straight ahead. 'I hear it's going to be cracking. There's a new band coming.'

'I've been meaning to tell you. I can't get the time off.'

175

He stopped, resting the deckchairs in the sand. 'You can't?'

'She needs me Friday.'

'What for?'

'His sister's coming.'

Arthur looked at his hands. 'Well. That is a pity.'

'Yes,' she said, and began walking again.

He caught her up. 'You do want to come still, though?'

Ahead, Mr Crane had stopped and was looking back. His hand was raised to his eyes, but she could tell he was looking directly at them.

'We'd better catch up.'

'Kitty. Wait.' Arthur gripped her arm tightly and she almost gave a yelp. 'I want you to come with me. Say you'll come.'

She glanced at Mr Crane, who was now sitting on the picnic basket, watching her, his image trembling in the heat.

Arthur pulled her towards him. 'Kitty . . .' His hand was warm, and softer than she'd expected. 'Say you'll come. If not this Friday, then next.'

His eyes were searching hers, his mouth, with its set-back teeth, hung slightly open. 'Come with me,' he said.

Then he put his other hand on her behind, and let it rest there. 'We could dance together all night.'

A hot pressure shot up her back.

'What's the hold-up?' Mr Crane was standing now, shouting, his hands cupped around his mouth. 'Get a move on, Arthur. We'll need that rug.'

'I'll try,' Kitty said, tugging free of Arthur's grip and walking towards the rest of the group.

Geenie pulled the white robe over her head, revealing an orange bathing costume with an anchor motif. With her smudged black eyes, gangly limbs and fuzz of blonde hair, the effect was pretty peculiar. A little like an overgrown doll, Kitty thought. Carrying Blotto in her arms, she ran down the sand. Diana followed, slowly, still wearing her shorts and blouse and holding her book, picking her way carefully through the seaweed and stones which edged the shore.

Mrs Steinberg was also undressing, bending over and using Mr Crane's shoulder as a balance as she stepped from her slacks.

Kitty stood for a moment, watching the woman's long legs appear.

Arthur removed his empty pipe from his mouth and cleared his throat. 'I'll go and fetch the rest of the chairs,' he announced, heading back for the car.

'Sit down, Kitty,' said Mr Crane, offering her a deckchair beside him.

She did as she was told, trying not to stare at Mrs Steinberg's naked thighs. The woman was wearing a very small black-and-white spotted bathing costume with a thin red belt around the waist. In it, her body looked as though it had been flattened: her chest and hips were wide rather than full. But her legs, every inch of them now revealed, were astonishingly long and thin. Kitty thought of the emu she'd seen in a picture book at school.

'Wonderful thing, isn't it, to be near the sea?' Mr Crane stared out at the water. 'So refreshing.'

She wasn't sure if he was expecting an answer. Mrs Steinberg, who was now lying on the rug, having placed a large pair of sunglasses on her face, was certainly ignoring him.

Kitty shifted her feet. Her shoes were full of sand and her toes were cramped and hot, but she could not think of a way to remove them without drawing attention to herself.

After a while, he said, 'Have you been on any walks lately, Kitty?'

'Not lately, Mr Crane.'

'No. Well, you've been busy. Looking after us. That's real work.'

Mrs Steinberg lowered her sunglasses and shot him a look, but said nothing. Above them, gulls were screeching like knives on china. In the distance, Kitty could see Geenie throwing Blotto into the waves, and Diana sitting in the shallows, reading.

'There's a lovely one, you know, if you don't mind hills. Straight out of the cottage, through the farmer's gate on the left, cut across the wheat field. You know there's a little patch of woodland there?'

Kitty nodded, trying to picture it, but failing.

'Well, there's a path right through the trees and up to the top. First-rate views all round.'

She said nothing. She was watching his bare wrists move as he gesticulated.

'Kitty's more interested in dancing, George.' Mrs Steinberg's glasses flashed. 'She's got real *swing*.'

Kitty brushed some imaginary sand from her lap.

Mr Crane turned to her. 'I didn't know you were a dancer, Kitty.'

Not in the way you think, she thought. Not like your ballerina wife.

'She has what you might call natural rhythm.' Mrs Steinberg kicked a leg in the air, scattering sand over the rug. 'Quite the showgirl,' she said, pointing her toes and wiggling her lower leg back and forth.

'Is that so?' He was smiling now, his left eye almost winking at her.

'Oh no, I—'

'Don't be modest, Kitty! Isn't it infuriating, Crane, the modesty of the working classes?' Mrs Steinberg's leg waved frantically. 'Why must they always bow their heads and mutter? Why do they never *admit* to anything? Take responsibility for themselves? In America, a working man's just proud to be alive, and to hell with the rest of them.'

Mr Crane ran a hand across his mouth. Kitty sat very still, staring at her mistress's slim leg as it swung back and forth.

'I don't think it's quite as simple as that, Ellen.'

'What's complicated about it? You either hold your head up, look the world in the eye, or you don't.'

Mr Crane shook his head and gave a short laugh. 'You can't compare the two in any level way. In America,' he said, his voice becoming louder, 'there isn't a long history of oppression. There isn't the same—ah—insidious class system, ingrained into the minds of the masses from birth . . .' He rubbed vigorously at his eye. 'It's not the same at all!'

'But nothing will ever change, will it, if the workers can't hold their heads up. They've got to do that, at least. They've got to say, *I've got swing, and to hell with the rest of them!'*

She hitched herself up on her elbows and grinned widely, but Mr Crane was scowling. 'You're being ridiculous.'

Mrs Steinberg looked at Kitty. 'Why don't we ask Kitty what she thinks? I'm sure she has an opinion.'

Kitty had taken her embroidery out of her sewing bag, and now she sat, clutching the frame, staring at her stitches, thinking of the way her mother went to the pub every night and left her and Lou to put themselves to bed. To hell with the rest of them had certainly been her motto. And, thought Kitty, it was Lou's too.

'Kitty? Am I being ridiculous?' Mrs Steinberg had taken off her sunglasses and was pointing them in Kitty's direction.

'Ellen . . .' Mr Crane pulled on his collar, as if it were suddenly too tight. 'Perhaps we should drop this—'

'I think,' said Kitty, surprised by the force of her own voice, 'it's not just about what class you are.'

They waited for her to continue.

She kept her eyes focused on the waves as she spoke. 'What I mean is, it's personality as well, isn't it? What a person's like.'

Mr Crane nodded. Slowly at first, but then more vigorously. 'Yes,' he said. 'Yes. That's—ah—one opinion. A good opinion.'

Mrs Steinberg laughed. 'I agree with you, Kitty. In the end, it's all about *personality*. What else is there?' She stood and stretched her arms above her head. 'Anyway. We're wasting bathing time. I'm going in.' She adjusted the straps of her costume. 'Aren't you two even going to take your shoes off?

180

It must be a hundred degrees out here.'

'I'd say that's a *slight* exaggeration, wouldn't you, Kitty?' Mr Crane flicked a smile at Kitty, raising his eyebrows as though in apology. Then he started to remove his scuffed brogues, impatiently tugging at the laces. Kitty bent down and began to do the same, tipping the sand from her upturned shoe.

Mrs Steinberg was watching her. 'You can take those stockings off, you know. Mr Crane won't watch, will you, George?'

Kitty looked at her lap.

'Go on, Kitty. Show him you've got *personality*.'

Mr Crane had removed his socks and turned up the ends of his trouser legs. He stood up. 'Look. I'll go for a stroll. Disappear for a bit. All right?'

When he'd gone behind the dune, Kitty hitched up her dress. Her mistress was still watching, a little smile on her face, whilst Kitty unrolled her stockings. The breeze whipped about her legs.

'That's better,' said Mrs Steinberg. 'Much better. Maybe we'll even get to see you in that bathing costume one day.'

Kitty watched the woman run into the sea. Then she took up her embroidery and began to work.

*   *   *

Ten minutes later, Arthur arrived with the windbreak and remaining chairs and began hammering in the posts. Kitty unpacked the hamper. That morning, she'd ironed and folded the checked tablecloth, washed out the flasks with bicarbonate of soda, and polished the silver cake forks. She'd boiled six eggs, wrapped the poppy-seed cake she'd baked yesterday, assembled the

181

shrimp paste sandwiches and cut off the crusts, packed a whole gala pie, and rinsed and hulled the first strawberries from the garden, wrapping them in a clean tea cloth.

Now she spread the tablecloth across the rug whilst Arthur assembled the windbreak. They said nothing as they worked, Arthur bending over the canvas, his brow knitted as he slammed the posts into place. Then he began on the deckchairs. Whilst he worked, she laid out the plates, the napkins and the glasses, and unwrapped the food. She glanced over to him. She'd never seen anyone handle a deckchair so confidently. The legs slotted into the right grooves first time round.

When she'd finished, she sat back on her heels.

'Let's have one of them strawberries.' Arthur reached across and plucked a fruit from the cloth. 'Proper scarlet,' he said, popping it into his mouth. 'Have one.' He held one in his palm for her. She looked around. Mrs Steinberg and the girls were still in the sea, and there was no sign of Mr Crane. She took the strawberry and held it to her nose: that sugary perfume was almost better than the thing itself. Taking a bite, her mouth was filled with acid sweetness. Arthur watched her, his lips open.

'Ah. Lunch.' Mr Crane sat on a deckchair. Kitty scrambled to her feet.

'Take a chair, there's enough for everyone. The girls can sit on the rug, I'm sure they'd prefer it anyway.' He looked out to sea and began waving both arms above his head. 'They'll be as wrinkled as prunes, staying in so long.' He waved and waved, but no one saw his signal.

'I'll call them, shall I, Mr Crane?'

'No, no, Arthur. No need. We'll wait.'

There was a silence. Kitty picked up her embroidery again. She meant to start work on the crab in the foreground of the scene. Looking at it now, she thought how the embroidered beach was much more pleasing than the real thing. There was no sand to get in your shoes, the little girls paddled elegantly, still wearing their white dresses, and the sun shone softly in the sky. Whereas here, on the actual beach, the light was so bright she could barely see to get the orange thread through the eye of her needle.

'Have you thought any more, Arthur, about what I mentioned to you the other day?' Mr Crane's face had become still, his voice hushed. 'I think it would be a really wonderful thing, you know, if you'd join us.'

Arthur tapped his pipe on the wooden frame of the deckchair and looked across the dunes. 'I've certainly thought about it, Mr Crane.'

'And what did you conclude?'

'I still haven't made my mind up, to be truthful, Mr Crane.'

'The party needs honest workers like you, Arthur. You'd be a valuable addition. Most valuable.'

Arthur produced a pouch of tobacco from his shorts pocket and tucked a tiny amount into his pipe. 'It's not that I don't think your lot have a point . . .' he struck a match, lit the pipe and sucked deeply on it. 'It's just I'm not sure if it's my thing, exactly.'

Mr Crane and Arthur regularly had discussions on the step of the writing studio in the late afternoon. Kitty had watched them standing together, Arthur on the lower step, nodding and tugging at his moustache whilst Mr Crane looked up to the sky and seemed to search for the right word. She'd presumed they were discussing the garden, or plans for the renovation of the cottage. But this seemed to be an entirely different matter. This seemed like politics, something that Bob always said women should never meddle in. Lou often pointed out that was a bit rich, coming from someone whose heroine was Queen Elizabeth.

'How do you mean?'

'Well.' Arthur took his pipe from his mouth and looked at it. 'I hope you won't take this the wrong way, Mr Crane, but I think it's more a thing for your intellectual type.'

'Intellectual?'

'Educated men, such as yourself.'

The crab was an odd shape. One pincer was definitely larger than the other. Kitty wondered if she could correct it.

'Come the Revolution, Arthur, we'll all be educated men. And women. That's the point.'

Kitty felt the men's eyes shift towards her and she focused hard on the crab's pincer. Her fingers were sweating in the heat, and her needle kept slipping. She'd have to be careful she didn't prick herself and let blood on the cloth. Then it would be ruined.

'Why,' Mr Crane continued, 'even Kitty here could join the Communist Party if she wished. She's a worker, a comrade, like you—like me— isn't she?'

Arthur sucked on his pipe and said nothing.

'It's my firm belief,' continued Mr Crane, 'that Kitty, and all her sex, have some very valuable views which should be heard.'

Mrs Steinberg and the girls were coming out of the sea. If the men would just keep talking for a minute more, the women would be back and Kitty would not be asked, for the second time today, for an *opinion*, when all she wanted was to finish embroidering her crab, eat some shrimp paste sandwiches (which would be turning crisp in this heat), and then cool her feet in the sea.

'I'm sure of that, Mr Crane,' said Arthur.

Bugger. She'd pricked her finger. Luckily there was no blood, yet. She sucked her reddening skin. If she didn't look up from her work, they might not ask her anything. They'd just keep talking as if she weren't quite there.

'Thank God! Lunch. I'm absolutely ravenous.'

Mrs Steinberg, still dripping from the sea, fell gratefully on the food. 'No Scotch eggs, Kitty?' There was a glint in her eye, but Kitty ignored this. If the woman had given her more than a day's notice, she would have been able to make both the Scotch eggs and the poppy-seed cake.

'I didn't have time, in the end, Mrs Steinberg.'

'*What* a shame. Well, tuck in, everyone. Don't stand on ceremony.' Mrs Steinberg took three sandwiches and a piece of pie, sat in a deckchair and began to eat with wet hands.

The girls helped themselves to the food, water dripping from their hair over the tablecloth. Diana sat near her father's feet and got to work on the crust of a piece of gala pie. Geenie helped herself to a strawberry and sat beside her, examining the fruit. Both girls' make-up had run down their faces, making them look like soggy chimney sweeps.

185

Mr Crane offered a sandwich first to Kitty, then to Arthur, and finally took one for himself.

When she'd finished her pie, Mrs Steinberg wrapped herself in a towel and stood to uncork a bottle of wine. Collecting four glasses together, she filled each one with red liquid, spilling some of it on the sand. 'Kitty, Arthur, have a drink with us.' She thrust a glass at Kitty, then took two cups and half-filled them. 'You too, girls. I have an announcement to make, and I want you all to have a drink in your hand.'

Mr Crane gripped his knees.

Mrs Steinberg was swilling her wine around, poking her large nose so far into her glass that Kitty imagined her mistress might begin to suck the drink up through her nostrils.

'An important announcement.'

Geenie stood and helped herself to a piece of poppy-seed cake.

'It's not time for cake yet, darling.'

'I hate shrimp paste.'

'Put the cake back. Only barbarians eat sweet before savoury.'

Geenie threw the cake down, but Mrs Steinberg was still wearing a clenched smile. Glass in hand, she knelt by Mr Crane's deckchair, shrugged the towel from her bronzed shoulders and gave her wet hair a shake. 'In fact, it's our announcement. Isn't it, George?'

Diana moved closer to her father, dropping her slice of pie as she did so. Only the meat was left. The girl had eaten all the pastry, the jelly and the egg. There was just a blob of pink pork with a hole in it, looking up at Mrs Steinberg. But the woman kept smiling. 'Never mind, Diana. Sit down,

Geenie.'

Geenie gave a heavy sigh before looking around and choosing to sit at Kitty's feet.

'Girls. I have some very exciting news for you.'

Mr Crane was staring down at the nibbled pork.

'Very exciting news.' Mrs Steinberg tossed her head back. Her wet cheeks were glowing.

'There'll soon be another person joining our family.'

Mr Crane passed a hand across his mouth.

Kitty would have liked to have taken up her embroidery again, to have something else to look at, but with the glass of wine in her hand, she didn't dare.

'Blotto! Blotto!' Geenie was suddenly on her knees, calling for the dog. Gathering her fists to her chest, as if in an effort to summon all her strength, she screeched again, this time at the top of her voice. 'Blotto!'

Everyone watched as the dog came running, its ears blowing behind. Geenie stretched out her arms to greet the animal, but Blotto ran straight past and through the picnic, his wet paws landing in the strawberries and knocking over the flask of tea. Then he doubled back, sat by Mrs Steinberg and plunged his head down to gobble the remains of Diana's gala pie.

There was a silence, but Mrs Steinberg was still smiling. She held her glass high. 'A toast, please. Raise your glasses. Kitty, Arthur. Join us.'

Kitty lifted her glass.

'To our new baby.' Mrs Steinberg tipped the wine to her mouth and swallowed, her throat contracting.

No one else drank. The girls were staring at

each other, their streaked faces dark. Mr Crane stood his glass in the sand and got up. 'Excuse me,' he said. 'I think I need some—ah . . .' he hung his head for a moment, and when he raised it again, his eyes were squeezed shut. 'I think I'll get my toes wet.' He walked towards the sea. Diana scrambled to her feet and followed him.

Biting her lip, Mrs Steinberg reached for the bottle and refilled her glass. 'Isn't it wonderful news, Geenie darling?'

The girl ignored her mother and raised her face to Kitty. 'Will you still make me a Pierrot outfit?' she whispered.

Kitty nodded. 'I promised, didn't I?'

The girl gave Kitty a weak smile. Mrs Steinberg drained her glass and filled it again.

TWENTY-THREE

Holding hands, the girls walked behind George. It was the morning after the picnic, and he'd announced over breakfast that he was taking them to see the bee orchids on Harting Down. 'You never forget your first bee orchid,' he'd said, gulping down his tea and pushing back his chair. 'We'll go at once, before it gets too warm.'

But it was already too warm. Geenie and Diana trailed along in the sun, their fingers sticking together, their sandals slapping on the dry chalk bridleway. George was striding ahead, his shoulders high, a dark patch of perspiration forming on the back of his shirt.

Geenie's eyes felt as if they'd been scratched.

She hadn't slept much last night, in Diana's bed. The two girls had stayed up for hours, whispering. It had been another sweaty, still night and the air under the covers was damp and heavy, but they'd huddled together beneath the canopy of the eiderdown, hair sticking to their foreheads, discussing the day's events, and what to do about them.

'We could say I'm very, very ill,' Diana had suggested. '*Gravely* ill. That might stop them.'

'How?'

'I could pretend to have an awful disease. TB or something. Then Daddy would have to take me home, and they could never get married, and your mother would have to—' she put her lips close to Geenie's ear, 'get rid of it.'

In the darkness, Geenie couldn't see her friend's face properly, but she felt her breath become quicker.

'I can make myself go awfully white when I want to. And if you go under the bedclothes and breathe really quickly for five minutes, you raise your temperature *and* your pulse. And I'm very good at coughing. Listen.' She flung her head back and hacked out something that sounded like Arthur's hoe scraping the garden path.

'It wouldn't work. You'd have to pretend for ages, and in the end they'd get a doctor and find out,' Geenie said, feeling pleased with herself for being so sensible.

'Couldn't you tell your mother you hate my father and you'll just have to kill yourself if they get married and have this baby?'

Diana, Geenie decided, had read far too many novels. 'She wouldn't believe me. And I don't hate your father. He's nice.'

Geenie listened to Diana chewing on a length of her own hair.

'I suppose,' said Geenie after a while, 'I suppose they might not get married.'

Diana shook her head. 'If there's a baby, my father will marry your mother, and I'll never get home to London. We'll both be stuck here in the middle of bloody nowhere forever.'

Geenie didn't really mind being stuck in the middle of nowhere. She'd become used to the cottage, the garden and the stream. She liked the way the willow trees whispered in the night. She liked the way the house was small enough for her to know the whereabouts of her mother, when Ellen was at home, at any time of the day. She liked riding her bicycle down the lane. She was even beginning to like Kitty, especially since the cook had agreed to make the Pierrot outfits. But the thought of her mother having a new baby was too much to bear. She would definitely be sent away to school then, and she'd probably never get to sit on her mother's knee and hear her read from *The Last Days of Pompeii* again.

'I've got it!' Diana clutched Geenie's arm with clammy fingers and gave a little squeal. 'Kitty!'

'What about her?'

'We'll say Kitty's having an affair with my father. Then your mother will throw him out, I'll go back to London, and your mother will have to, you know, not have the baby.'

'But—Kitty isn't having an affair with your father, is she?'

'I know that! Really, Geenie, you're most awfully literal sometimes. We'll have to pretend.

Like in a play.'

'How?'

'It'll be easy. It's a perfect, perfect plan. It's like I said. Cooks and housemaids are flighty. Everyone knows that. Your mother will believe us, not her.'

'Can we wait until she's made the Pierrot outfits?'

Diana let out a huff. 'I suppose so.'

*　　*　　*

'Keep in step!' Diana said, and Geenie put her right foot forward in time with her friend's. Left, right, left, right. They bobbed along the bridleway, shoulders occasionally bumping together. Geenie had never seen Diana look so happy. She smiled as she walked, swinging Geenie's hand in hers. No more details of the plan had been discussed, but just the knowledge of a plot was enough to make them giggle whenever they looked at each other.

'You two are very gleeful today,' said George, holding a gate open for them. Beyond him, the wheat swayed in the sunshine.

'We're happy, Daddy, about the new baby.'

George frowned.

'Won't it be wonderful, Geenie, to have a little brother or sister?' Diana reached for her father's hand and gave him a brilliant smile.

'Well.' George looked into his daughter's face. 'It's lovely to see you looking more cheerful, darling, but don't get too—ah—excited, will you?' Dropping her hand, he closed the gate and walked ahead.

The hill was very steep, and Geenie's fingers kept slipping from Diana's as the other girl marched on, breathing heavily. They were walking through long grass now, and all around the grasshoppers were scratching, scratching, scratching. Geenie could feel the weight of the sun's heat on her hair. As she walked, the grass whirled round her bare legs. 'Can we stop?' she asked.

Diana didn't seem to hear. She'd let go of Geenie's hand and was following her father to the top, her black hair swinging.

If Jimmy were here, he would stop. Jimmy had been keen on walking, and had taken Geenie with him sometimes. One night, at Heathstead Hall, they'd climbed the hill at the back of the house to look for badgers. Jimmy always wore walking britches and long woolly socks, whatever the weather, and carried a special stick which he said had seen him across the desert in the war. Ellen told Geenie never to ask Jimmy about the war because he'd killed a German and he hated himself for it. He'd held Geenie's hand and pulled her along after him, so she hardly had to move her own legs through the damp grass. Occasionally she thought her arm would come loose in its socket, but she'd said nothing. When they reached the top, they stood and looked back at the house, its lights winking in the darkness. Geenie could imagine her mother down there, her face at the window, waiting for them to return.

'You're not frightened, are you?' Jimmy had said.

Geenie shook her head. 'Only if I look this way.' She turned towards the black mass of trees on top of the hill. 'As long as I can see the lights, it's all right.'

Jimmy had held her hand, tightly, all the way back down to the house.

*   *   *

'Right.' George stopped and wiped his brow. They'd reached the top, and were standing on the edge of a clump of gorse. A warm wind blew around them, and they all stood for a moment, watching patches of cloud shadow inching across the fields below. 'They're up here, somewhere. Careful where you stand, girls.' Bending towards the grass, George began to study the area. 'They're delicate specimens.'

Geenie could see the whole village, the green spire of the church pricking the air, the sweep of the main street, their own cottage standing slightly apart, surrounded by trees. She wondered which one Diana had climbed, and thought of Kitty taking off her shoes and stockings, her face serious and pink.

'Daddy?' Diana sat on the grass and hugged her knees to her chest.

'Yes, darling?' He didn't stop studying the ground.

The girl shot a look towards Geenie and winked. 'You know Ellen said she was going to have a baby . . .'

George straightened up.

'How does that happen, exactly?'

He blinked. 'How does it happen?'

Diana put her head to one side and widened her black eyes. 'How is a baby made? We were wondering, weren't we, Geenie?'

Geenie knew how babies were made. Ellen had

related the facts years ago, demonstrating with a pair of Red Indian dolls. She'd said she didn't want her daughter to suffer the same 'agonies of ignorance' she had as a young girl, and asked Geenie to repeat all the information back to her when she'd finished. Geenie had always presumed Diana knew, too. They'd never discussed the afternoon noises, but Diana had read enough novels, even grown-up ones like *Tess of the D'Urbervilles* and, she'd boasted, things by D. H. Lawrence.

George ran a hand over his mouth and looked to the sky. 'Hasn't your mother told you?'

'How could she?' said Diana, looking straight at him. 'Mummy's in London.'

'Well. Ah. Yes.' He'd begun to pace up and down.

Diana sat on her hands and waited. Geenie stood beside her, watching.

'Well. Yes. No point in being kept in the dark about these things. Much better to be in full possession of the facts.'

There was a long silence, broken only by the busy song of the larks.

'Well. If we observe nature, for example . . .' he stopped pacing and looked around him. 'It's a question of an egg being—ah—germinated. Just like those buttercups there. Well, not exactly like them. The lady has an egg, you see, and that egg must be germinated by the man's seed.'

'What egg?' asked Diana. 'Where does the lady keep the egg?'

'It's in the tummy, darling. Deep inside. That's where the baby grows.'

Diana placed a hand on her own stomach and

swallowed. 'How does the seed get there?'

The larks were still singing. Jimmy had told Geenie that the males went as high as they could, singing all the time, before plunging to the earth, to impress the females. 'Like men talking clever, clever, cleverer,' Ellen had said, 'until they can talk no more.'

George wasn't talking now. He was sitting on the grass next to his daughter, looking out at the village, a deep frown on his face.

'Daddy? How does the seed get there?'

If Diana really did know, then she was very good at pretending she didn't, thought Geenie. She wondered if her friend was practising, for when she'd have to pretend that Kitty was having a love affair with George.

'Well. It's quite complicated. And yet simple,' his face brightened a little. 'Wonderfully simple, really. And—yes—beautiful.'

Diana waited.

'You see, what happens is. Ah. A man and a woman are in love, and probably married—'

'But you and Ellen aren't married.'

He looked at Geenie and sighed. 'No. No, we're not. It's not necessary to be married, you see, but most people are, because that's what society demands, marriage, and family. It's a way of sort of keeping people in order. The Soviet peoples have a different view of it, of course; there it's *community* that counts, not family, not some archaic, superstitious idea of religion—'

'But you have to be in love?' Diana asked.

'Yes. Yes, it helps to be in love. Personally speaking, I'd say that helps. Is necessary, in fact. Although not everyone agrees.'

195

The girls looked at one another. Diana arched her eyebrows. 'So how does the seed get there? Is it through *kissing*?' She giggled.

'Well, yes, that's a part of it. There will be kissing, yes, and touching, touching each other, holding one another. And then—and then—'

'The man puts his thing up you,' interrupted Geenie. 'The man puts his penis in the lady's vagina and he produces semen which makes her pregnant. If she's started menstruating, that is.'

George stared at her. His bad eye twitched. 'Yes. That's it,' he said, finally. 'Exactly.'

'Urgh,' said Diana. She jumped to her feet and gave a shudder.

'We ought to get back,' said George. 'It must be almost lunchtime.' He walked ahead. The patch of sweat now covered his back.

'What about the bee orchid?' called Geenie.

But he didn't reply. He just waved a hand in the air and carried on down the hill.

When he was so far in front that they kept losing sight of him, Geenie turned to Diana and said, 'Didn't you know that?'

'Of course I did.' Diana trailed one hand through the long grass. 'Aunt Laura told me, ages ago.'

'Why did you ask, then?'

'Because I wanted to see what he'd say.' As she squinted against the sun, her dark eyes looked small but bright. 'Now I know we're going back to London, I don't have to be nice to him all the time, do I?'

Geenie tightened her grip on her friend's hand and tried to keep in step.

TWENTY-FOUR

Dearest Bird, Ellen typed.

> *If I were another man, I would write of what*
> *a tonic the country air affords, of how I am*
> *getting better, whatever that means, out here on*
> *the bleak hills, being blown into goodness by the*
> *unforgiving wind; but all I can think of is how*
> *long it will be before I am home again in*
> *London with you and Flossy.*
> *Mother, of course, occasionally tries to bring*
> *up the subject of Rachel (whom she now knows*
> *is, in name at least, my wife—it seems Rachel*
> *has written to tell her), but those tweed skirts*
> *and double strings of pearls seem to keep her*
> *from speaking too plainly, and she won't allow*
> *herself to become emotional with her only son,*
> *who, she can see, needs rest and quiet, to*
> *recover from his nerves.*

She stopped. James had sent this one whilst visiting his parents' home in Northumberland. It was one in a series of letters she kept separate from the others, in a folder marked 'personal'. She'd never thought of publishing these. But, today, something had compelled her to begin work on them. They were, she realised, the key to the collection. Without them, the book would be incomplete.

> *I will stop drinking, darling; I know I've*
> *promised before, but now I am away from*

London, all that madness, all that pressure to perform, *I do feel I can do it.*

The library window was open but the air refused to move. She was sitting in her nightgown at three o'clock in the afternoon, and she could smell her own skin in the heat. Burying her nose into the fleshiness of her upper arm, she reflected that Crane hadn't really touched her since their al fresco encounter. Last night, after the picnic, he'd come to bed late after spending all evening in his studio, and she'd pretended to be asleep. This morning, she'd heard him rise early, but she'd stayed in bed as long as she could, counting the boatmen on her curtains. How could he have abandoned her in that damned dramatic fashion on the beach? She'd had to sit there with Arthur's silence and Kitty's infernal fiddling with needle and thread. In the end she'd plunged into the sea again and swum until her eyes were stinging. She didn't notice the ache in her arms and legs until she was sitting beside him on the silent drive home, watching his long fingers grasp and wrench the gear knob into place.

Pushing her hair back, she began typing again.

It's partly for the physical pain (I won't go into the mental pain; it's too tiresome even to consider), you know that, don't you, darling? Whisky seems to be the only thing that stops my blasted ankle hurting, but when I return, and have had the operation and it's all re-set, I know I will feel one hundred per cent better.

There was something about hitting the keys that

soothed her. It wasn't about re-living the past. It was about typing it up and putting it away. Getting it all onto clean white sheets. Seeing it as it was, in black ink, for one last time.

She ripped the page from the typewriter and placed it on the pile with the rest. Then she riffled through the folder. It was a while before she found what she was looking for: the letter she'd received from Crane after James's death.

She knew this one couldn't possibly go into the book, but, scrolling paper into the machine, she began again.

My adored Ellen,

I do not know how to begin this letter. It is so sad and strange. I am so sorry for your loss. I cannot imagine what you are feeling now. I can hardly imagine what I myself am feeling. It's a terrible shock for all of us. You most of all.

Everything has happened so suddenly—all of it—that it's hard to know how to act, what to do.

I did not mean to write this letter.

Please forgive me for still wanting you. This is hardly the time to write about such things, but our afternoon in Laura's flat was quite the best thing to have happened to me.

If you choose not to come again, I will respect your wishes. You will not hear from me any more.

But if, when the time is right, you decide to live again, to love again, please live with me.

I can be patient.

He hadn't had to be, of course. Two weeks later,

she'd been here, in this library, holding his arm and telling him she was going to buy the place, despite its cramped, dim little rooms. He'd kept calling her his Cleopatra. On the train back to London to pick up Geenie, her thighs aching from three days of sex with Crane in the White Hart Hotel, she'd found she couldn't stop weeping. A woman in a bright yellow hat with a greasy Yorkshire terrier on her lap had moved carriages in disgust. Ellen had lain on the seat, beaten her fist against the antimacassar, and wailed. She'd thought she would never be able to catch enough breath to cry even harder, but somehow she'd managed it, the snot running into her mouth, her throat clenching. When she'd reached Waterloo, the tears had stopped, and she hadn't cried again. She'd told herself it was for her daughter's sake. It was necessary to begin anew, wipe the slate clean, for Geenie.

She'd long suspected that her daughter knew. Geenie must know, surely, that James's death was Ellen's fault. Her daughter would have heard, of course, the terrible row the night before the operation. James had been drunk again, and it was just after she'd first slept with Crane, but it was all over some silly thing—James saying they should try to persuade Dora to keep working after she was married, at least until she had children of her own, Ellen insisting she could bring up her own daughter perfectly well. It was when James had faced her and said, 'You have no idea who that girl is,' that she'd snapped and thrown her tumbler of whisky at him; he'd ducked, and the glass had smashed on the wall and dripped down one of his maps, soaking the countries and the seas, staining

200

everything brown. James had brought back his hand and slapped her like a child. What she'd felt, she remembered now, was relief that finally he'd done it, just as she'd always known he would, just as Charles had hit her almost every week for the last year of their marriage. She'd sunk to her knees and started to pick up the pieces of glass from the leopard-skin rug, the short hairs bristling beneath her fingers. James stood above her, watching in silence. When she was finished she'd gone to bed, knowing he would sit in his study all night. She'd never thought, not for a moment, that there would still be enough alcohol in him to react so badly with the anaesthetic. It simply hadn't occurred to her to mention it to the anaesthetist the next morning, when he'd arrived with his leather bag, warm hands and onion breath. James was going to stop, after all; he'd promised her he'd stop, just as soon as the operation was over and all the pain was gone. And, she remembered, her own head had felt as though a knife were stuck in her scalp, her tongue was coated and her stomach tight, and all she'd wanted was to close the door of the sitting room and lie down in the dark.

Still. It was, she felt even now, sitting at her desk in this strange little house in the wilderness, looking out onto a garden blighted by fierce heat, entirely her fault.

She left the sheet of paper in the typewriter and went upstairs to bed. The only thing to do on an afternoon like this was to close her eyes and hope sleep would take her somewhere else.

*   *   *

201

At half past seven, she managed to comb her hair into some sort of shape (there was nothing left, now, of that sculpture of waves and light created so carefully by Robin), dust her nose with powder without looking too closely at the evil thing in the mirror, and put on her cream silk dress, all without crying. Laura was already downstairs. Ellen could hear the click of her heels on the wooden floor, the slow, confident timbre of her voice. She'd have to go down and face them all: the girls, Crane, his pregnant sister and her drip of a husband. And the dinner, of course, instructions for which she'd left scribbled on the back of an envelope last night: *KITTY: Tomorrow's dinner menu. Pea and lettuce soup. Chilled poached salmon and new potatoes. Strawberries and cream.* Then she'd added: *I won't be available to help so have kept it simple. E.S.*

They were all seated when she arrived downstairs. Kitty had extended the mahogany table to its full length. Ellen had brought it with her from the London house, and even with the two rooms knocked into one, it was a squeeze to fit it in comfortably. Crane seemed very far away, sitting on the other side of the room, studying his napkin. The feeble central light hung too low over the table, giving the room a rather shadowy feel. For once, she was glad of it: her reddened eyes wouldn't be so obvious in the gloom.

'There you are,' said Laura. She was wearing a jade shot-silk tunic with metallic blue feathers for earrings. Everything about her looked fuller: her curved lips and eyes, her black bobbed hair.

'Here I am,' agreed Ellen, trying a smile.

Next to Laura was a girl of about twenty, wearing a man's paisley waistcoat and no blouse.

She stood up and bowed her head towards Ellen.

'This is my new friend, Tab,' said Laura, stretching a hand towards the young woman's elbow. 'She's a singer. Awfully talented.'

Ellen looked Tab up and down. Her bare arms were sleek and muscled; her small breasts seemed to be holding themselves up without any support, apart from the waistcoat, and her hair—dyed red to the point of being almost purple—was short and set in neat waves.

'Where's Humphrey?'

'Where indeed?' replied Laura.

Ellen glanced at Crane, but he was still studying his napkin. She pulled out a chair at the opposite end of the table and sat down. 'Welcome to Willow Cottage, Tab. Do sit.'

The wall seemed to be very close behind Ellen's back, hemming her into place. 'A singer. How interesting. What sort of thing?'

Tab cleared her throat. When she spoke, her voice was high and reedy. 'Anything, really,' she said, gazing at Laura. 'I mean, I love the French songs . . .'

'She does a marvellous "Mômes de la cloche", interjected Laura. 'Extraordinary.'

'I'm working on widening my repertoire.' Tab's accent was hard to place. It was a bit like the barmaid's in the Wheatsheaf, but not quite that coarse.

'She's been a great success at the Café Royal, haven't you, Tab darling?'

Ellen smoothed her napkin over her lap. 'I rather thought it had all blown over for the dear old Café now.'

'When was the last time you were there?' asked

Crane, looking up.

Ellen laughed. 'Oh, I don't know. I've been stuck here in the wilderness with you for an age.'

'It's lovely here,' said Tab. 'A right breath of fresh air.'

'Tab's a Brighton girl,' said Laura, sliding her eyes sidelong. 'Isn't it a blast? A fisherman's daughter singing in the Café Royal.'

The colour rose in Tab's face.

'She used to help her father haul the nets up the beach,' said Laura.

'How interesting,' said Crane, putting down his napkin and leaning towards Tab. 'Wasn't it wonderful work, though, Tab, out there? There's something so—ah—rewarding about physical work out of doors, isn't there?'

Tab shrugged her shoulders. 'I prefer the Café Royal.'

'Shall we eat?' said Ellen, ladling herself some soup from the tureen and passing it to Tab. She could tell the stuff wasn't nearly hot enough as soon as she lifted the lid: there was hardly any steam. Taking a breath, she decided to let it go. She would have to ignore these little things in order to get through this evening. It was strange; despite being so upset this afternoon by re-reading the letters, she found what her mind kept returning to was the image of that cow being dragged along Petersfield High Street. She saw again the huge open wound of its stomach, the way it had seemed to sink helplessly into the road.

Picking up her spoon, she looked around the table and forced herself to focus. Geenie's normally pale face was, she noticed, now quite tanned, which made her appear somehow more defined; her chin wasn't pressed so far into her chest, and her hair had been bleached almost white by the sun. Instead of eating her soup, she was studying the prongs of her fork, holding the silver close to her nose. Next to Crane, whose eyes were fixed on his soup, was Diana. She, too, was tanned. Dark as an Italian, thought Ellen, and eating like one, too: nothing could stop Diana once she'd started on her food.

'Tell me,' Ellen began. 'Did you girls have an interesting day?'

Crane swallowed. 'I was just telling Laura. We went up Harting Down, looking for bee orchids.'

'But we didn't find any, did we, Daddy?' said Diana, between mouthfuls. 'So we had a very interesting discussion instead.'

Geenie gave a giggle.

George ducked his head.

'Fascinating,' said Laura. 'You're so lucky, living here in the country all year round. I long for it whenever I'm in London.'

Ellen was silent. In the half-light, she was trying to make out how much Laura's stomach had grown since she last saw her. Beneath her silk tunic, there was a sizeable bump.

'Have you been in town lately, then?'

'Heaps. I have to occupy myself. Can't seem to get my mind off this damn pregnancy. Tabs has been an absolute tonic.' Laura pushed her bowl away. 'Sorry, darling, I can't eat anything this green at the moment.'

'You must be very excited,' said George.

'Must I?'

Crane reached across the table for more bread.

'Can't you ask for that to be passed?' flashed

Ellen.

There was a pause before Laura gave a little laugh and said, 'Don't mind me. I'm not the slightest bit bothered by manners. I've been teaching Tab: just because everyone else does these silly things—ladies first, endless apologising and all that—doesn't mean we should. She was *terribly* polite when I first found her.'

Tab grinned.

Ellen filled her own glass with wine. 'Your brother is usually such a stickler for manners, Laura. He's really surprisingly bourgeois, for a Bolshevik.'

There was a long silence, throughout which Diana continued to slurp her soup.

'Has everyone finished?' Crane stood and began to collect the bowls.

'What on earth are you doing?' demanded Ellen.

'Clearing the table. Kitty's had a lot to organise this evening, and we always said we didn't want her waiting on us.'

'How is the little thing coming on?' asked Laura.

'She's coming on very well,' said Crane, carrying the stack of bowls out of the door. 'Very well indeed.'

Ellen bit her lip. The lukewarm soup had left her stomach feeling bloated and oddly empty.

'We must have some light,' she said, suddenly pushing back her chair and squeezing herself free from the table. 'It's too damned dark in here.'

She left the room and went into the library. Ignoring the bespectacled gaze of the stuffed fox (why had she allowed Crane to keep that thing?), she rummaged in her desk drawer for some matches. When she'd found them, she flung open the window, sat on the ledge and looked out into the evening. The sky was a deep pink, and the house martins were circling. There was no air, even here: just the smell of the baked earth after another boiling day. She told herself to concentrate on that. To breathe in the earth. To not think about the hot stink of cow. She glanced over at her typewriter and the folder of letters. She should get back, she knew, but first she had to re-read one part of Crane's letter.

But if, when the time is right, you decide to live again, to love again, please live with me.

I can be patient. Who knows how two people should act, at a time like this? All we can know are our feelings for one another.

She'd known her feelings, hadn't she? It had seemed to be the right thing to do at the time. There must be some way to make it the right thing to have done.

She placed the letter back in the folder, rubbed her scalp, and returned to the dining table, clutching the box of matches.

Crane had brought the potatoes through, and provided everyone with a dinner plate. Ellen struck a match and leaned across to light the long candles in the centre of the table. Her fingers were trembling a little and she had some trouble getting the last one going.

'Are you all right?' asked Geenie, looking up at her mother.

'I'm perfectly fine.'

'You do look a little odd, darling,' said Laura.

'It must be the heat.'

'You were always complaining that it was cold before,' said Crane.

'But this heat—it's too close, isn't it? It gets under your skin.'

'You ought to try carrying a damned baby around in your stomach,' said Laura, lighting a cigarette. 'That really warms things up.'

Kitty came in with the salmon. She was still wearing her apron, and her face was round and pink about the cheeks. Ellen watched her as she placed the fish down. The girl really wasn't bad looking: a tidy little figure and a neat waist. A shine on her lip. She seemed to be standing straighter, too, and her hands no longer shook when she put something on the dining table.

Kitty made a small bob, then backed out of the room.

'How many times must we tell that girl not to do that?' asked Ellen, standing to dish up the salmon. It looked passable: its eye still firm, its skin lightly crisped, garnished with parsley and lemon. Using a fork and spoon, she peeled back a strip of silver to reveal the rose-coloured flesh beneath, thanking God it wasn't beef.

'Pass plates, please.'

'Have you told Aunt Laura the good news, Daddy?' Diana was looking at her father with a bright face.

Crane's eyes met Ellen's. He looked very tired. She thought again of the wounded animal being dragged along the street.

'We'll tell Aunt Laura later, Diana dear,' she said, firmly.

'Tell me what?' Laura had her elbows on the

208

table and was leaning towards Diana, cupping a hand around her ear. 'Whisper it to me. I love secrets.'

Crane put a hand on his daughter's shoulder. 'Yes, it is good news, actually. I've been offered some work. With the Party. Lecturing.'

As soon as Ellen plunged the knife in, she knew the fish was overdone. There was no give to the flesh, no room. It was dry, and when she lifted a slice and dropped it on Crane's plate, it stood absolutely still.

'Didn't I tell you?' Laura said, blowing out a stream of smoke. 'I'm a vegetarian now.'

'Lecturing?' said Ellen, slicing another piece of fish.

'Don't vegetarians eat fish?' asked Geenie.

'I don't eat anything that's drawn breath.'

Tab held out her plate. 'I'd love some. Salmon's my favourite.'

'She's such a carnivore.' Laura traced a line along Tab's jaw with one finger. 'Or should that be a pescivore? I've never met a girl with such a taste for the sea.'

'Lecturing? Where?'

'I want to be a vegetarian,' said Geenie loudly, folding her arms across her plate.

Ellen stuck a fork into the fish and let it stand there, stiffly upright. 'Where will you be lecturing, Crane?'

He was helping himself to potatoes. 'All around the country.'

'You'll be travelling?'

'Quite a bit, yes.'

'And when were you going to mention it?'

'I thought now might be a good time, seeing as

Diana brought up the subject of good news. I'll be speaking to the people about the importance of politics in great literature.'

'Can I have some fish?' asked Diana.

Ellen ignored her. 'The importance of politics in great literature.'

'That's right.'

'And what's happened to the great literature you're supposed to be writing?'

'Haven't you finished that blasted novel yet, Georgie?' Laura laughed. 'What's he been doing all this time in that studio of his, Ellen?'

Crane began to dissect his fish. 'The novel is not as important.' His voice was low and steady. 'This is real work. Work that can change people's minds. Work that can change the way things are.'

Ellen snatched Crane's plate from the table. 'Don't eat that.' She began clearing everyone's plates and cutlery. 'In fact, don't eat any of it.'

'Ellen—'

'It's awful. Ruined. I'm going to have to do something about that girl. She can't cook anything. She never could.'

Crashing the plates down on the table, she shouted, 'Kitty!'

Crane put his hand over his eyes.

'Kitty! Come here please!'

'Ellen, don't—'

'Kitty!'

There was the sound of a door slamming and footsteps along the corridor. Kitty appeared in the doorway, her face flushed.

'What have you done to that poor fish?'

Kitty's mouth moved but no sound came out. The sight of her downcast eyes made Ellen even more furious. 'It's ruined!' She couldn't help yelling. 'Absolutely ruined! What did you think you were doing? Incinerating it? The point is to cook it, not kill it.'

There was a loud bang as Crane smashed his fist on the table. 'Ellen! Not here. Not now.'

'Why not? It's my house. I want to know what this stupid girl thinks she was doing. I want this explained.' She stepped closer to Kitty. 'Do you think I didn't know you weren't a cook when you first came here? Do you think I couldn't see right through you? I gave you a chance, and this is what I get in return. Fucking incinerated fish.'

Kitty was staring at the floor.

Crane went to her. 'Kitty,' he said, softly, 'you can go now. We'll talk about this in the morning.'

Ellen's hands were shaking. She brought them to her scalp and rubbed at her hair to try and still them.

'Leave the washing-up,' added Crane. 'We'll do it.'

Ellen looked at Laura. 'Give me a cigarette.'

Laura took one from her silver case, lit it against her own, and handed it to her.

'I did it like it said in the book.'

They all looked up. Kitty was staring at Ellen, her chin trembling but her eyes fierce. 'Mrs Steinberg. Madam. I did it how it said.'

Crane put his hand on her elbow. 'You can go now, Kitty. Take the rest of the evening off.'

But the girl was still staring directly at Ellen. Then there was a sudden crackle, and the room went dark.

'Blasted generator,' muttered Crane. 'I'll see if Arthur's still about.' He stepped from the room and held the door open for Kitty to follow him, but she remained where she was, staring at Ellen.

'Nothing works in this damned house,' said Ellen, sinking into a chair.

'Just like it said in the book,' Kitty said again before turning to go.

The girl's footsteps echoed down the corridor. Ellen's cigarette smoke evaporated into the air.

TWENTY-FIVE

Kitty had been sitting on her bed for the last hour, staring at her embroidery. It was no use, she knew, trying to tackle the girl's face now. Without the electric light, she couldn't see enough, and her fingers felt too large and hot for the work. It was partly that the blood was still thick in her head; she could feel it pumping down her neck, along her shoulders and through her arms. Anger made her body want to move, to lash out at something, but still she sat with the embroidery on her lap, her work-box open at her feet, and tried to concentrate on the stitches.

The embroidery was heavier in her hands now. She brought it close to the paraffin lamp she'd placed by the bed. The sky and the sea, the crabs, starfish, pebbles and rocks were done. She'd unpicked and corrected the wonky claw, and the crabs looked almost solid, she'd been so careful to keep her satin stitches absolutely even and close together. Each one was snug up against the next. Kitty was particularly pleased with the contrast of the burnt orange thread she'd used for the shells

212

with the black French knots of the creature's eyes. She was now halfway through the girl stooping with her net in the foreground. The outline of the girl's face, which Kitty had begun in stem stitch, was tricky: she knew that if she got it wrong, the whole thing would be skewed. With hair a few extra stitches were all right, but you had to be careful with faces. One stitch too many and a face could turn into a shapeless blot.

She put the embroidery down on the counterpane beside her, stood up and went to the wardrobe. Opening it, she smelled cinnamon and decided she must scrub the whole thing clean. There was something wrong with having another woman's perfume in your wardrobe. The emerald frock was still hanging there, unworn, above the single green shoe given to her by Mrs Steinberg on her first day. What had the woman been thinking? No one could do anything with one shoe. She should have refused it straight away.

It was no good. She was thinking again of them all sitting round their dinner table, watching her. Of Diana with her little smile. Of Geenie with her worried eyes. Of that strange woman with the purple hair who looked like a lovely boy; she'd been the only one who hadn't stared. Of Mrs Steinberg's face, like Lou's was when Kitty had told her just before Mother died that she should've come sooner. Like a child who'd been smacked. Knowing they're in the wrong, but willing you to be the one to blame.

After Mrs Steinberg had shouted, Kitty went into the kitchen and, still feeling the touch of Mr Crane's fingers on her arm, removed her apron and hung it on the door. The generator hadn't yet

213

got going again, so she'd lit a paraffin lamp she'd found in the larder and washed the soup bowls he'd brought through for her earlier, thinking *he carried these for me*, not thinking of Mrs Steinberg's face, of her voice, of *fucking incinerated fish*. It was almost funny, wasn't it? Getting that annoyed over a bit of salmon. Mrs Steinberg had told her she wasn't to spend more than two shillings a week on the MacFisheries order—so what did she expect? She wasn't a miracle worker. Lou would have pointed that out to her employer, quick as you like. *Well, what do you want? Bloody miracles?* And Arthur would have laughed. Shrugged his shoulders. *Whatever you say, Mrs S.* Walked away. Neither of them would have stood there trembling, only managing to squeak something about doing it like the book said.

When she'd finished washing the bowls, she'd fetched her sharp scissors from her work-box. Back in the kitchen, she'd sliced straight through the Chinese lantern's tassel and thrown it in the bucket she kept by the door for the compost peelings.

Now she glanced at the clock on her chest of drawers. Only nine. He might be out there, in his shed, even now.

She peeled off her old work frock and changed into the blue lily print. Looking in the glass, she noticed that her hair had lightened in the sun, and her cheeks were still flushed from the incident. That wasn't a bad thing. She bit down, hard, on her bottom lip, to bring the colour up, dipped her finger into her pot of Vaseline and ran it round her mouth. It was a trick Lou had shown her, years ago: not quite lipstick, but almost as good. Should Arthur ask her again, she decided, she would miss

214

tea at her sister's on Sunday afternoon in favour of the dance she knew they held at the Crown and Thistle Hotel in Petersfield. It was mostly girls dancing with one another, of course, and only tea to drink, but maybe that would be for the best.

Then there was a knock at the door.

Kitty stood very still. If the woman was coming to start on again about the bloody fish—

Another knock. Quite a light knock. A bit of hesitation in it.

She held her breath, wondering how long it would take for Mrs Steinberg to retreat.

Then there was a voice—'Kitty. It's Mr Crane. May I come in, please?'

She looked around. Her room wasn't untidy—it never was—but the embroidery was on the crumpled counterpane and her work-box was open on the floor. Hurriedly, she stuck her old frock on a hanger and closed the wardrobe.

'Kitty? Are you in there?'

Taking a breath, she pulled the door open. He was holding a candle. As soon as she saw his face— lined and a bit startled looking in the wavering light, as if he hadn't expected her to actually open up—she turned away and sat on the bed, trying to hide the work-box under her feet.

'Sorry to disturb—may I come in?'

She nodded.

'Thanks.' He stood for a moment, looking around. 'I thought you might need this,' he said, pointing at the candle. 'But I see you've sorted yourself out.'

'Yes. Thank you.'

He put the candle on her chest of drawers. 'Look here,' he began. 'I—ah—sorry it's a bit

215

late—but I thought . . .' he trailed off.

She waited.

'Are those your parents?' he gestured towards the framed photograph.

'Yes.'

'May I?' Picking up the photograph, he held it at arm's length, inclining his head first this way, then that, as if studying some exquisite object he might be about to buy.

'Your father has a very fine look about him.'

Kitty glanced up. 'Does he?'

'He appears—full of humour. Doesn't he?'

Kitty thought about her father going up the passage to fart. *Don't tell, Kitty-Cat.*

'And what a smart jacket.'

'Oh, that's not his.'

Mr Crane raised his eyebrows.

'He didn't have a suit. I expect he hired it, from the photographer.'

'Quite. Yes, I see.'

He put the photograph down and dug his hands into his pockets. 'I'm so awfully sorry, about earlier.'

She focused on the place where his grey flannel trousers were going thin at the knees. There would be a hole in the left one soon. What would it take to make him a new pair? She'd never made a pair of men's trousers before, but she estimated three yards of a light gabardine—perhaps navy blue, it would go with his dark hair—and a high waist, with a slimmer fit. She could run them up for him on Lou's machine in no time.

'You see, Ellen—Mrs Steinberg—is a bit out of sorts at the moment. Not that that's any excuse. But I'm sure you'll—ah—understand.'

216

Had she sent him here, to apologise on her behalf? Kitty knew she should say *it's all right*, but couldn't bring the words into her mouth.

He sat down heavily then, right next to her on the bed. 'I want you to know that I'm very pleased with your work, Kitty. Very pleased indeed.'

It didn't seem to get cooler any more, even at this time in the evening. She could smell the sweetness of his sweat. There was still that pulse of blood in her neck and shoulders, making her body warm, making her want to move, to lash out. She swallowed it down.

'Is this your work?' He was looking at the embroidery she'd left on the counterpane.

She nodded.

He picked it up and held it close to the candle to examine it, just as he'd examined the photograph. 'It's the most accomplished craftsmanship, Kitty. It really is.'

'It's just a bit of sewing, Mr Crane. Something to pass the time.'

'It's much more than that, surely! Look at the detail in it!' His voice had become hushed, urgent. 'It's, well, it's remarkable.'

She fixed her eyes on his hands as they held the cloth, but she knew he was looking at her face now.

'Kitty . . .' His fingers were stroking the Cretan stitches she'd made for the clouds. Then he ran the flat of his hand over the surface of the rocks and the sand. He brushed the French knots of the crab's eyes, the gentle zigzag chain she'd sewn for the surf of the sea. 'You really care about your work, don't you?'

'About the house and the cooking, Mr Crane?'

'No, I don't mean that. I mean this. Your craft.'

217

She looked into his face. His eyes were so bright that she had to look away. 'Yes,' she said. 'I suppose I do.'

'That's a gift, Kitty. You know that, don't you?'

His voice was soft, and she was sure he would touch her now. He would touch her arm again, that would be how it would start. She moved her elbow closer to his hand. All along her forearm, her skin seemed to prickle, despite the heat. She steadied her breathing. If she could just wait a moment longer—if her skin could just move a little closer to his—surely he would respond to that pulse in her—surely they would move together—

He stood up, making the bed springs creak.

'Are you going?' As soon as she'd said it, she put her hand to her mouth.

'I'd better get back, see what the others are up to.' He smiled faintly from above. 'I'm glad we had this talk, Kitty.'

Once more, she fixed her eyes on the worn place at his knees.

'Keep up the good work, won't you?'

He left the room. Kitty listened to his footsteps over the kitchen flags, followed by the sound of voices in the sitting room. He'd gone back to them, then. Telling Mrs Steinberg, no doubt, that it was all sorted out. Probably the others had forgotten about it by now, anyway. She continued to sit, staring at her open work-box. There was the slap of bare feet on the flags, and the clink of bottles. Mrs Steinberg fetching more wine. Eventually, the electric light came back on, laughter started, and there was a woman's voice wailing a song. The girl who looked like a lovely boy must be singing. Kitty listened to the song for a few minutes—it wasn't

218

one she recognised, and the girl's voice was too cracked to be really beautiful—then she stood, opened her door, walked through the kitchen and, without even a glance at the washing-up piled in the sink and sprawled over the table, went outside into the night.

It was cooler in the garden, and she was suddenly aware that she should have washed. She'd been cooking most of the afternoon, and she could smell the tang of salmon grease as well as her own sweat. But at least now she was moving, the blood in her head thinning, her limbs growing lighter as she walked towards the shed.

A line of light leaked onto the grass from the open door. She decided not to knock. Instead, she stood in the doorway and said his name.

Arthur looked up from where he was sitting, a book on his knee. He didn't appear to have been sleeping this time.

'Do you sit here every night?' she asked.

He spread his hands on his lap and yawned. 'What makes you think that?'

'Your lamp's often burning.'

'Have you been watching, then?'

'Don't you want to go home?'

'Not especially.'

There was a pause.

'What's for me at home?' he asked. 'Empty chair on the other side of the table. Tin of Skipper's. Nothing on the wireless.'

'But you have to go home, eventually.'

'Eventually,' he agreed. 'But here there's folk about. And they needed me tonight, didn't they? The beast needed a kick.'

She shifted from foot to foot. 'Arthur—'

'Are you coming in or not?' He dragged a camp stool out from behind his deckchair and patted the top to show her where she should sit.

'Why have you got that shoe?' She pointed at the green high-heeled shoe, which was still beneath Arthur's deckchair.

He narrowed his eyes. Then he took his pipe from his top pocket and began tapping it on the frame of the deckchair and brushing away the debris.

When he'd re-loaded his pipe with fresh tobacco, placed it in the side of his mouth and got it lit, he reached beneath the chair and brought the shoe out. 'I was keeping it for you,' he said. 'I thought I might find the other, one day, but it hasn't turned up.' He knocked the heel on the floor and mud flaked from its sides. 'Don't suppose one shoe's much good to you, is it?'

'Let's go to the tea-dance Sunday,' she said.

He gave a short laugh. 'This Sunday afternoon?'

'Yes.'

'You're sure you want to?'

She let out a sigh. 'I said, didn't I?'

He replaced the shoe beneath the deckchair and patted the stool again. 'Come and sit, then. Sit with me for a bit.'

'Sunday,' Kitty repeated, ignoring his offer. 'Three o'clock. The Crown and Thistle. I'll see you there.'

She turned and walked back to her room, knowing his eyes were following her.

TWENTY-SIX

Ellen's face was closed. Geenie knew the signs: chin tucked tight to her chest, eyes unblinking.

'I've got a hairdresser's appointment and you're coming with me.'

'Kitty could look after me.'

'I'm not leaving you with that girl.' Ellen pressed her lips together. She was wearing orange lipstick, which made her look as though she'd been sucking on a lolly, a green shiny dress, and a string of orange glass beads. Geenie could see where the powder had settled in the pores of her mother's large nose. Something important was going to happen in town. Her mother's orange handbag and matching shoes with heels and straps—rather than laces—confirmed it.

Alone with Ellen. All summer Geenie had wished she and her mother could be alone together, but now it was just the two of them, she wanted Diana and George back. This morning they'd caught the train to London; George had stated over breakfast that he'd some urgent work to attend to and was taking Diana to stay at her mother's for a few days. Ellen, still wearing her dressing gown, had stood at the window, looking out and saying nothing. Geenie had groped for Diana's hand, but her friend had jumped from the table, knocking her toast to the floor. Then she'd run straight upstairs to pack, leaving Geenie gazing at her mother's back.

'Go and put something decent on.' Ellen stared down at her daughter. 'And wash your knees.'

'It's too hot for something decent.'

'Just hurry up.' Ellen snapped her handbag closed. 'Please, darling. We don't want people to think we're completely hopeless.'

*   *   *

Geenie lay on the back seat of the car and let herself roll around as her mother drove. Instead of looking out of the window—she knew the sky was white with heat and the fields would be crisped and dusty—she stared at the stitching on the inside of the roof. If she counted each stitch, they might get there quicker, and whatever was going to happen would be over, and Diana would be back.

Ellen held her by the upper arm as they slogged through the market place. Smells of old cabbage and rabbit cages rose up from the Saturday stalls. No one was buying much in this heat. Outside the pub on the square, men were sitting on the steps in their shirtsleeves, fanning themselves with their hats, sipping from pint jugs. They watched Geenie and her mother as the two of them walked by. Geenie stared back, and one of the men, wearing thick glasses and no tie, nodded to her.

Ellen quickened her pace. 'Don't stare.'

'Why not? It's interesting.'

'English people don't like it.'

'Can we stop for a lemonade?'

'Later.'

They walked down the cobbled lane to the hairdressers'. Next door, flies were buzzing around the butcher's chain-link curtain and there was a solid, meaty smell. Geenie tried to peer through the gaps as her mother dragged her past. There

222

was always blood and sawdust in butcher's shops, which was all right to look at, as long as you didn't have to touch it. It was like the Italian paintings Jimmy had taken her to see in the National Gallery. All flesh and blood. It looked strange and sort of lovely, but you wouldn't want it on your hands.

The front door of the shop was open and an electric fan was groaning in the corner. The air, heavy with a chemical smell, seemed thicker, coarser, inside the shop.

A man in a white coat came to greet them, holding out a strong-looking hand.

'Hello, Robin,' said Ellen, smiling and touching his fingertips. 'I'm afraid I've had to bring my daughter with me.'

The man glanced down at Geenie. The skin on his face looked like cheese.

'That's quite all right, Madam.' He narrowed his eyes but did not smile. Instead, he knelt on the green tiles beside Geenie and whispered, 'How would you like to look like Garbo?'

His breath reeked of milky tea. Geenie kept a tight hold on her mother's hand.

'She'd love it,' said Ellen. 'What girl wouldn't?'

'Then I shall arrange it,' said the man, still kneeling, still breathing tea. 'Hilda will take off all the excess weight . . .' here he plunged a hand into Geenie's hair and lifted it away from her face— 'and then set it for you. How about that?'

Geenie snatched a long strand of her hair away from Robin's fingers, placed it in her mouth, and began to chew.

Between chews, she said, 'Cut it off, do you mean?'

223

'I mean, lick it into shape.' He winked. 'Hilda will make you look very sophisticated. It's her speciality.' Straightening up and facing Ellen, he added, 'It will take about an hour. Enough time for a special treatment for yourself, Madam.'

Ellen pulled her hand free of Geenie's and gave her a little shove forwards. 'You'll look beautiful, darling,' she said, her eyes still on Robin. 'Think how jealous Diana will be when she comes home.'

*   *   *

Hilda held out a pink paisley gown. 'Slip this on love, and we'll get you washed.'

Pushing her arms into the scratchy material, Geenie asked, 'Are you going to make me look like Garbo?'

Hilda gave a short laugh. 'You and all the others.'

The basin was cold against her neck. Hilda's fingers sprung about Geenie's scalp as she rubbed in the shampoo. She wore very red lipstick and had a splodge of freckles on her nose. Her hair was shiny yellow and her curls bounced as she rinsed the soap away. 'What a lot of hair,' she said.

'Some people call me Flossy, because it looks like candyfloss.'

'Do they now? Come over to the mirror, then, and we'll see what we can do about that.'

It had been a while since Geenie had studied her own reflection. Sitting in the curtained cubicle, she looked in the large round mirror before her. Her hair now reached her waist and her face looked darker than before.

Hilda pulled a metal comb through the ends of

224

Geenie's hair, making her yelp.

'This is a right old tangle. Doesn't your mother brush it for you?'

Geenie shook her head.

Hilda frowned as she tugged the comb through. 'We might have to cut some of these out I'm afraid, love.'

The metal teeth sang as Hilda tackled another knot.

'Cut it all off.' Geenie stared at her own mouth as she formed the phrase.

Hilda stopped combing. 'All of it?'

'Really short.'

Hilda ran her fingers through the thick mass. 'It would be a shame to lose *all* of it . . .'

'I don't want it any more. Get rid of it.'

'Are you sure, Miss? What'll your mother say?'

'She won't say anything.'

Hilda hesitated. She put one hand on her hip and held the comb in the air. 'How old are you, if you don't mind me asking, Miss?'

'Thirteen,' Geenie lied.

Hilda sighed. 'And you're sure you want it short?'

'Yes. Quite sure.'

'Right.' Hilda reached for the scissors. 'Put your head forward.'

And she began to cut.

The hair sprayed down to the floor. Once cut, it twisted helplessly to the ground. It was like when Kitty lifted the pie dish to trim the edge of the pastry. The stuff fell cleanly from the knife, as if relieved to be set free.

Hilda's bosom pressed against Geenie's shoulder as she angled the girl's head. Geenie

225

closed her eyes, breathed in Hilda's currant-bun scent, and stayed absolutely still in the chair, waiting to be transformed. It would be like the dancing princesses being set free by Jack. Everything would be different, after this; once the yellow curtain was drawn back and she stepped out into the shop, everything would change. When Jimmy was alive, she'd been Flossy. But Jimmy wasn't coming back.

'Short enough?'

Geenie opened her eyes. Her hair brushed the tops of her shoulders.

'Shorter,' she said, closing her eyes again.

Throughout the cutting, Geenie heard only one noise from the back room: it was a familiar, long 'yes'.

*   *   *

After an hour, it was done. Hilda had cut a bob so short that the lobes of Geenie's ears were partly exposed. She felt her hair prickling the skin there. Turning her head to the side, she saw how white her neck was, and reached up to touch it.

Hilda laughed. 'Nothing there any more, is there?'

Geenie looked in the mirror again. She wasn't sure who was staring back at her. The reflection didn't seem to be one she quite recognised. Instead of a mass of hair, there was her face: her pale blue eyes, her receding chin, her small mouth, all looking strangely prominent.

Hilda swept the blonde strands into an enormous pile. 'Do you want to take it home?' She swished the curtains back so Geenie was exposed.

Geenie looked around, expecting to hear her mother's shocked response to her new look. But there was no sign of Ellen.

'Miss? I can put it in a bag for you, if you like.'

Geenie looked at the mound of dead hair. 'My mother might want it,' she said.

*   *   *

When Ellen eventually emerged from the back room, she was no longer wearing orange lipstick, and her hair looked exactly the same as before, but the green shiny dress was creased across her thighs and bottom.

Geenie sat in the chair by the reception desk with a paper bag full of hair on her lap, and waited for her mother to notice.

'Robin said my daughter's hair would be included in the price.' Ellen leaned across the desk and spoke to the top of Hilda's head.

Hilda glanced at Geenie, and Ellen's eyes followed.

There was a tiny silence, during which Geenie listened to the groaning of the electric fan. Her head felt light and cool. Gripping the bag tightly, she knew she was ready for whatever happened.

'What have you done?' There was a tremble in Ellen's voice which Geenie hadn't heard for a very long time.

'What,' Ellen repeated, staring at her daughter's head, 'have you done?'

Holding out the open bag, Geenie shook it in her mother's direction. Then she watched as Ellen closed her eyes very slowly, put a hand to her mouth and shook her head. 'Your beautiful hair!'

227

she whispered.

Geenie placed the bag back on her lap, expecting Ellen to take a swipe at it, but instead Ellen came and knelt on the floor before her. It was a moment before she spoke, and, when she did, her voice was so quiet Geenie had to lean forward to make out what she was saying. 'Jimmy loved your hair! You were his Flossy.'

Geenie studied her mother's eyes. They were smaller, greyer, than her own. They looked, she thought, washed out.

'Don't you remember, Geenie?'

Slowly, Geenie put the bag of dead hair on the floor. 'Of course I remember,' she said. 'I remember everything about Jimmy.' Her voice sounded loud in the empty shop.

Ellen reached out and touched the new, blunt ends of her daughter's hair. She took a strand between her finger and thumb and rubbed at it, as though it were a fine fabric.

Then Geenie said, 'But he's gone, hasn't he?'

Ellen pulled Geenie into her arms and held her. Geenie pressed her cheek into her mother's shoulder and felt her shuddering breath on the back of her own naked neck. They both held on tight.

When Ellen let go, she scooped up the bag of hair, carefully folded the top over, and tucked it under her arm. 'I'll keep this safe,' she said.

TWENTY-SEVEN

Arthur said they should have tea before dancing, and Kitty was relieved to have an excuse to put off the moment when he'd touch her, remembering the way he'd placed his hand on her backside at the beach. He led her through the quiet hotel and out into the tea garden. The Crown and Thistle wasn't nearly as upmarket as the White Hart: there was no revolving door, the girl on the desk didn't have a uniform, and it was a smaller place altogether, in the centre of town rather than out by the lake; but it was, Kitty thought, quite posh enough, and much better than the Drill Hall for dancing, even in the afternoon. Most people seemed to be sitting outside in the small garden, under the shade of the hotel's blue umbrellas, and she'd been right: the place was full of young women—some of them probably worked at the Macklows'. She didn't look too closely at individual faces in case there was one she recognised. Over the tinkle of 'Tiptoe Through the Tulips' there was the clatter of teaspoons on porcelain. As they crossed the lawn, there was a limp round of applause between numbers.

She was wearing her lily-print dress and a neat white tricorne hat, to the front of which she'd appliquéd a violet. It was her only hat besides the beret, and she was fond of it, even though Lou always said it looked like a boat washed up on her head. She'd pinned the hat so tightly to her hair that she could feel it pull every time she nodded to Arthur as they tried to find a table.

229

Arthur got out his hankie and wiped the lattice-work chair before Kitty sat. There was a blob of jam on the cloth and no parasol. Kitty removed her hat and wondered if she should have worn gloves to hide the fact that the tips of her fingers were damp.

'Well,' said Arthur, squinting at her. 'This is nice.'

He straightened his jacket sleeves. He was wearing the same suit she'd seen him in at the pictures, and she saw, now, that the fabric was shiny with wear on the elbows. His face was ruddy and he'd put something on his hair to keep it down. What with this, his flushed cheeks, and his damp brow, his whole head looked as though it had been covered in a film of grease.

Taking out his pipe, he twisted round, searching for the waiter. 'I'm parched,' he announced.

'Have you been here before?'

'Couple of times. In the evenings.'

Kitty was surprised but tried to hide it by looking down at the tablecloth.

'It's what you do, isn't it? With women, I mean.'

She'd never heard him say that word, *women*, before. It sounded slightly obscene.

'No doubt you've been here plenty, Kitty. Dancer like you.'

Kitty thought of the times she'd been to the Sunday tea-dance with Lou when she was younger: the two of them had clutched at each other's dresses, and Lou always hissed that Kitty should lead in case any boys were watching them.

She lifted her head. 'What do you mean, with *women*?'

Arthur tucked some tobacco into his pipe and

smiled. 'You know. Girls and that. *Ladies*. A twirl around the floor in some hotel. It's what they expect, isn't it?'

Kitty wiped her palms on her skirt and raised her chin. 'What do *you* expect, then?'

Arthur lit his pipe. 'Oh,' he said, 'I don't know. Bit of company, I suppose.' He paused before looking straight at her. 'Someone to share things with. Doesn't really matter what they are, does it? As long as you do them together.'

Kitty looked across the lawn. The sun blazed down, bleaching everything in sight.

Arthur put his hand up for the waiter, but the boy didn't seem to see them.

'Do you want to stay in service, Kitty?'

The question caught her off guard. It wasn't something she'd thought much about. She'd just been glad not to have to live with Lou and Bob any more, and it didn't seem like there was any choice other than to stay in service—at least until she was married. Not that getting married seemed very likely to Kitty. She didn't allow herself to picture that scenario very often, and when she did, she always thought of the wedding photograph, with herself in a tidy marocain silk frock, perhaps, and a feather in her hat, which would bear no resemblance to a boat. But she couldn't imagine the man at her side at all.

'It's not a bad life, is it?' she answered.

'Well,' said Arthur. '*I'm* all right. Come and go as I please really: do a bit of gardening, see to the beast. They don't seem to mind, as long as I show my face and things keep going. It's better than slogging it down at the rubber factory, at any rate.' He sucked on his pipe. 'But I don't know about

231

you. Seems to me you're wasted, with them lot.'

The waiter was near them again, and Kitty raised her hand a fraction of an inch. But he swept straight past.

'You could be cooking in some proper house,' Arthur continued. 'For proper gentry. Have some girl do the skivvying for you. Those cakes of yours are smashing. Especially the—what is it? French sponge.'

'French buns.'

'That's it. Smashing.'

She smiled. For a while now, she'd had an idea that perhaps she'd be able to move and get a position as a real cook somewhere else, somewhere there'd be a kitchen maid to help her. But after the salmon incident, she knew she wouldn't get anything like a decent reference from Mrs Steinberg.

'Or, of course . . .' he licked his bottom lip. 'Of course, you could decide to go off and get married to some lucky Joe.'

'Didn't we ought to dance?' she said, standing up so she wouldn't have to look at his shining eyes. 'It's getting on. The band only plays until four.'

'What about your tea?'

But she was already heading for the open patio doors.

*   *   *

As they walked to the floor, Arthur let his hand rest on Kitty's hip. In between the mopping of brows, the band was playing a drowsy 'Continental'. Kitty noticed that the lead trumpeter's shirt was wet through; you could see

232

the outline of his vest. A few girl-couples limped through the dance, gazing over each other's shoulders, but there were no men in sight, apart from an old gentleman still wearing his jacket, who was guiding his wife slowly around the floor, his eyes half shut.

She let Arthur pull her quite close before they began to move to the music. His hand was warm and dry as it clasped her fingers. He'd left his jacket on the chair outside, and his chest was against hers; she could feel its rise and fall. She thought again of the movement of Mr Crane's shoulders as he put on his shirt. The leap of his muscle.

Forwards, backwards, turn. Arthur wasn't a bad dancer at all. His waist was stiff, but his feet knew where to go. The trumpets let out a long blast in an attempt to get some life into the tune. No one here would dance on the tables, Kitty thought. She tried to concentrate on following Arthur and not think of how she'd danced in the kitchen with Mrs Steinberg, how she'd let her hips lead the way. Here she must sway, rather than swing. She mustn't force him with any sudden movement. His breath was on her forehead. He smelled slightly of his shed: warm mud and fraying string.

'That girl's very fond of you, you know.'

Kitty looked up.

'She told me what happened the other night, with Mrs S. Damned liberty, if you ask me.'

Kitty stopped moving, but Arthur swung her round.

'You should be careful, though. It's never good to let them get too close.' He was looking over her head. 'Better to stick with your own.'

'How do you mean?'

He swung her round again. 'I mean, they're all right and that, but in the end they'll always be them, and we'll always be us.'

The only reply Kitty could think of was, 'Geenie's just a girl.'

Arthur ignored this. 'Take Crane. He's on at me to join the Bolshies, but I know it's not for me, it's for them. I listen to what he has to say, and I even agree with some of it, but I keep my distance.'

The music stopped for a moment. He released her and wiped the back of his neck with his handkerchief.

'It's not as if I'm really close to—to any of them—'

'Didn't say you were. But the girl was gabbing about you making her some costume or other. Rang alarm bells, that's all.'

The music started again. He took her hand and smiled. 'Just looking out for you, Kitty. Seeing you're all right.'

She said nothing.

'Told you I could dance,' he said, dropping his hand lower on her back and pulling her in closer.

'I think it's good,' said Kitty, keeping her fingers taut in his, 'the way Mr Crane stands up for the working classes.'

Arthur gave a loud laugh over her head. 'He's just playing at it. Underneath all that talk, the *Daily Worker* and all that claptrap, he's like the rest. He's one of them.'

'At least he cares.'

Arthur pushed his hip into her body and moved his mouth close to her ear. 'Crane doesn't know anything about the working classes, Kitty. Have you ever seen him do any actual *work*?'

She tried to move her face away from his breath. 'He did that room, didn't he? Knocked it through?'

'I did that, with a mate who's a brickie. Crane just handed us some tools now and then.'

'He's writing a book.'

'That's not work, is it? Sitting at a desk making up stories.'

Kitty didn't reply. She didn't mention Arthur's love of Westerns. Instead she closed her eyes and remembered the feel of Mr Crane's fingers on her elbow, and was glad Arthur hadn't touched her there.

'Ladies and gentlemen, I'm sorry to announce this will be the last dance of the afternoon. I thank you.' The trumpeter made a salute and let out a loud blast, and the band began a new tune with more vim. Yelping girls suddenly squeezed through the patio doors and piled onto the dance floor. They began spinning each other around and laughing. Arthur kept his back straight and squeezed Kitty's hand.

But Kitty had decided to let her hips lead the way. Her thighs took the strain as she dipped, then straightened, taking Arthur with her. She hardened her jaw and looked to the right, then the left, aware of Arthur watching her with a slight frown, his feet stumbling in an attempt to keep up with hers. The floor itself seemed to be moving with the rhythm. Everything was much too hot and fast, but the only thing to do was keep dancing. It was the last number and you had to keep dancing. The girls bounced around them, giggling, overheated, swinging.

Arthur hooked his knee between her legs and

235

swiped it to the side, almost causing her to topple. 'You're leading,' he hissed.

Regaining her balance, Kitty continued to dance, gripping his fingers in hers and twirling him around. Their feet tangled but she carried on.

'Kitty!' As he tugged his hand free of hers, she span out of his path; Arthur lunged forward, arms flailing, and she watched him and thought, *he's going to fall*, but she made no move to save him. He batted his arms in the air, as he'd done when trying to fend off that wasp in the garden, and somehow, through this frantic windmilling action, managed to stop himself going down.

The music stopped and a great wave of chatter and applause broke over their heads. Immediately, waitresses appeared and began to move through the crowd, pushing their way out into the tea garden with trays.

They stood apart in the bustle, staring at each other.

'You were leading.'

She put a hand to her hair. 'Was I?' she said, panting slightly from the heat and the exercise. 'I didn't realise.'

He seemed to be waiting for some sort of explanation, but she couldn't think of anything to offer him.

'We'd better go,' he said eventually, starting for the doors.

Standing in the middle of the dance floor, she watched him leave. She was sure he would turn around when he reached the doors and call for her to follow; he'd extend an arm, his trimmed moustache would twitch, and he'd say, 'You coming?' She waited, her eyes fixed on his short

236

back. But he stepped right through the doors without so much as a glance over his shoulder.

The room had emptied around her. Kitty looked up at the stage. The band was packing up, but the trumpeter was still sitting back in his chair, his shirt soaked. Raising his hand to his brow, he saluted her.

TWENTY-EIGHT

It was incredible how close the girl could be. As Ellen walked down the garden path in the Sunday afternoon sunshine, she was sure she could hear Geenie breathing. It was almost as if the girl were trying to stick herself to Ellen's own skin. When they reached the stream, Ellen stopped abruptly, and Geenie crashed into her back, her face crushing against her mother's spine. Blotto nosed Ellen's ankles.

'Is it possible,' asked Ellen, 'that you could walk *beside* me, like a normal human being?'

Dog and daughter looked up with big eyes. She sighed. 'Right. All off.' She began unbuttoning Geenie's blouse, but the girl pulled away.

'I can do it.'

'Suit yourself.'

Ellen was wearing a knitted sleeveless top with nothing beneath, so was naked to the waist with one peeling motion. She unbuttoned her linen slacks, stepped out of her knickers and kicked them aside. They landed under the willow tree.

'Ready?'

Geenie had undressed, and was standing with

both hands clenched around her backside.

'What are you doing that for?'

'In case anyone sees my bottom.'

Ellen laughed. 'It's the front you want to worry about,' she said, looking her daughter up and down. Over the summer, Geenie had filled out a little: there was now a definite curve to her hip, a fullness to her nipples; even a few pubic hairs were beginning to show.

Ellen stretched her arms above her head, swivelling her hips around and bending at the knees before balancing on the edge of the bank. It was what James had always done before bathing. After weeks of sunshine, the earth was powdery between her toes. She looked over her shoulder and held out a hand. 'Come on, Flossy. Nothing matters when you're naked.'

Geenie stepped to her side, and together they launched themselves into the water.

It only came up to Ellen's thighs, but it was cold enough to make them both yelp, which set Blotto off. The dog ran back and forth along the bank, yapping hysterically, ears bobbing and throat jerking with effort.

'Watch this!' Geenie cried, and there was a great splash as she threw herself backwards into the water, her limbs splaying, her newly shorn head going under. She held herself there, her face warped and silvery beneath the surface, and Ellen watched her daughter, wondering how long she would hold her breath this time. Ellen counted thirty seconds, concentrating on the sticklebacks pulsing around the girl's waist. Blotto's yaps turned into howls. Sixty seconds. Geenie's cheeks ballooned and her eyes were squeezed tight. A minute and a half. Longer than she'd ever done before. The dog's howls reached a higher pitch, and, in the shade of the willows, Ellen felt the top half of her body begin to cool and prickle.

'Geenie,' she said, trying to keep her voice steady. 'Come up now.'

Two minutes.

'Come up.'

Two and a half minutes.

'Come up.' Ellen plunged her hands into the water and grasped her daughter by the shoulders. 'For God's sake—'

But Geenie twisted away, burst out of the water, sucked in a huge breath, and, using her hands as paddles, began to scoop the stream in her mother's direction, almost knocking her down.

It took Ellen a moment before she steadied herself and fought back. She ran the length of both arms across the surface of the stream, pushing water over her daughter's head. The stream was a white fury of crashing foam as the two of them shrieked and splashed, and Blotto rushed around the base of the willow tree, barking.

*   *   *

Ellen spread a towel on the lawn and they lay down to dry themselves in the sun. Next to Geenie, Blotto flopped on his side, panting hoarsely. Overhead, the sky throbbed blue. Ellen closed her eyes and let the sun warm her from head to toe. She'd always loved to sunbathe, and believed the sun's energy penetrated her very core. She smiled to herself, remembering the heat in the back room of the hairdressers'. When Robin unhooked her bra he'd made a sort of dive straight for her nipples, which had been tiresome, but she'd soon guided him back to her face and slowed him down. Then he'd carried her to the divan, which was something she hadn't expected. No one had carried her anywhere since she was a child.

'When are George and Diana coming back?' Geenie had buttoned up her blouse and pulled on her skirt, and was kneeling on the towel, looking down at her mother.

'Soon.' Crane hadn't said anything specific about his return when he and Diana left yesterday morning. He'd just mumbled something about being away 'a few days', and, at the time, Ellen hadn't the will to tackle him about it. He'd hardly taken a thing with him, though, so he'd have to come back, if only to pick up some clean underclothes.

'How soon?'

Ellen shielded her eyes from the sun and peered at her daughter. 'What would you say,' she asked, 'if I told you that it might be just you and me, for a while?'

'Aren't they coming back?'

'I didn't say that.'

Geenie tucked her chin into her chest and looked towards the house.

'But if they didn't come back for a while, it would be all right, wouldn't it?' Ellen continued. 'We'd get on all right, wouldn't we? The two of us.' She sat up and put a hand on her daughter's arm.

'Why did we come here?'

'You know why, darling.'

'I don't.'

Ellen's head began to feel tight with heat. She

drew the towel around her shoulders so she wouldn't have to answer her daughter's question while fully naked. Then she looked at her hands and tried to think how she should begin.

Geenie sat very still. Blotto had begun to snore.

'When Jimmy died,' Ellen said, 'when he died, I didn't know what to do. I know it's hard to understand, but I needed to get away . . .'

'Will we go back?'

'To London?'

Geenie nodded.

Ellen pulled the towel tighter. 'I don't know, darling, maybe—'

'Because I don't want to go back. I want us all to stay here.'

Ellen caught Geenie's chin and twisted her daughter's face towards her own. 'So I did the right thing, didn't I?'

There was no response.

'Geenie? Don't you think I did the right thing?'

There was a pause, during which the dog's snores grew louder.

Geenie closed her eyes and replied in a flat tone, 'Yes, Mama.'

Ellen's head was aching now; she could feel her pulse behind her eyes. She'd have to go and sit inside, in the dark. The sun's energy was too much for her today. A gin and it would help. She removed the towel and reached for her clothes.

'How did he die?' Geenie's voice was quieter, but she still spoke in the same flat tone.

Ellen dropped her clothes on the grass. The dog woke with a piercing yap and tore down the garden towards some unknown crisis.

'How did who die, darling?'

241

'Jimmy.'

Ellen took a breath. Blotto was rushing around the willow tree again, barking with abandon.

'You know how he died, darling. I told you. He died during the operation on his ankle.'

'Why?'

'Operations are very dangerous—'

'People don't usually die of a broken ankle.'

'Well, Jimmy did. The operation went wrong. Sometimes it happens.' Ellen stood up and shook the towel out. She must get inside before the dog started howling again. 'Jimmy was unlucky. We all were.' She dressed quickly, being careful not to look directly at Geenie, who was staring at the house, her blank face steady and unblinking.

Leaving her daughter on the lawn, Ellen walked to the writing studio. The door wasn't locked, and she went straight inside and managed to close it before the tears came. The afternoon sun had made the studio like a glass house, and she leant back on the door and wept and sweated silently, one hand across her mouth, the other clenched tight across her belly.

When she'd managed to stop, she sat in Crane's armchair and steadied her breathing by telling herself, over and over: *he will be back*. She could smell the muddiness of the stream on her hands. Her nails were full of it. *He will come back*. He'd sit here again and look at her while she scolded him for not getting on with his novel. He would have to come back, and when he did, she would make it all right. After all, hadn't she been thinking of him, of their first time together, even when Robin had been inside her yesterday? It was amazing how one man could seem like another during the sexual act,

242

how you could almost forget who the man was entirely, and become lost in the act itself. Robin had been a sure-touched and attentive lover, but hadn't she been thinking of Crane's trembling hands? It was outside the bedroom that men were so very different.

Perhaps if she waited long enough, Crane would arrive and find her in the chair, and she could say she'd been sitting there, waiting, all the time he'd been gone. Then he'd call her his Cleopatra, and they'd make love on his desk. Perhaps there was still some hope for a pregnancy.

Wiping her wet cheeks with the heel of her hand, she stood and, telling herself that she didn't mean to, opened his top desk drawer. She didn't think about what she was doing, or of what she was about to do; she just clasped the brass handle and pulled. Inside were several photographs of Diana as an infant (one in a knitted bonnet on her mother's slim lap); a couple of pens with broken nibs; a letter from the publishing house saying they would always welcome him back; and a dirty handkerchief. Ellen pulled the second drawer open. Apart from a clutch of rubber bands and a few pencil shavings, it was empty. The final drawer was the deepest, and felt heavy as she pulled. She knew this was it: the manuscript. And sure enough, there was a pile of paper, the top leaf of which read:

LOVE ON THE DOWNS
a novel
by G. M. Crane

What did that M stand for? He'd never used a

middle name before. She stepped back from the paper and swallowed, becoming aware of how very quiet it was in the studio. Briefly she remembered Geenie, still sitting outside, staring blankly at the house, and thought that she should push the drawer back into place and go into the house to fetch them both some barley lemonade. Or maybe a gin and it. But instead she reached in, dragged the pile of paper from the drawer and placed it on top of the mess of papers on his desk. Then she stood a moment, looking at the top sheet, the rush of her blood making her feel light-headed. She gave a small laugh—how bad could it be? It was only the story of their love affair. It wasn't like she didn't know what had happened. What was happening.

She turned over the title page. The second page was blank, apart from an inscription typed halfway down the sheet: *For my dear Diana*. Ellen stared at the words for a full minute, not quite believing it wasn't her own name there, before turning two more blank pages and coming to the heading: *CHAPTER ONE: The Arrival*. Turning another page, she finally found a whole typed paragraph, which she held before her and read.

It was going to be an endless summer. Georgina Chance had arrived at the Sussex cottage with her family two days ago. As soon as she set foot in the place, she'd left the crashing of teacups and the clatter of servants carrying goodness knows what up and down the stairs behind, and had climbed to the top of the green hill which rose up from the end of their long garden. For she was a young woman with scant respect for

*the oppressive gentility of her generation. Born
into the aristocracy, she longed for one thing:
escape from manners and money, and all that
went with it.*

So it *was* about her, albeit in a roundabout way.
Realising that her fingers were sweating, making
the thin paper wilt, Ellen sat in the armchair,
placed the page flat on her lap, and read on.

*No one could have been more relieved than she
to be out of London. The Downs were there,
wetly beckoning from every window.*

She'd have to challenge him on that. 'Wetly
beckoning' wasn't right at all.

*What bliss it had been to walk barefoot through
the grass, with no care for convention, and no
one to see her shapely white ankles!*

Yes, that was right. Although Ellen herself had
yet to walk the full height of the hill.

*She'd allowed her thoughts to wander to her
great love: poetry. Her father was against poetry,
caring only for money and commerce, and her
mother said it was 'all right until you get
married'. But for Georgina, poetry was the life
force itself, and out there, on the green hills, she
could feel its power in her very bones . . .*

Ellen rose and went to the desk to find the rest.
But the next page was blank. She placed the typed
page on top of the ones she'd already read and

lifted another page. That was blank, too. And the one after that. And the one after that. She picked up the whole pile of paper and flicked through its corners with her thumb. But there was nothing. Not one more word. Just page after page of white, blank paper.

Perhaps this was a false start. The rest of it would be somewhere else, hidden. She bent down and looked beneath the desk, lifting the edge of Blotto's hair-matted old blanket. A ripe whiff like stewed meat came up, and she moved away, holding her nose. She looked around the room. Of course. The filing cabinet.

On her knees, she wrenched up the wooden shutter. The top drawer was stuck; as she tugged it open it made a squealing sound which reminded her of the lorry she'd seen dragging that poor cow down Petersfield High Street. But she blinked that thought away. When she'd finally got the thing fully open and delved her hand to the back, it was empty. The next drawer opened easily, but there was nothing in there apart from a copy of *The Socialist Sixth of the World*. Ellen threw it on the floor in disgust. The other drawers yielded only dog-eared envelopes and stray photo-corners. Then she looked beneath the low table with the wireless on top; all she found was the wastepaper basket, so she rummaged in there, too, fingering a drying apple core and a screwed-up piece of paper. She was about to move on when she noticed that the paper had something typed on it, so she smoothed it flat and read the words: *Sunlight. Shadow. The girl brings him cakes on a tray. His blood is heavy with wanting.*

She almost screwed it back up and threw it

away—she was thinking about looking behind the filing cabinet now—but something made her read it again. *Sunlight. Shadow. The girl brings him cakes on a tray. His blood is heavy with wanting.*

Ellen stood, holding the page in her damp fingers. She smoothed it out once more, trying to get rid of all the creases this time, to make it completely flat, thinking that perhaps she'd missed something. She read it again. *The girl brings him cakes on a tray.*

There was no mistake, no hidden word, nothing missing in the creases of the paper. *Sunlight. Shadow.* Who else could it be? Who else could it be, this girl with cakes who made his blood heavy? Her stomach squeezed tight, and she felt a hot liquid at the back of her throat. She leant on the desk to steady herself until the nausea had passed. *The girl brings him cakes on a tray.* How had she not seen it before? His novel was nothing, the story over before it had begun, the heroine ridiculous, and nothing like her—apart from those ankles; it was clear to Ellen now that Crane had been sitting in this place for months doing absolutely damn all; but *who was this*? She heard herself saying it aloud. 'Who is this?' Her voice was small, strangled. 'Who is this?' she repeated, knowing the answer full well.

TWENTY-NINE

They came back in the middle of the night. Geenie was twisted in her bed, waiting for sleep, when she heard the front door open, the low sound of George's voice, and Diana's quick footsteps up the stairs. She sat up and listened. The clack-click of Diana's door closing was louder than usual, and was followed by several bangs and crashes. Then there was George's even tread along the landing. A rumble—that would be him putting his case down. A couple of thumps—taking his shoes off. The squeak of her mother's bedsprings. And then— silence.

She threw back the covers and climbed out of bed. Tiptoeing to the door, she listened. Not a sound. Keeping close to the wall, she edged along the landing to Diana's room. Once inside, she could make out Diana's suitcase, still buckled, sitting by the window. There was also a large lump beneath the bedclothes. A large lump which didn't move when Geenie hissed, 'Diana!' So she sat on the edge of the bed, flicked on the lamp, and poked the lump. It twitched. 'You're back!' she whispered.

'Go away,' said a muffled voice, and the lump shifted.

Geenie sat a while longer, looking at the lump, wondering whether to leave it alone. Then she thought of the saggy centre of her own bed, and how lonely it was there, and she said, 'Something exciting happened, while you were away.' She stretched out a hand and tried to find the edge of the sheet so she could peel it back. Grabbing a piece of smooth cotton, she pulled, but a hand appeared and gripped the sheet hard, preventing it from moving.

'Please come out.'

'No.'

'What's the matter?' Again, Geenie tugged at the bedclothes. This time she caught Diana off guard, and the sheet came away suddenly, revealing Diana's back. The girl was curled in a cramped ball, and was still wearing her blouse and skirt. Her hair was pulled into a tight plait so intricate in design, and so securely knotted, that it must hurt to wear it. 'What happened to your hair?' Geenie whispered.

'My mother did it.'

Geenie tapped Diana's tense shoulder. 'Look at mine! Look at my hair, Diana!' She crawled around the bed, trying to see her friend's eyes. But Diana remained scrunched tight, her face pressed to the mattress.

'Please look.'

Diana covered the back of her head with both hands, as if ducking a blow, and curled into an even smaller ball.

Geenie sat on her heels and sighed. Deciding she may as well wait, she stretched out along what was available of the bed, and tried to stay as still as possible. Her friend couldn't remain in that position forever, she reasoned, and, in the end, her curiosity about the exciting thing that had happened would surely get the better of her.

Eventually, Diana stirred. Very slowly, she removed her hands from her head and caught hold of Geenie's wrist. Geenie waited a moment before whispering, 'I'm glad you came back.'

'Daddy said we had to. I could've stayed with Mummy.'

'Why didn't you?'

Diana lifted her head. 'It just wasn't the right time. Mummy's got a very important show on and it wasn't the right time for her. Any other time, I could've stayed.'

Geenie put her other hand on top of Diana's. 'I'm glad you came back,' she repeated.

After a while, Diana uncurled herself and knelt next to Geenie on the bed. 'What happened to your—'

'I cut it,' said Geenie, sitting up.

Diana clamped her fingers around the top of Geenie's scalp and twisted her head this way and that so she could examine the bob fully. Finally, she nodded her approval. 'Was it awful here without me?'

'Yes,' said Geenie, without thinking. 'Quite awful. Apart from the haircut. And Ellen and I bathed in the stream and I soaked her.'

'Well,' said Diana, yawning, 'I don't mean to stay long.'

'What does your father say?'

'You know Daddy. He hardly says anything. Unless it's about the workers.' She looked Geenie in the face. 'We have to carry out the plan, so I can get home.'

Geenie had almost forgotten about the plan.

'We have to start as soon as possible,' continued Diana, lying flat on the bed, stretching her arms and closing her eyes. 'We'll begin first thing in the morning.'

Geenie remained sitting upright, watching over her friend until Diana's plump bottom lip fell away from her teeth and she began to snore, softly.

*   *   *

'Keep still, Miss.'

Kitty looked peculiar with all those pins in her mouth. Her face was set, her voice louder than

250

usual.

'Now turn around, please.' She pressed the cool steel tip of the inch tape into the nape of Geenie's neck and ran the length of it down her spine. 'Two pompoms, was it?'

'Yes. And they must be black,' interjected Diana, who was sitting on a kitchen chair, watching, having already been measured for her costume.

'You said, Miss.'

'How long will it take?' asked Geenie.

'That depends.' The tape was now around Geenie's waist. Kitty held the ends together for a moment, then let it go and began spinning it around her hand, winding it back into a ball.

'On what?' asked Diana, swinging her legs and scuffing the tiles.

'That's you done, Miss,' Kitty said to Geenie. When she'd finished winding the tape, and had written some numbers down on a little pad, she turned to Diana. 'It depends on how busy I am, Miss.'

'Can you hurry?' Geenie pressed her palms together and gazed up at Kitty from under her brows. 'Please, Kitty? Can you?'

Kitty laughed. 'Well. I suppose it shouldn't take me so very long . . .'

Geenie hopped on the spot.

'Especially if I borrow my sister's machine.'

Diana stood and, with her hands behind her back, aimed a dazzling smile directly at Kitty. 'That would be really super of you.'

Kitty took a step back. 'Yes, well. I'll see what I can do.' She turned to the table and picked up one of the long white cotton nightdresses Geenie had dumped in her lap that morning. 'Are you sure it's all right for me to use these, Miss?' She held one up to the light from the window. 'They're very nice stuff.'

'They're old,' said Geenie, standing at her side and gazing at the fine cotton.

'But your mother said we could use them?'

Geenie nodded. 'She hasn't worn them in years.' One was from Geenie's dressing-up pile, the other she'd pinched from her mother's drawer this morning. But she hadn't told even Diana about that.

Kitty looked from Geenie to Diana and back again. 'Well, if you're sure—'

'When can you do them?' asked Diana.

Kitty gathered up the fabric, her notebook and her work-box. 'We'll see.'

Diana shot a look at Geenie. 'When?' asked Geenie, standing in front of Diana and grasping Kitty's hand. It was smaller than her mother's, and much rougher to touch, but she squeezed it as tenderly as she could. 'When do you think you might?'

Kitty looked down at her fingers, and Geenie gave another squeeze.

'I'm going to my sister's tomorrow, so I might be able to make a start then—'

'Oh, please do!' said Diana.

'But I can't promise anything, Miss. Now, I really must get on.'

Geenie could tell by the little flush rising in Kitty's cheeks that they would have the costumes soon enough.

*　　　*　　　*

252

They began rehearsals right away in Geenie's bedroom, wearing just their knickers and vests (because no other costume would have been right), and with their faces painted white. Diana had appointed herself writer/director, and Geenie was in charge of costumes and set.

'First of all,' said Diana, standing on the bed with her hands on her hips, 'we'll both do a song.'

Geenie was sitting cross-legged on the paint-stained rug. 'I can't sing.'

'You can do a dance, then.'

But Geenie didn't think she could do a dance, either. 'Can I do Cleopatra?'

'You want to do *Shakespeare*?'

'No—just Cleopatra.'

'What will you do?'

Geenie thought. 'I'll die on stage. I'll collapse in a swoon, and I'll die. I'll wear my white robe.'

'But we'll be in Pierrot costumes. That's the point.'

Geenie was silent. From here, Diana looked rather frightening: her hair, now released from its complicated plait, had gone kinky and wild.

'I'll do a dance,' said Diana, kicking up one leg and managing to keep her balance perfectly whilst the earrings wound around Geenie's headboard rattled in a mad dance. 'You don't have to do anything. Anyway. That's just the *prelude*.'

'What's a prelude?'

'It's like an introduction. Something to whet the audience's appetite.' Diana strutted from one side of the bed to the other then launched herself to the floor, landing before Geenie with a quiet thud, her hair shuddering around her bare shoulders.

'What's important is the Main Act.' She licked her lips. 'Now. It's a one-act play called *What the Gardener Saw*. You'll be the housemaid, Ruby, and I'll be the great poet, John Cross.'

'Can't I be the great poet?'

'No. My father's a poet and I know much more about it.'

Geenie lay on the floor and looked at the ceiling. 'Can't we do another play?'

Diana slowly walked around her friend before leaning over and looking into her face. 'You get to kiss me.'

Geenie sat up and the two girls' noses almost touched. 'What happens?'

'I'll show you.' Diana giggled and pulled the other girl to her feet. 'It's *hopelessly* romantic. We open with me.' She jumped into position, sitting at the end of the bed. 'I'm at my desk, composing, like this.' She crossed her legs and, resting an elbow on one knee, put a fist to her forehead. 'Then you come in with your duster—'

'Duster?'

'It could be a feather one, I suppose, or a tea cloth—'

'I'll have a feather one.'

'So you come in, and you say, *Oh, sorry to disturb you, Sir*—'

'How do I say it?'

'How?'

'You're the director.'

'Well. Sort of—quiet, you know, and hesitant. Look at the floor a lot. Just think of Kitty and copy what she does. Like this.' Diana stood, hunched her shoulders, and shuffled towards the door. '*Oh*,' she said, her voice barely a whisper, '*I'm so sorry—*'

254

'Kitty isn't like that.'

'But that's more or less it, isn't it? Anyway, you're not Kitty, you're Ruby. It's a general impression of a housemaid sort that we're after.'

'Kitty's not a housemaid. She's a cook.'

Diana sighed. 'Do you want to know what happens next, or not?'

Geenie nodded.

'Now we come to the good part.' Diana sat back on the bed. 'I'm struck by the thunderbolt, you see—'

'What thunderbolt?'

'The thunderbolt of love. I'm struck with love, and I just sit and stare at you, like this.' Placing her hand flat on her heart, she opened her eyes as wide as they would go, then closed them slowly and let her neck go limp before saying, in a deep voice, 'I am inspired as never before—inspired by love.'

'Oh,' said Geenie, 'that's good.'

Diana smiled. 'Isn't it?'

'Do you kiss me then?'

'Not yet. In the next scene, you're kneeling on the floor, scrubbing, like this.' Diana got down on all fours and rubbed furiously at the rug with her knuckles, pausing to wipe her forehead in a long sweeping gesture.

'We'll need some props for that,' said Geenie.

'Of course—that's your department. So you're scrubbing, working really hard, and I—the great poet John Cross—come up behind you and start reading my love poem.'

'How does it go?'

Here Diana looked suddenly shy. She sat back on her heels and tucked her frizzy hair behind one ear. 'I haven't finished it yet.'

'Never mind. What then?'

'Then I kiss you, passionately.'

'Show me,' said Geenie.

'All right.' Diana stood, readjusted her knickers and vest, and took a step towards her. Geenie closed her eyes and waited.

'Don't close your eyes yet.'

'Why not?'

'We have to build up to the *moment*.' Diana stretched out a hand and let it rest on Geenie's shoulder. She moistened her cushiony top lip with her tongue and opened her mouth very slightly. Geenie began to giggle.

'You can't laugh when we perform it for real, you know.'

Geenie covered her mouth with one hand and took a deep breath.

'In fact,' Diana said, 'when I touch you, I think you should swoon.'

'I can do that.'

'Go on then.'

Geenie closed her eyes, put her forearm to her brow and let her body buckle. As she went down, Diana caught her, spreading one hand flat in the centre of Geenie's back, cupping the other beneath her naked neck, and pulling her close. 'Pretend you love me,' she said, moving in for the kiss.

When it came, the kiss was dry and hard, and both girls stayed completely still as their lips locked. Geenie squeezed her eyes tighter and wondered if she really would faint: her knees were weak, her neck twisted, her heartbeat loud in her ears; she could taste the sweat on Diana's top lip. At first, she held onto her friend with a fierce grip to keep from falling, but as the kiss went on,

Geenie let her lips go soft, and she found herself relaxing into Diana's arms.

Finally, Diana came up for air. 'Very good,' she said, a little breathlessly. 'I'll tell Daddy that we have a play to show them on Friday morning.' She reached past Geenie, grabbed her skirt from the bed and began to dress. Geenie did the same, her fingers slipping on the mother-of-pearl buttons on her blouse, her heart still jumping inside her vest.

THIRTY

When Kitty arrived at Woodbury Avenue on Wednesday afternoon, Lou was waiting for her in the doorway, wearing a lilac crepe frock with matching hat, and cradling a lilac bag beneath her arm as if it were a small, fashionable dog. She peered through the net which half-covered her eyes with lilac crosses. 'We're going to the White Hart for tea.'

'Now?'

'It's your birthday, isn't it?'

Kitty hadn't expected her sister to remember. 'Tomorrow. Tomorrow's my birthday.'

Lou shifted her bag to the other arm and stroked it. 'It's nearly your birthday then, isn't it? I've booked a taxicab and everything.'

'Where's Bob?'

Lou didn't answer this. Instead, she looked her sister up and down and said, 'I'd have thought you'd make more of an effort, on your birthday.'

'It's not my birthday,' Kitty replied, running a hand over the skirt of her lily-print frock. 'Anyway,

Lou, I really need to borrow your sewing machine this afternoon. Can't we go another day?'

Lou tutted. 'Don't be an idiot. Come inside. We'd better get you kitted out, quick.'

*   *   *

In the back of the cab, Lou stared out of the window at the sun-stunned streets. Her face was flattened by white powder, and her hands wouldn't stay still. It was unlike Lou, Kitty thought, to keep fidgeting with her hat, her gloves, her handbag; but all the way to the hotel, Lou's fingers were busy with some clasp, seam, or pin. Kitty held on instinctively to the straw hat attached to her hair. It was pink, to match the pink frock with the white bib front Lou had donated to Kitty for the afternoon. The frock was too small for Lou ('that's what marriage does for you,' she'd said), but wasn't too bad a fit for Kitty. The crispness of the organdie on her skin made up for the slight sagginess around her bosom. Lou had also persuaded her to experiment with her Tangine lipstick, and Kitty could taste the stale-sweetness of it on her mouth.

'Perhaps I could run up the costumes when we get back,' Kitty thought aloud.

'You'd better not.' Lou patted her handbag. 'I'll have to get on—Bob's dinner . . .'

'I won't get in the way.'

'Why are you so set on these bloody costumes?'

Kitty said nothing.

'It's not like they do much for you.'

'It means a lot to Miss Geenie.' Kitty looked at her sister. 'I don't give a fig for the other one, but,

258

well, you have to feel a bit sorry for Geenie.'

Lou huffed. 'Poor little miss millionaire. It must be awful, having all that money, and never having to lift a finger.'

'She's lonely, though,' said Kitty.

'Aren't we all,' Lou stated.

*　　*　　*

It was cool and silent in the hotel reception. Yellow chintz armchairs were plumped and ready, but no one was sitting in them. A gleaming coffee table displayed a fan of expensive magazines, untouched. Kitty stepped across the deep pile towards the woman at the desk, whose head was bowed over a snowy white register.

'It's through here,' said Lou, taking her sister's arm and leading her through a pair of glass doors.

They came into a large, light room which smelled strongly of beeswax. Pictures of ships on stormy seas covered the walls, and in the middle of the room was a grand piano. All the tables, each one displaying a tight white rose arrangement at its centre, were empty. An electric fan at the back of the room puffed over a parlour palm, but apart from that, the air was absolutely still.

Lou took the table next to the open windows, sticking her face in front of the fan for a moment and blowing out her cheeks before sitting down. 'This place is like the morgue. The morgue in a heatwave. Not very good for the dead, this kind of temperature. We'll have a cocktail, liven things up. Where's the boy?'

'Tea for me, please,' said Kitty, noticing the softness of the cushioned chair, the yellow and scarlet monogrammed antimacassar: WHH, the two Hs entwined in fish-bone stitch. 'And cake. Victoria sponge, if they have it.'

'No you won't. You'll have a White Lady with me. It's your birthday.'

'Not until tomorrow.'

'Where did you get your damned uptightness from? It's certainly not from Mother.'

A waiter crossed the carpet noiselessly and stood over them, one hand behind his back. He was young, with a spray of spots up one side of his neck, but his cuffs were crisp, and his face did not move.

'Two White Ladies, a pot of tea and some cakes, please,' said Lou, the dots of rouge on her cheeks crinkling.

'Would Madam like the afternoon selection? Or a particular cake?'

Lou hesitated. She looked down at the tablecloth, then enquired in a quieter voice, 'How much is the afternoon selection?'

The waiter's top lip twitched very slightly. 'The afternoon selection is three shillings, Madam. It consists of a selection of our best sandwiches, cakes and dainties.'

'All right,' said Lou, looking up at him with a wide smile. 'That's what we'll have.'

'Very good.' The waiter moved away as silently as he'd arrived.

Kitty leant across the table and touched her sister's fingers. 'Can you afford it, Lou?' she whispered.

'Of course I can,' snapped Lou, taking a packet of Player's from her handbag and lighting one. 'It's always good to check the price in these places

260

beforehand, that's all. Then they don't swindle you when it comes to the bill.' She drummed her painted fingernails along the tablecloth and blew smoke towards the windows. 'So. What's new in Bohemia?'

· Kitty had been dying to tell someone—anyone—about the row over the salmon for days. But she couldn't think of a way to explain it that wouldn't make her sister angry, so instead she offered, '*He* left for a few days, all of a sudden. It was quite peculiar.'

Lou took a long drag on her cigarette.

Kitty couldn't help adding, 'I think it might have had something to do with me.'

Lou gave a short laugh. 'What could it have had to do with you?'

'Maybe it didn't. But she shouted at me—and he didn't agree with it—and then, next day, he left.'

Their cocktails arrived in long-stemmed glasses. Lou thanked the waiter, who looked over their heads and gave a quick, stiff bow before retreating.

Kitty took a sip of her drink. The gin scalded her throat. 'It was all over nothing, really . . .'

'Don't give me that. What happened?'

Kitty swallowed another mouthful of White Lady. Her insides were suddenly cooled by the alcohol. It was lovely, like a cold, soft tongue flicking through you.

'Something about the fish being overdone. She got very upset over it.'

'What did she say?'

Having first checked over each shoulder to see if anyone else had come in, Kitty leaned across the table towards her sister and whispered, 'Fucking incinerated fish.'

261

Lou almost spat out her drink. 'No! She said that?'

Kitty giggled. 'They had this dinner party, and she went off her head, saying I'd overcooked the salmon—she called me in and said that it was—'

'Fucking incinerated?' asked Lou, wide-eyed. Kitty nodded. Both sisters took another drink, and then exploded with laughter.

Kitty was laughing so hard that she didn't notice the waiter had taken up position behind her chair. 'Oh!' she said, and giggled again as he placed the three-tiered silver tray and a silver teapot on the table.

'Will you require anything else, Madam?' he asked the air.

Lou shook her head.

When he'd gone, Kitty hissed, 'Did he hear us?'

'Don't think so,' said Lou, bypassing the sandwiches and helping herself to a cream slice. 'Happy twentieth birthday.' She held up her glass in a toast, and they clinked and drank. A happy flush of gin spread from Kitty's stomach to her thighs.

'So he didn't like it, then, when she shouted?'

Kitty's hand hovered over the sandwiches. Egg and cress, tomato paste, ham and mustard. Each one as flat as an envelope.

'I don't think he did, no,' she said, choosing a glistening éclair instead. 'He apologised to me.'

'He *apologised*?'

'Yes.' Kitty took a bite of éclair and licked a dollop of cream from her lip.

'He apologised to *you*?'

'Yes.' Two bites and the éclair was gone. She moved on to the pineapple meringue.

Lou sighed. 'He sounds *gallant*. I wish Bob was more like that. I don't think he's ever said sorry to me. Not once.' She pushed her plate away and lit another Player's.

'He is—polite,' said Kitty, through a mouthful of sugary crumbs. 'Very polite.' Then she dared to add, 'And thoughtful. He's the sensitive type, you know.'

Lou was staring at the tablecloth. 'Bob's never apologised. Not even now. After everything.'

'What do you mean?'

'Nothing.' Lou drained her cocktail.

Kitty swallowed the last of the meringue and eyed the thin slice of strawberry gateau still on the silver tray. Before she could get it onto her plate, though, Lou sighed again, loudly.

'What's the matter?' asked Kitty, abandoning the gateau.

'Sorry.' Lou put a hand to her mouth and shook her head. 'I suppose I might as well tell you.'

'Tell me what?'

'I didn't mean to mention it, not now.'

'Tell me what, Lou?'

Lou opened and closed the clasp of her handbag. 'Bob and me have been having a spot of trouble.'

'What kind of trouble?'

'The marriage kind.' She smiled weakly. 'We might—separate. For a bit.'

Kitty stared at her sister.

'He's going to live—somewhere else.' Lou looked out of the window. 'With someone else.' She ground out her cigarette. 'I'll be glad to get shot of the old bastard, won't I?' Then she added, 'Sorry to spoil your birthday.'

Picking up the silver teapot, Kitty poured tea into Lou's cup, added milk and two knobs of sugar, and pushed it over to her sister. 'It's not my birthday.'

'Fucking incinerated fish,' said Lou, with a dry laugh.

*   *   *

They travelled back to Woodbury Avenue in silence until, passing by the cemetery, Lou put a hand on the back of the driver's seat. 'You can drop us here, please.'

They hadn't been here together since their mother's funeral. Kitty stood on the path, watching a heatwave shimmer over the rows of gravestones fanning out in neat lines on either side of them. It was a new cemetery, and the trees had yet to grow large enough to offer any shade. The smell of the rubber factory, which was just behind the cemetery wall, was at its worst in this spot, and the sickly, burning aroma rose around them.

Lou pulled the net of her hat down lower. 'I hate cemeteries,' she said. 'Especially ones that stink.'

Kitty scanned the rows of crosses and slabs. She knew exactly where the grave was, but she wondered if her sister would. As they walked, Lou's heel caught in the crack of a paving stone. 'Bugger it.' She twisted round and yanked the shoe from her foot. 'It's come right off,' she said, showing the damage to Kitty.

'You could stick it back on.'

'It'll just come off again.' Clenching the heel in one hand, Lou limped on, and Kitty followed. To her surprise, Lou went straight to the right plot, over in the left-hand corner, by the wall nearest the factory. There was a small stone which read: *Douglas Allen, 1875–1921; Mary Allen, 1881–1934; At Peace with God*. The sisters stood before it in silence. It didn't matter how many times you read it, Kitty thought, it never became any more familiar, or comforting. She considered uttering her usual quick prayer—something about hoping they were both in heaven, and asking God to look over them—but she didn't want to kneel, not in front of Lou, and not in the organdie frock.

'It's been two years, almost,' said Lou.

'I know.'

'She would've been disappointed with me, wouldn't she? Her eldest daughter—the divorcee.'

Kitty remembered the way their mother had always referred to Bob as *The School Teacher*. It was a kind of reverence, but also a kind of scorn. 'She'd have wanted you to be happy.'

'No she wouldn't. She would've wanted what looked best on her.' Lou turned to Kitty. 'Not that she had to put up with Dad, did she? He went and died before she could get really fed up with him.'

Kitty said nothing.

'Listen,' said Lou, suddenly grabbing Kitty's elbow. 'Bob's going to let me stop on at the house, and pay me a bit. It's all agreed. I've just got to take the blame in the divorce. He gets to keep his reputation, but I get to keep the house. It's the least he can do, considering he's the one who's gone off with that old trout . . . do you know what he said to me? That he'd found paradise!' The net on Lou's hat quivered with anger. 'As if he'd know paradise if it came up and bit him on the arse.' She

265

jabbed her broken heel in the air. 'But what I thought—just last night—what I thought was, why be on my own? Why be on my own when Kitty could come back?'

'Come back?'

'To live at the house. With me.'

Kitty took a step away from her sister. 'But—my job—the cottage—'

'You don't have to live in, do you? Anyway, you could get another, now you've the experience. The Macklows'—'

'I hated it at the Macklows'.'

'At least it was work. It got you out of the house, didn't it?'

Kitty gave a laugh. 'I still had to go home every day and get Mother's tea, while you were—' She stopped. The sisters faced each other. Lou's cheeks were puffy with heat and her lipstick had a tiny crumb of cake stuck to it.

'While I was what?'

Kitty concentrated on the crumb and kept her voice even. 'Married. In your own house. With your own things. Away from us.'

They were silent for a while. Then Lou said, 'She had an all right life, when you look at it.' She gestured towards their mother's name on the gravestone with her handbag. 'Did what she liked, didn't she?'

'Not in the end, she didn't,' said Kitty. Then she added, feeling the heat and the gin in her limbs, 'I know I should have fetched the doctor, but you should have come sooner. We were waiting for you.'

Lou turned her face away. It was a minute before Kitty realised her sister was quietly crying.

There was a long pause before Kitty managed to say, 'I'm sorry about Bob,' and hand Lou her hankie.

Lou sniffed and nodded. 'Come back to the house with me?'

'What about Bob's dinner?'

'He's already gone. I just didn't know how to tell you, earlier.' Lou blew her nose loudly, three times. Kitty recognised the sound from their childhood: Lou's three blows in the morning, and three before bed.

'That was loud enough to wake the dead,' Kitty said.

Lou smiled briefly. 'You'll think over what I said? About coming to live at the house?'

'Maybe.'

The sun was getting lower and the yellow evening light was sneaking into their eyes. Kitty took Lou's arm, and the two of them walked back to Woodbury Avenue together, Lou hobbling, still carrying her broken heel in her hand.

*   *   *

It was late when Kitty got back to the cottage. With the Pierrot outfits she'd run up on Lou's Singer bundled under one arm, she let herself in the back door. There was no light on in the kitchen, and she almost tripped over Blotto, who was snoozing on the mat. The dog groaned and stretched before tucking his head back into his chest and letting out a long, creaky sigh. Kitty turned on the kitchen light and looked up the hallway: no sign of any life there, either, so she fetched herself a glass of water and sat at the kitchen table to drink it down in large, grateful gulps. As she drank, she stared at the lantern's trimmed tassel. No one else seemed to have noticed that it was much shorter than before. She wondered, now, if she could remove the whole thing without anyone saying anything. The kitchen would be much brighter in the evenings if she did.

She wiped her mouth, took off her shoes, rolled down her stockings, laid her bare feet on the cool flags and closed her eyes. It had been a long evening, and she'd been glad of work to do while listening to Lou's story of Bob's affair with the older woman. Apparently she was a widow who lived in one of the big houses by the lake; they'd met at the local historical society and shared a passion for Queen Elizabeth. Lou said he was welcome to her, that she was glad to be rid of him, but as she spoke, she'd kept plucking at her collar and cuffs, and smoked a chain of cigarettes. Kitty had tried to listen while focusing on getting the seams of the outfits straight. They'd been quite simple—a bit like baggy pyjama-suits, with wide circular collars attached. All she had to do now was make the pompoms. She was sure she had some black wool somewhere in her work-box. She could even, she thought, get Miss Geenie on to making the pompoms herself. The girl might enjoy that.

After rinsing her glass in the sink, she turned off the light and opened the door to her room. Although it was quite dark, she knew immediately that someone was in there.

'Kitty—forgive me.'

On hearing his voice, she dropped the Pierrot costumes to the floor.

'It's the most unforgivable intrusion—please

forgive me.'

She took a couple of deep breaths. She could see the outline of him now, sitting on her bed in his shirtsleeves. And here she was, standing before him, with no stockings on and a pile of silly costumes round her bare feet.

She snapped on the light and he flinched. His sleeves were rolled up to the elbow, and his hands—those beautiful long fingers—touched his hair, hiding his face.

'Forgive me,' he said again.

'What do you want, Mr Crane?'

He nodded. 'Quite. What do I want? What do I want?' He hung his head, his hands still in his hair.

'Have you been—drinking?' She knew he hadn't, but she couldn't think of anything else to say. A man was in her room without her permission, and she should be outraged.

He lifted his head. 'Kitty,' he said, and his voice was suddenly loud and deep, as if he were addressing an audience, 'Kitty, when I came here the other evening, I wasn't entirely straight with you.'

She should scream, shouldn't she? Scream and throw him out.

'I didn't say what I meant to say.' He nodded his head again. 'Yes, that's it. I didn't express what I wanted—needed—to express.'

Kitty didn't move. She was watching those fingers. They were on his knees now, each one evenly spread over the thinning fabric as he sat up very straight and nodded again. 'What I want, what I'd like very much, is for you to sit here beside me for a minute.'

He looked at her for a long moment, his eyes

steady, his face pale and thin in the electric light, and Kitty knew she'd have to do as he asked. She was shaking as she sat on the edge of the bed, her stomach pulling inwards as if a thread were being stroked and gathered inside her.

'Let me see your ears,' he said.

She looked at him.

'I've never seen them—the whole of them.' His fingers reached out and touched her ordinary hair, and he moved his face close to her neck. His breath was on her exposed skin, and she thought of how even she had never really looked there, behind her ear, in that hidden place. They were both very still, and the thread in her stomach pulled tighter. What was he seeing as he looked there, at that secret spot of white skin, which must be knobbled and strange? What shape were her ears? She tried to picture them, their folds and bumps, but could not. She felt a sudden urge to laugh as he moved closer, but then his face was in her hair, his lips on her earlobe, and the thread in her stomach snapped and everything came loose.

'They're lovely.'

'Mr Crane—'

'Please call me George.'

His lips touched her again, this time just below her ear, and her hand went up, first to her own throat, then to his. She wrapped her fingers around the back of his neck, and she held his head there while he kissed her.

THIRTY-ONE

The letters were finished. It was Thursday morning, and Ellen sat back in her chair, flexed her aching fingers, and gazed out of the library window. On the lawn, the girls were laughing together. A minute ago Geenie had looked like she was scrubbing the grass clean: she'd been on her hands and knees, knuckles working the dusty ground, while Diana stood over her, proclaiming something with one arm stretched elegantly into the air. Some game or other, Ellen thought: it was good to see her daughter so engaged with another girl; it certainly made a change from hanging around rooms, waiting for her mother to do or say something. Not that Geenie had been hanging around much since they'd had the conversation about James's death. Ellen wished she'd been able to say more to her daughter on that subject, but somehow there were no words for it. And there was also the sense, she reflected now, taking another swig of her gin and it—a pre-lunch drink wasn't so out of the ordinary, was it?—that James wasn't much to do with Geenie. He wasn't her father, after all. He was Ellen's lover. His death was her business.

Pulling the final page from the typewriter, she set it on the pile. Then she finished her drink, pushed back her chair, and carried the manuscript from the room.

She was so surprised to find Crane's studio empty that she marched directly to where the girls were playing on the lawn. They saw her coming and Geenie pressed her lips together.

'Where's your father?' Ellen asked Diana.

For an answer she received a shrug and a smile. She looked from girl to girl, and Geenie slid behind Diana and began to laugh.

'What's the matter with you?'

'She's just excited,' said Diana, 'about the play.'

'What play?'

'The play I've written. We're performing it tomorrow morning. Eleven o'clock sharp. On the lawn.'

'Everyone's invited,' said Geenie, peeping over her friend's shoulder.

Ellen gazed at Diana, and the girl gazed back, her dark eyes amused, her face composed. Eventually Ellen turned and walked back to the studio, leaving the girls whispering behind her like lovers.

*   *   *

Inside, she sat in Crane's armchair with the manuscript on her lap and wished she'd thought to fetch another gin. She had a notion that she would wait here until Crane returned, and she might need another drink. Ellen hadn't given much thought to what she would do when he did arrive; she only knew that she wanted him to see the letters, now they were finished. They'd managed to avoid each other almost completely since he'd got back from London on Monday night. By the time he'd climbed into their bed in the dark, she'd had time to think, and her urge to scream and slap him very hard had waned. Anyway, what would she have said, exactly? *I was snooping in your wastepaper basket and I found this*? Or, *I was looking for the novel you obviously haven't written and I came across these—words*? She couldn't admit she'd been prying, and even if she did, he would have said it was just a poem, something he'd made up. So she'd clenched her body into a tight bundle on the edge of the bed and pretended to sleep.

Crane had hidden in his studio for most of the next day, and she'd locked herself in the library, brooding over the letters, drinking too much gin, and then falling asleep in her chair, waking to find herself covered in sweat and ravenously hungry. At dinner she'd concentrated on filling her gasping stomach with Kitty's admittedly rather tasty chicken pie while Crane's eye twitched like some trapped insect. But by Wednesday morning Ellen was thinking of going to Robin again. After lunch, during which Crane revealed his busy schedule of talks for the Party, telling her they were to begin next week in Rochdale (where was that? she hadn't even bothered to ask), she'd taken the Lanchester into Petersfield and parked by the market square. Walking down the lane to the hairdressers' shop, smelling the mixture of carbolic and blood from the butcher's open door, she told herself that perhaps she would just book another appointment after all, then go straight back and face Crane and tell him it was over. Or perhaps she could cry a little, and relations would thaw. But when she walked through the door and saw Robin sitting at the back of the empty shop, a penny paper spread across his solid knees, she'd known exactly what would happen. If Crane's blood was *heavy with wanting* for the cook, why shouldn't she spend a little time with Robin? In the back room, he'd kept the wireless on, and his knowledgeable hands had slowly stroked her breasts to the rhythms of the *Afternoon Band Hour*. Just as he was sliding his fingers beneath her French knickers, she stopped him and said, 'I want you for the whole night.'

It had been expensive, of course. There was the room at the Royal Oak in Midhurst, where—after she'd telephoned Crane and told him she was too drunk to drive home and was spending the night at Laura's—they'd signed in as Mr and Mrs Crane; and Robin had still charged by the hour. But it had been worth it, she decided, as she rose from the chair to place the manuscript on Crane's desk, over his latest copy of the *Daily Worker*. It had been worth it, because since she'd got back to the cottage at ten o'clock this morning (and Crane hadn't been anywhere to be seen, even then), her head had been marvellously clear. Clear enough to finish work on the manuscript, and to add a note between the title page and the first letter:

To the memory of James Holt, my greatest love.
With this book, I ask for forgiveness.
—Ellen Steinberg

James's memory was the most important thing, after all. It was the thing she had to keep safe from now on. Crane had distracted her from it. At least, that was how it had seemed when she'd typed the dedication. She could always, she thought, change things later.

Leaving the pile of paper on the desk, she walked out of the studio and into the sunshine. She wouldn't wait for Crane, she decided. Let him find the letters there, just as she'd found his scrap of a poem. She wouldn't even wait for lunch. She'd drive into Petersfield straight away, buy flowers for the cottage from Gander's, perhaps stop at the White Hart for a drink, and then, if she still felt like it, drop by the hairdressers' once more.

THIRTY-TWO

Kitty woke early on Thursday, the morning of her birthday, still wearing Lou's pink organdie frock. The skirt was pressed against her thighs, as if something were pulling it back. She reached behind and smiled to herself as she felt Mr Crane's knee there, pinning her frock to the bed. It wasn't much past dawn: the birds were raucous outside her window, their songs clambering into the air. And he was still here. He was still here. She tried to stay unmoving on the edge of the bed so as not to disturb him. He was still here. She closed her eyes again. All night the feeling of his kiss was there, even when she'd turned from him and eventually reached something like sleep. They'd kissed until her lips were dry and her neck tired. Sometimes the kisses had been long and light; at other times he'd kissed her so hard she'd felt his teeth on hers. His hands were in her hair, on her throat, then his arms were crushing her to him and she thought, this is what they mean when they say *breathless*. He'd kept murmuring 'lovely', and she wasn't sure if he meant her or the kisses. Eventually he'd lain back on the counterpane and said 'come to bed now', and she'd frozen, thinking that he must want her to undress and not knowing how she could possibly start. But instead he pulled her to his side and cradled her head on his chest, and then he'd slept. Kitty stayed awake for hours, listening to his breath, inhaling the scent of him and staring at his chin, at all the little ticks of stubble there, so close to her face. And here he still was. She still had him. In her small room, on her small bed.

She opened her eyes again. It was already light and warm in the room. The Pierrot costumes were on the floor, where she'd dropped them last night. She wished the picture of her parents wasn't so visible from the bed. Her mother's face stared directly down at her, and she shifted her eyes away. The clock on the chest of drawers said six. She closed her eyes again and inched a little closer to him. No one would be up before nine. There were hours to go. Hours of just lying here, knowing he was next to her. If she could move slowly enough, she might even be able to turn over and watch his face while he slept.

Then the thought hit her hard and she sprang upright: Mrs Steinberg. *Fucking incinerated fish* would be nothing compared to this. She stole a look over her shoulder at the sleeping man on her sheets, taking in the length of his legs, the way one hand was thrown over his head, the muscle of his upper arm filling his shirt sleeve, the shapely wrist resting on her pillow. Just one more kiss, she thought, and then I'll tell him he has to go. She bent close and studied his face: the long nose, the black lashes, the slightly sunken cheeks. She was just about to touch his forehead with her lips when his eyes flicked open.

'Good morning,' he said.

Kitty drew back.

He gave a huge yawn and stretched his arms. 'I slept so well. I haven't slept so well in ages.'

Sitting on the edge of the mattress, Kitty fixed her eyes on the door and waited for him to move from her bed. It would all be over soon: he'd get up, stretch again, say something about what a night of madness it had been, he didn't know what he'd been thinking, it was an unforgivable intrusion and could she forgive him, could she? Then he'd walk out without waiting for her answer, and she'd have to pretend nothing had happened, put his tea down without glancing at him, watch Mrs Steinberg casually touch his thigh beneath the table, listen to them laughing together in the sitting room, picture her dancing for him while that man's sweet, rasping voice unravelled from the gramophone. She didn't think she could do it. There was nothing else for it: she'd have to go back to Lou's.

'Kitty? Did you—ah—sleep well?'

'I think you should go.'

'What time is it?'

'After six. I think you should go.' It wouldn't be so bad at Woodbury Avenue, without Bob there to rattle the newspaper in her direction.

Mr Crane sat up.

'You should go,' she said again, keeping her voice low.

He rubbed his eyes. 'What's wrong?'

'You should go. You should go, otherwise— she'll know.'

He came to the edge of the bed, placed his hands on her shoulders and turned her towards him. One collar was dented, striking him in the chin, and his shirt was badly creased. His eye gave

277

a twitch. 'Listen to me. It doesn't matter. None of that matters, not really.'

She twisted away from him. 'Not to you, maybe—'

He reached for her again. 'Kitty. Ellen—Mrs Steinberg—didn't come home last night.'

'How do you know?'

'She telephoned me. She stayed at my sister's house last night. And she'll have the most dreadful hangover this morning, so I'd be surprised if she came back before lunchtime.'

'Oh.' Kitty stared at the floor. 'You should still go though, shouldn't you?'

He smiled. 'Let's go for a bicycle ride.'

'Now?'

'Now.'

'I don't have a bicycle.'

'You can borrow Geenie's. She's almost as tall as you. I'll adjust the saddle.'

Kitty let out a laugh. 'At six in the morning?'

'Why not? You told me, didn't you, that time I met you on the road. Don't you remember? You said you liked riding bicycles.'

'What about the girls? The breakfast . . .'

'We'll be back before then,' he said, springing from the bed and and holding out his hands to her. 'I promise.'

*   *   *

It was exactly as she remembered: the breeze on your cheeks as you pedalled, the way the saddle made you sit upright and almost proud, the wheels throwing the road carelessly behind. Even now, the hedgerows were drying out in the early morning sun and heat was beginning to rise from the asphalt. Yellow wheat danced in the fields on either side of them, but the hills in front were a flat, grey green, yet to be touched by the sun. Mr Crane, still in his creased shirt and with his slick of dark hair splayed on the crown of his head, cycled on while Kitty kept a short way behind, in case anyone should see them. Not that she could think of any reason she should be cycling at this time in the morning at all, let alone so close behind Mr Crane, who was, to outsiders' eyes at least, her master. What was he in her eyes, then? Was he— she dared hardly think the word—her lover? Her lover, who was also a poet, although he didn't look like one. She smiled to herself at that.

When they came into the village, she saw it was deserted, the High Street stretching emptily ahead and the windows of the houses utterly blind, and she pushed down hard on the pedals to overtake him, calling quietly over her shoulder, 'Follow me.'

As she opened the gate to the churchyard, it seemed smaller than she remembered. She didn't look at him as they abandoned their bicycles by the wall and walked through the damp grass, past the Fetherstonhaughs' private enclosure, towards the back of the church. It was very cool here, just as Kitty remembered it had been on her picnics with Lou years ago. She gave a shiver, partly because of the cold dampness of the place, and partly because she knew what would happen if she kept walking deeper amongst the graves, away from the road and the church, to the stones in the back corner, by the flint wall. He was close behind her, and she knew he was watching her body move in the crumpled organdie frock, and he'd seen that

279

place behind her ear which no one else—not even she—had seen; but she was going to follow through.

She stopped when she found what she was looking for, a long headstone beneath a large yew tree. Mary Belcher, who had died young and been alone underground all this time. There it was, the grave where she and Lou used to sit, still lying flat in the grass, splattered with lichen.

'This place,' she began, 'I used to think it was haunted.'

He was approaching her, a smile on his lips.

'I used to think,' she said, 'that the devil might hide here.'

'And does he?'

'Perhaps.'

He looked behind him in mock fear. 'Well. It's— ah—just you and me at the moment.'

She moved closer to the grave. The ivy and moss were thicker now, but the place had that same stillness, that same smell of mould.

'Today's my birthday,' she said, quietly.

Mr Crane stopped smiling, and for a moment she wondered if she'd said the wrong thing, but then he stepped forward, took hold of her waist and kissed her, pulling her in so close she could feel all the buttons on his shirt pressing through the bib front of her frock. Inching her hands down his straight spine, she felt for that dimple of flesh she'd seen when she'd spied on him getting dressed, and, feeling the indent, she tugged his shirt from his trousers, reached behind his braces and found his soft place. He gave a little moan as her fingers touched his naked skin. Thinking of Lou stretching out with her knees showing, waiting

280

for someone to come along, Kitty broke away from him. 'Wait,' she said.

Mr Crane watched as she lay down on Mary Belcher's grave. The cold stone sent a shocking jolt through her skin, but she hitched up the hem of her frock and extended a hand to him. 'Here,' she said. 'Here.'

THIRTY-THREE

It was past seven o'clock when Ellen returned with half a dozen bunches of canna lilies on the back seat of the car, a gnawing hunger in her stomach, having skipped lunch, and a buzz in her thighs from her hour with Robin. Getting out of the car, she groaned to herself as she noticed Crane waiting in the front porch. She gathered up the lilies so he wouldn't be able to see her face and pushed past him without a word.

He followed her into the sitting room and closed the door behind them. 'I need to speak with you.'

Ellen stood in the middle of the room, her arms still full of flowers. '*I* need to put these in water.'

She made for the door, but he blocked the way and clutched her arm. 'Ellen. Please.' His voice was low, his face grey.

She laughed. 'You haven't needed to speak to me for the last few days, Crane; I don't see why you should start now.'

'It has to be now. But not here.'

'You're hurting my elbow.'

'Come for a walk.'

'Don't you think these will look sublime in here,

281

darling?' She pushed the lilies into his face. The over-rich scent rose between them.

'Come for a walk, Ellen.'

'You know I loathe walks.'

He looked at her through the petals. 'Do you? You never said.'

She sighed. 'Does it have to be now?'

He pulled the lilies from her arms, dumped them on the dining table and held the door open.

*   *   *

They crossed the field. Broken ears of wheat poked at Ellen's feet through her peep-toe shoes—there'd been no time to change. Crane walked ahead, saying nothing. His shirt was very creased, and was sticking to his back in streaks.

'Is that a grass stain on your shoulder?'

His hand leapt to the place. 'I was—lying on the lawn, earlier.'

A smear of swallows flew over them, circling and screeching across the field. Ahead, Harting Down was still brightly lit. Its chalk paths, gnarled bushes and scrubby grass glowed in the evening sun.

'When are we going to talk?' she asked. 'I thought it was urgent.'

'When we get to the top.'

She stopped walking then, put her hands on her hips, and was about to refuse, loudly, to climb to the top of that hill. But he ignored her actions and kept walking ahead, and she had a feeling that if she didn't follow him he would simply continue on his own. Then this thing, whatever it was, would never be said. So she trudged behind him, watching the sweat grow on his back, her feet swelling, her head beginning to pound heavily. Picking another sharp stone from her shoe, she wished she'd had time to wash the smell of Robin from her hands.

When they'd passed the little patch of woodland and gone through the gate, they reached the narrow chalk track. But instead of following it, taking the gentler route up the hill, Crane broke from the path and began climbing straight up the grassy slope, using his hands to help him.

'Crane!' shouted Ellen. 'This is ridiculous!' But he continued his ascent, almost leaping up the hill with irritating sprightliness.

Puffing with the effort, she followed. Her fingers clutched at dry grass, her feet slipped on stones. Once she fell, scraped both knees on the dirt and cried out for him. But he did not look back. Her head began to feel heavy and light at the same time: the blood still pulsed in her temples, but there was also a pressure in her nose which made her vision swim a little. Her throat was dry (she'd had nothing since those gin and its earlier on), her stomach empty, and the buzz in her thighs had become a dull ache. 'Crane!' she croaked, but still he pressed ahead.

When the hill had levelled out a little, she stopped to rest, sitting on the grass and gazing down at the village. She'd never seen the cottage from this high up before; from here it looked compact and insignificant: no more than a brown lump in the landscape. Inside, she thought, Kitty would be in the kitchen, fretting over potatoes; Arthur would be dozing in his shed (she knew he spent a lot of time doing this, but she'd never objected, since she only paid him for a few hours a day anyway); and Geenie—where would Geenie be? She realised that she had no idea. Her daughter might be anywhere at all.

'Crane!' Ellen shouted up to his disappearing legs. 'No further! Do you hear me? No further!'

She waited. She wouldn't allow herself to fully imagine what he might be about to say, when he'd worked himself up sufficiently; but she told herself that if it looked as though he were about to break it off, she would do so first by pointing out that she knew all about him lusting after the cook, and she, Ellen Steinberg, was not a woman to tolerate such betrayal.

She heard him stepping carefully down the slope towards her, and knew he would be avoiding treading on any flowers.

'It's really unforgivably dramatic of you to drag me all the way up here,' she said.

He sat down next to her, breathing hard.

To her surprise, he didn't pause long to catch his breath. Instead, he began to speak almost immediately. 'I'm glad you've typed James's letters,' he said, taking little gulps of air between words, staring all the time at the village below. 'Thank you for letting me see them. They're exceptionally interesting and I'm sure they'll be published.'

'Yes—'

'And I think the dedication you've added is wholly apt, and absolutely right.'

'Yes—I wanted to talk to *you* about that—'

'There's no baby, Ellen, is there?'

The possibility of lying to him flashed into her mind. But how much time would that buy her?

'No,' she said. 'There's no baby.'

'Then I think we should part.'

She tried to speak but he continued in the same quiet tone, his eyes still fixed on the village below. 'It's been over a year now, hasn't it, since James died, and I've given it a lot of thought and I think now is a good time to end it. We both need to move on. I'm going to leave as soon as I can.' Then he added, in a warmer tone, 'I'm sorry, Ellen.'

He was so decisive, so calm, and he'd stolen her thunder so completely, that she almost laughed. She'd never heard him sound so resolute. It was as if he were reading out a letter he'd carefully composed weeks before.

Ellen gripped a handful of grass, pulled it from its roots and tossed it into the air. 'What have you been doing all summer?'

His head drooped a little. 'What do you mean?'

'Well. You certainly haven't been writing a novel.'

'No,' he said. 'I haven't . . .'

'Any poetry?'

'Not really.'

'Well,' she said. 'That's that, then.'

'That's what?'

'It's all been a waste of time, hasn't it? Being here, I mean. It's been a colossal waste of time for you.'

'Of course it hasn't.' He was looking at her now, but she refused to meet his gaze. 'I've been with you—'

She snorted.

'And I've been—ah—reading. Getting ready. Preparing myself for more important work. For the Party . . .'

She pounced. 'So *that's* where my money's been

going. The development of the damned Bolsheviks. And there was me thinking I was a patron of the arts.'

'Ellen—' he reached for her hand, but she snatched it away.

There was a pause before she said, 'I meant what I wrote, you know, in the dedication.'

'I know you did. I know James was the love of your life—'

'Not that. I meant what I wrote about forgiveness. About asking for forgiveness.'

He sighed. 'Ellen, you shouldn't waste time with guilt. After all, we didn't do much, did we, until after his death—no one could blame you for getting on with life.'

She turned to him. 'I knew he was still drunk,' she said. 'I knew it, and I let them operate.'

Crane stared at her.

'Do you understand? It was my fault, George.' Her voice had become high and shaky. 'James's death was my fault, and Geenie knows it.'

He shook his head and put his hand over hers, gripping her fingers tightly. 'Geenie loves you,' he said. 'She loves you, Ellen.'

Suddenly there was an immense pealing of church bells. Thursday practice had begun. The chimes rose and fell, scattering sound over the village and echoing around the valley. Ellen had always hated the clanging racket of those bells, which went on for hours, drowning out her records and prohibiting any decent conversation.

'Damn those bells to hell,' she said.

He squeezed her hand. 'I'm so sorry.'

'You already apologised.'

They sat together, listening to the chimes racing

up and down the scales, never quite making a tune.

After a few minutes, she said, 'I'd better get back. It's dinnertime. The girls will be waiting for me.'

He lay on the grass and squinted at the sky. 'I think I'll stay here a bit.'

Running a finger along his cheek, she looked at him, this slim and elegant man who was leaving her. Then she left him there and stumbled down the hill, sprinting in places, slipping on the grass but righting herself before she fell, her face blasted by the last rays of the sun, her stomach groaning for the food that was waiting for her.

THIRTY-FOUR

That night, Kitty waited for Mr Crane to come again. She told herself that this was not what she was doing. What she was doing was finishing her embroidery, just as she would have done if nothing had happened. She was sitting on her bed—where he'd held her head to his chest, where he'd kissed her earlobe, and then her neck—with the embroidery in her lap, and she would finish it tonight. Looking towards the window, she saw there was a light in his studio. Her ears strained for the sounds of his door opening, his footsteps along the gravel path. It was half past eleven, and he hadn't had any dinner. Surely he'd come in soon. She threaded her needle with red silk. He hadn't said he would come. He hadn't said anything much as they'd lain in each other's arms on the grave, looking up at the patches of blue flickering between the yew's needles. He'd stroked her hair and said *Kitty*. *Kitty* he'd said, as if it were a beautiful sound.

She would fill the stripes on the girl's gown with fern stitch. Gripping the needle, she forced it through. The picture was almost complete, and the cloth had stiffened. How could he come? He'd left her as soon as they'd got back to the cottage, saying nothing about when he would see her again. He hadn't been at the dinner table when she'd left the cutlets and retreated without looking anyone in the face, not even Geenie, who'd kept thanking her for the Pierrot costumes. The thread creaked as she made the last stitches on the girl's sash. But how could he not come again? How could he not come, when he'd touched her between her thighs, running his forefinger along that secret nub of skin, building a fierce heat low down in her, a pressure that had to be released. It had been painful when he'd pushed himself into her, and she'd kept her eyes on his face and gripped the sides of the grave as her lower back pressed against the uneven stone. But she wanted it to happen again, now that she knew the pressure was possible, now that she suspected he would be able to release it.

She secured the stitch with another at the back of the calico, removed the frame, shook out the fabric and examined her work. Everything was correct—she'd managed to pick out the faces and the rocks well; the French knots were all even; the loop stitches of the fishing nets were almost perfect; the fern stitching was so close you could hardly see it was stitched at all—but the work seemed flat and bland to Kitty now. What was it *for*? There was no life to it, and no purpose in it: she realised that she'd sewn the whole thing without knowing what its use would be. She flung it down on the bed beside her, scooped her silks back into her work-box and slapped the lid shut.

The pink organdie frock was hanging on the door of her wardrobe. There was a long grass stain down the back of the skirt; a few stitches at the waist were broken, and a button on the bib front had been lost, leaving a trailing thread. She thought of that stray white button, buried somewhere in the grass and the fallen yew needles of the churchyard. Then she drew handfuls of the material to her face, covering her nose and mouth with it, inhaling the dampness of the grave, the salt of his skin, the musk of her own body.

Still holding the frock, she went to the open window and fixed her eyes on the light in the studio. If she concentrated hard enough, he might come. That's what lovers did, wasn't it? Called each other up out of the night. She waited, but there was no sign. There was just the gurgling sigh of the stream, and the willows, huge and quiet in the darkness. She would have to send a signal. Gathering up the frock, she hooked a button hole over the window catch, and threw it out into the night like a flag. For the next hour Kitty stood at her open window, touching the organdie and watching for him. But the light in the studio remained constant.

THIRTY-FIVE

On Friday morning, Geenie jumped from her bed to put her costume on again. She'd found both the outfits hanging on the back of her door yesterday afternoon, with a note from Kitty: *Dear Miss Geenie and Miss Diana. Here are your costumes. I could not do the pompoms as I had no wool. Kitty Allen*. She'd called Diana, who'd suggested they 'run through a dress rehearsal' immediately, so they'd clambered into the pyjama-like trousers and white tunics and, after a moment spent congratulating each other on the effect, Diana stood on the bed, declaiming the poem she'd now finished, which was very good and all about the *turmoil of love*. It was full of words like *tranquil* and *tremulous*, and also featured a unicorn. The odd thing was, now that Geenie was standing before the mirror in her costume, she couldn't remember one word of the play; all she could picture was Diana closing her eyes as she moved in for the kiss.

*　　　*　　　*

They were to perform in front of the rose bed, which was now in full bloom. They'd placed four kitchen chairs in a row on the cracked lawn, adding cushions as an afterthought; Geenie had fetched a bucket, feather duster and scrubbing brush from Kitty's cupboard beneath the stairs, and now they were in Arthur's shed, which they'd claimed as their dressing room, waiting for the audience to arrive. Geenie had been wearing her costume since

290

she'd got out of bed, and by ten o'clock they'd both been fully made up, their faces sticky with white pan-stick, and two tears pencilled on each cheek. Geenie had drawn Diana's for her with a shaking hand.

'Where is everyone?' asked Diana, peeping round the shed door. 'I hope they're all coming, now we've gone to all this bloody trouble.'

All morning, a large, round pebble had been growing heavier in Geenie's stomach. Now it expanded a little and she gave a whine, like Blotto did when teased with food. When she put a hand on her friend's arm and tried to see past her huge white sleeve, she noticed that her own fingers wouldn't quite keep still. 'We could just do it for Kitty and Arthur,' she suggested, hopefully.

'What would be the point of that?'

'They might like it.'

Diana squealed. 'They're here!' Slamming the door shut, she turned to Geenie. 'Right. This is it. Plan into action.'

Geenie stared at Diana. With great clarity she suddenly saw that the costumes were all wrong. They should have pompoms. The black circles Kitty had sewn on instead were not the same. And Pierrot clowns were supposed to wear black skull caps, weren't they? All they'd done was scrape their hair back and tried to keep it in place with soapy water. Their tears were smudged. And their ruffs were really just wide, flat collars, not the stiffened pleats that real Pierrots wore. 'It's not right,' she said, clutching Diana's arm. 'I don't think we can do it. It's not right—'

'I'm on,' said Diana, pulling away and opening the door.

In the earthy gloom of the shed, Geenie looked at Arthur's neat rows of tools. Perhaps no one would notice if she just stayed in here. It was airless and hot, but she could stand it. It would be better than facing the four adult faces out there in the bright sunshine. She sat on Arthur's deckchair, twisted her hands together and sweated. Outside, Diana was singing *those charming, alarming, blonde women!* in her best Dietrich voice. Geenie closed her eyes and tried to remember what she had to do. Was she supposed to scrub the floor first, or pretend to be dusting?

As Diana was nearing the end of the song, Geenie gathered enough courage to crack open the shed door and take a peek. Her friend was bobbing around on the lawn, kicking her legs in the air. She'd pulled her black hair into a bun and her head looked small and determined on top of her baggy white costume. Ellen, George, Kitty and Arthur were sitting in a row. Her mother looked rather bored, which cheered Geenie a little. George had his hands behind his head and a smile on his face, but his eye was twitching. Kitty's cheeks were very pink, and she was looking at her knees, which was where Arthur's eyes were also fixed.

Diana gave a twirl and a bow, and everyone clapped.

'And now for our main attraction, which is a play written by me, Diana Crane. Ladies and gentlemen, *What the Gardener Saw*.' Diana bowed again and extended an arm towards the shed, her white sleeve gaping in Geenie's direction.

It was too late, now, to escape, and impossible to hide. Geenie's blood fluttered in her veins as she

292

pulled open the door. She knew she *was* walking—she could see her feet stepping across the lawn—but she felt as though she were swimming. Was it the lawn, or the sky, that was wobbling? She stopped beside Diana and anchored her eyes on Kitty, who gave her a small smile.

'Oh!' said her mother. 'You both look so theatrical!'

'*What the Gardener Saw*,' said Diana again in a more urgent tone, gesturing to Geenie. This was a cue, but for what? Everything wobbled again. There was another small round of clapping, and Arthur began to chuckle.

The sun glared. Geenie stood and blinked. If she could just keep standing, things might stop moving around and glowing a ghastly pink.

Diana gave a short sigh before announcing in a loud voice: 'This is Ruby, the housemaid. And I am the great poet, John Cross.'

Arthur chuckled some more. Geenie stood very still, staring at Kitty's flushed face and searching her mind for some sort of command, some memory of the play, of the plan. What had it all been for? She could hardly recall.

Kitty nodded and smiled again, and Geenie let out a breath: she could see what she had to do now. Falling to her knees, she began to scrub the grass, not caring that her props were still in the shed.

'That's not the start,' Diana hissed from above. But Geenie continued rubbing her knuckles in the dirt.

'You've missed out the whole of the first act!'

'Just carry on, darlings,' laughed Ellen. 'The show must go on and all that.'

Geenie could hear Diana puffing out a series of snorts, but she continued to work at the grass with her invisible scrubbing brush.

There was a long pause before Diana stepped behind Geenie, threw an arm over her own face and began to speak. 'Who is this wondrous creature? What beauty there is to be found in a lowly housemaid! I am inspired as never before—inspired by love!'

Geenie heard her mother's high-pitched laugh again, but it was quieter this time.

'You beautiful creature! I must have a kiss!' Grabbing Geenie's arms, Diana hauled her to her feet, pinching her flesh so hard that Geenie winced. The pain seemed to reduce the size and weight of the pebble in her stomach, and stop everything from wobbling quite so violently.

'Kiss me now, and then I will declare my poem in your honour!' Diana's hot breath was on Geenie's face as she lunged forward for the kiss. 'Do not resist me, maid! I am struck by the thunderbolt!'

Planting both feet firmly on the ground, Geenie pushed her hands into her friend's chest. 'No,' she said.

Diana tried to hold her tighter, moving her hands to Geenie's waist and pulling her in, but Geenie struggled and pushed harder. The two of them almost toppled. 'My beautiful darling, my muse!' gasped Diana, closing her eyes and puckering her lips. 'One kiss is all I ask!'

Summoning all her strength, Geenie shoved Diana away. Just as the girl was regaining her balance and coming for her again, Geenie dodged sideways. 'Leave me alone!' she shouted.

Diana stood, staring at Geenie, who was faintly aware of her words echoing round the garden. Before the other girl could speak, Geenie turned to their audience. 'The end,' she panted, bobbing slightly.

There was no applause. George had his hand over his eyes. Kitty's mouth was hanging open. Arthur was looking at the ground, chewing his lip.

Ellen got to her feet and put an arm around her daughter's shoulder. 'Well done, girls. I'm not quite sure what that was all about, but I'm sure we all appreciated it.' She began to clap, but no one else joined in.

'I haven't done my poem,' said Diana in a small voice.

George stood and cleared his throat. 'Well done, girls. Most—ah—inventive.' He took Diana by the arm. 'Come and tell your poem to me,' he whispered, leading her across the lawn to his studio.

Geenie glanced up at her mother. 'That wasn't how it was supposed to be,' she said.

'Wasn't it, darling? I'd never have guessed.'

'It was better this way, though.'

'You improvised, darling, which is very clever. And I like your costume.'

'Kitty made it.' She turned to the chair where Kitty had been sitting, but it was empty. Looking towards the house, Geenie caught a glimpse of the cook running through the back door, one hand pressed across her mouth, the other frantically cutting the air.

THIRTY-SIX

Kitty sat at the kitchen table, struggling to control her breathing. She'd been so preoccupied with the sensation of being next to Mr Crane on the lawn—once his knee had touched hers and the thudding in her chest had become so strong that she thought she would have to go inside—and with not looking at him, despite the burning in her face and the irritation in her fingers, that she hadn't concentrated on what the girls were doing at all. It was only when Diana had declared *What beauty there is to be found in a lowly housemaid!* in that strange, hollow voice she'd adopted that Kitty had begun to pay attention to the play. And from that moment on, she'd prayed for the thing to be over.

Taking a deep breath, she laid her hands flat on the table, trying to steady her trembling fingers. The girls couldn't know, she thought, what had really happened. They couldn't. If they did, Geenie would never have pushed Diana away. But still. They must know something.

'Tea?'

She swung round to see Arthur filling the kettle. He hadn't come in for his late morning tea since they'd danced together that Sunday afternoon at the Crown and Thistle. As he measured out the leaves, tapping the spoon three times on the edge of the caddy, he whistled 'The Continental' under his breath. Setting the pot and two cups on the table, he pulled up a chair next to Kitty and sat down with a loud sigh.

'Weather's going to break soon,' he predicted,

taking the lid from the pot and stirring the tea with considerable force.

She tried to say something suitable, but her mind couldn't settle on any one word. Arthur poured tea, then milk, into a cup and pushed it in her direction. 'That was a proper spectacle, wasn't it?'

She brought the cup to her face and blinked.

'Those girls.' He gave a laugh, leaning back in his seat and rubbing his eyes. 'When Miss Geenie gave the other one a shove! It was all I could do not to laugh. I thought they were both going over. Splayed out on the lawn like a couple of wrestlers.' He took a long slurp of his tea and ducked his head to catch Kitty's eye. 'You all right?'

She looked at her lap.

Then he said, in a low voice, 'What the gardener didn't see would've been more like it, eh?'

Kitty put her cup down. The china clattered and some liquid spilled into the saucer. She looked at Arthur, at his ridged brow, his neatly trimmed moustache. His eyes searched hers, and she knew he was waiting for her to deny it. But she could not.

A small smile passed over his lips. 'Well, it's like I said. It's never good to get too close to them.' He finished his drink and stood up. 'Better get back to it. I'm a busy man.'

'Arthur—'

He stopped, tea still glistening on his moustache.

Kitty swallowed. 'Will she sack me, do you think?'

Arthur gave a loud laugh. 'Well, I wouldn't wait around to find out, if I were you. If I were you, I'd get it over, before she does.' He laughed again, shaking his head. 'Bloody women!' he muttered, striding through the door.

* * *

The weather did not break that day. Kitty spent most of it in the kitchen, her mind veering from one thought to the other. At first she'd vowed to find Mrs Steinberg right away and tell her she was leaving. Then she'd heard the crackle of tyres on the gravel, and looked out to see both cars disappearing down the drive. Going back to the kitchen, she decided she would wait just one more day—it was only a day, after all, since he'd kissed her, and she needed to see him again before making any firm decision. Standing in the larder, wondering why she'd gone in there in the first place, she decided she should disappear herself: just up and leave without a word. She imagined Mr Crane appearing at Lou's gate, looking for her, his thin face drawn. Washing lettuce leaves for the girls' lunch, she decided she'd pretend nothing had happened. If Mrs Steinberg tackled her about it, she'd deny everything.

In fact, the only decision she really managed to make was to bake a quiche, as she'd now learned to call it, after lunch. The bringing together of the pastry, having first run her fingers beneath the cold water tap, soothed her, and she found it was possible to concentrate on each small task. Then her heart would leap only when she heard what sounded like a car coming close to the cottage, rather than with every other breath. Leaving the pastry to rest in the larder, she scrubbed out the sink with Jeyes and wiped down all the shelves. She

298

rolled out the pastry and put it in the oven to bake blind. Still only half past four, and no car in the drive. So she set to work on the kitchen and larder windows, rubbing them to a shine with a little vinegar. Whilst doing this, she noticed for the first time that the girls had been silent all day. Remembering Geenie's face as she'd stood before her on the lawn, her features stiffened with fear, Kitty considered going upstairs to check on the girl when she'd finished her chores. But after she'd swept out all the downstairs rooms with the soft broom, it was time to scrape the potatoes and shell the peas. And her heart was still flipping in her chest with every noise from the road.

The girls came down at half past seven to feed themselves, and Kitty left them to it, sitting alone at the kitchen table to try to eat the slice she'd put aside for herself. Although the bacon was crisp, the pastry softly crumbling, and the cream and egg filling shivered on her fork, she didn't swallow more than three bites. Going into the sitting room, she found the girls had left the table. She cleared the things away and washed up, running the water so hot that the geyser knocked against the wall and her fingers turned the colour of crabs in the sink.

It was past ten o'clock when she heard a car return, and by that time she'd decided what she would do. She even smiled to herself as she sat on her bed and listened to Mr Crane's deliberate footsteps along the path to his studio. The lamp's glow grew in his window. There was no time to waste. Unbuttoning her apron and taking off her dress, she changed into a clean pair of knickers, the ones with the lace trim that she'd sewn around the legs herself. Then she removed the emerald

299

green Macclesfield silk dress that Lou had given her from its hanger. It was slippery and cool on her forearms as she lifted it and slipped it over her head. The heavy fabric rested on her hips and breasts and followed the curve of her thighs. It was a little long, but that didn't matter now. She combed her hair, tucking it behind her ears, pinched her cheeks and smeared Vaseline over her lips. Then she realised she'd no shoes. The green shoe—if it had had a partner, and if it had fitted—would have matched, but one shoe was worse than no shoes, and she couldn't very well ask Arthur for the other now. She'd have to cross the lawn barefoot. In a last-minute rush of daring, she left her stockings off, too.

She tiptoed through the kitchen and out into the night. The roses smelled their best at this time, but she didn't think about that. The damp grass licked her toes as she headed straight across the lawn towards the studio, her dress swishing behind her.

Pausing before the door, she gulped several mouthfuls of cool air and pressed the dress down around her hips. Her heart was rushing, her palms moist, her throat dry, but she couldn't stand here, exposed in her emerald silk dress and no shoes. She kept her eyes closed as she pushed on his door, and it was only when it was almost fully open that she thought: what if he's not alone in there? But it was too late. She was standing on the threshold looking in, and he was sitting in his armchair, looking back at her.

'Good grief,' he said. They were both frozen for a moment, Kitty grinning at the sight of him—he was real, breathing, here—Mr Crane's mouth gaping. Then he jumped to his feet, pulled her inside, and slammed the door closed. She came easily, stepping very close to him. He held her wrist and their hips pressed together, the dress crumpling between them as she looked into his face. Her hand reached for the back of his neck, but before she could kiss him, he said, 'Wait.'

She hadn't planned words. She'd planned only the dress, and the taking off of the dress, and their bodies moving together again.

He let go of her wrist and took a step back. 'Kitty, I—ah—I've been meaning to talk with you.' Then he looked her up and down and added, a smile growing, 'I'm glad you came. And in such a dress.'

'It's the first time I've worn it,' she said, wishing her voice didn't sound so small.

'It's lovely.' He touched her elbow.

'I wanted to wear it for you.'

'Did you?' His eyes were following the curves of the dress, of her body in the dress.

She smiled, and had to stop herself from twirling in front of him. Instead, she moved towards him again and looked up.

He cleared his throat, then said, very quickly, 'Look here. It's the most awful timing, but I have to go away tomorrow.' He held on to her elbow, as he had on that first day when she'd stood in his studio and almost curtsied. His fingers were very white against the green silk.

'It's a lecture tour, you see, with the Communist Party. Up and down the whole country. Very important work. Damned awful timing. But I have to take this opportunity.'

She blinked, and swallowed hard, before managing to ask, 'When will you be back?'

There was a silence. He dropped his hand to his side and looked away. 'I'm not altogether sure. But when I am, I hope we'll—ah—see one another again. Don't you?'

She fixed her eyes on the pile of old blankets beneath his desk. Blotto's bed. Picturing the dog curled up at his feet, warm and snoozing, she began to shake.

'It's important work,' he said again. 'And it's really very exciting. This country is going to change. Everyone says so. The working classes are going to rise up—'

'You should wash those,' she said, staring at the blankets. 'They smell.'

He drew a hand across his mouth. 'Kitty. I'm so sorry.'

Clasping her fingers behind her back to stop them trembling, she glanced around the room. His desk was empty. The typewriter was in its carrying case, by the door. A pile of books was stacked on top of the filing cabinet, and there were no pictures anywhere. 'How long have you known?'

He sat in the chair and patted the leather patch on its arm. 'Sit with me.'

'How long have you known?'

'Some weeks.'

The shaking became stronger, forcing its way from her knees to her stomach, then up her spine and out of her mouth in a short, audible gasp of air. She covered her face with her hands.

'Kitty. Dear Kitty. Sit with me. Please.'

She didn't move.

'Kitty. Please.' His hands were on her waist, pulling her towards the chair. 'Lovely Kitty,' he said, slowly drawing her hands from her eyes, 'It

302

was lovely, wasn't it?' He slipped his fingers up her naked forearm. 'And this dress is—quite beautiful. You're quite beautiful in it.' He planted a kiss on her wrist, but she was looking over his head at her own reflection in the darkened window. The shaking had almost stopped now. The emerald dress flashed in the lamplight, her eyes were large and empty-looking, her mouth shining. She let him go on kissing the soft skin of her arm, all the way up to the elbow. He nudged the green silk sleeve higher. 'Kitty,' he said. 'Kitty.' He tried to rise from the chair, but she pushed him down again, grasping his hair and holding his head to her stomach so his cheek pressed against the heavy fabric. She gazed at her own reflection in the window, absorbing the image of herself with a man's face buried in her waist, and she kept him there until she was ready to leave.

THIRTY-SEVEN

Geenie did not go to Diana's room that night. Instead she slept in the soft centre of her own bed, and dreamed of the maps on Jimmy's wall. In her dream, she drew all the countries and the seas on the floor of Jimmy's study, and when he came into the room, he was carrying his walking stick, and he was ready to take her anywhere.

In the morning, she rose early. Sitting at the dining table, rubbing sleep from her eyes, she watched Diana bring in a plate of toast, a pot of tea and two cups.

'Where's Kitty?' Geenie yawned.

Diana spread the toast with butter, being careful to get it in all the corners. 'There's no baby, you know,' she said, taking a bite.

Geenie had almost forgotten about her mother's announcement. The day on the beach seemed long ago, now. 'Isn't there?'

'Daddy told me yesterday.'

Geenie nodded. Then she asked again, 'Where's Kitty?'

'Haven't seen her. Daddy made me toast, and I made the tea.' Diana sipped her drink.

'You can make tea?'

'It's far better, actually. Not so strong. Want a cup?'

Geenie shook her head and watched in silence as Diana ate two more slices of toast, thickly smeared with raspberry jam.

The door opened. 'Five minutes, darling. We've got to catch the eight-forty.' Spotting Geenie, George stepped into the room. 'Don't look so worried,' he said, giving her a pat on the head. 'You two will see each other again. You'll have to visit Diana at her mother's. Won't she, Diana?'

Pushing past George, Geenie ran from the room and took the stairs two at a time. Dragging all her dressing-up things from the bottom of the wardrobe, she plunged her arms into the pile and threw stockings, hats, shoes, dresses and waistcoats over her shoulder until her fingers touched the cool sleekness of fur.

Diana was standing in the hallway with her suitcase by her feet when Geenie made it back downstairs. Geenie thrust the coat towards her friend. 'If you're going,' she panted, 'you'd better have this.' It weighed down her arms and draped on

304

the floor about the two of them, like a king's cloak.

Diana hooked her hair behind one ear. 'But it's yours.'

'Take it.'

From the driveway, George was calling his daughter.

'It's Jimmy's,' said Diana. 'You have to keep it.' She stroked the fur collar. 'It suits you best, anyway.'

When the front door had closed, Geenie wrapped herself tightly in the coat and went in search of her mother.

*   *   *

As far as Ellen was concerned, they'd already said their goodbyes on Harting Down, and there was little point in getting up this early in the morning. She burrowed beneath the bedclothes and closed her eyes. What she really couldn't stand was the thought of another drama. She'd spent all yesterday avoiding it. After the play, Crane had gone to Laura's to meet with Lillian and make the necessary arrangements for Diana, who was going to stay with her mother while he went on his lecture tour, and Ellen had gone to the hairdressers'. She'd actually had an appointment this time, and Robin had spent hours dyeing her hair jet black and then styling it in the same Hollywood wave as before. While she was sitting in the chair, watching his steady fingers move around her face, she'd thought again of Crane's scrap of poetry. *His blood is heavy with wanting.* Ridiculous. It had to be make-believe, Ellen decided, just like that amusing little play the girls had put on.

305

Geenie had shown a lot of nerve, barking back at Diana like that, and almost pushing her over. It was actually very promising.

Once she was polished and set, Ellen couldn't quite face going back to the cottage in case he'd returned, so she went for tea at the White Hart before meeting Robin again, this time in the back room. It had been, as always, vigorous and refreshing, but she meant to make it her last visit. Since she'd decided her daughter should go to the local school in September, she should make the most of the few remaining weeks of summer with Geenie. Perhaps she could teach her to dance. Besides, Robin was getting to be an awfully expensive habit.

Ellen shifted in the bed. Crane had come up late last night, but she hadn't pretended to sleep. Instead, she'd opened her eyes and said, 'In the morning, will you just go? I don't think I can stand it, otherwise.' He'd brushed her hand with his, and she'd caught it and held fast. But now, as she lay between the sheets, looking at the little boatmen on her curtains, she did think about going downstairs and blocking the doorway. Forbidding him to leave. Begging him to stay. She covered her head with the pillow, but still she could hear the muffled sound of his careful tread on the hallway boards, the click and shudder as he pulled open the front door. She put her hands to her ears and closed her eyes, as she'd done as a girl when her father was leaving the house to visit his mistress. It was surprisingly comforting, especially with the pillow draped over your head and shoulders and your body curled in on itself. Almost like someone was holding you.

When she unfurled her arms and legs, the cottage was quiet. She lifted the pillow from her head. The sun was warming the sheets, and her daughter was opening the door and throwing herself on the bed beside her, wearing a beautiful fur that Ellen hadn't seen or touched for a long time. With a laugh, she recognised it: Jimmy's sable coat. Accepting it from the girl's hands, Ellen draped it across the bed, and she and Geenie lay down together and slept on top of the coat until lunchtime.

*   *   *

Kitty was too exhausted to cry any more, but she wasn't refusing to get out of bed. It was just that she didn't see why she should. George (she thought of him as George for the first time, and it was less painful: *George* was not the man who'd kissed her goodbye last night) had said Mrs Steinberg knew nothing of their love affair (was that what it had been?), but Kitty couldn't believe him. The woman was sure to throw her out. She may as well try to sleep for another hour, and then, when she was stronger, she could face it.

But it was no good. Although her body was heavy, her mind was still alert. She peeped over the sheets. The green silk frock was sprawled on the floor, where she'd kicked it off last night. The best thing to do would be to give it back to Lou and tell her it could be altered after all. With enough determination, you could make anything fit.

Rolling over, Kitty covered her eyes against the sun, which was glaring through a gap in the curtains, and gave a little groan. Sounds were

307

coming from the kitchen, quiet ones at first: shoes on the flags, the larder door creaking. Then louder: drawers opening, cutlery chiming. Pots being clashed together. Kitty turned over again, trying to ignore the row. Let the woman get on with it, she thought. She wouldn't know butter from margarine, or a skillet from a saucepan. Let her pull the kitchen apart, if that's what she wants. See how she fares.

Then she noticed something poking between the wall and the mattress. She reached for the corner of the material and tugged. Her embroidery. Sitting up, she spread it across her lap, flattening out the creases with her hands and remembering the day at the beach, how she'd felt the embroidered scene was so much better than the real one. Running a finger along its surface, she felt the thickness of the rocks, the pinched knobbles of the crab's eyes, the fine filigree of the girls' fishing nets. She'd had a thought that she might give it to George—Mr Crane—as a gift. But now she was glad she hadn't. Perhaps it was good enough to put on the wall. She could use it to replace the awful painting of the woman at the waterfall.

Then she remembered that by the end of the day she'd be back at Lou's, among her sister's things, where anything homemade was not tolerated.

There was a knock at the door. Kitty gathered the embroidery to her chest and turned her face to the wall.

'Kitty.' It was Geenie's voice. 'Kitty?'

She waited for the girl to go away.

'Ellen says, will you have lunch with us?'

So that was it. Even now, they couldn't make themselves a meal. Kitty threw off the bedclothes and, still in her nightgown, pulled open the door. 'Can't you get your own lunch, just for once?' She was almost shouting. Geenie stepped backwards, and Kitty looked beyond her into the kitchen. Mrs Steinberg was standing at the stove, stirring something. Her hair had changed colour: it was glossy and black, like oil, and it made her nose stand out even further. There was a smell of burnt toast, and a pot of tea was steaming on the table.

'It's only scrambled egg,' the woman said, frowning at the stove, ploughing her wooden spoon into the pan. 'Well, you can make up for it tomorrow, Kitty, I'm sure. But for now, we'll have to put up with my effort.'

'I helped,' added Geenie, hopping on one foot. 'I cracked the eggs.'

Kitty folded her arms across her chest. 'I'm not—dressed.'

'What does that matter?' Mrs Steinberg was dolloping mounds of egg onto plates. 'Sit down and eat.'

Kitty could tell by the way the egg fell with a heavy splat that it would be rubbery. The toast in the rack looked limp and cold. But her mouth filled with water.

Taking a chair, she sat at the table.

'Just a minute.' Mrs Steinberg disappeared from the room. Kitty looked at Geenie. 'The costumes were lovely,' the girl said. Then the cottage was filled with the thump and soar of music, and a man's sweet, rasping voice began to sing.

Mrs Steinberg returned. 'Much better,' she said. Pushing a plate of egg over to Kitty, she sat with

Geenie at her side. Kitty took up her knife and fork. Together, the three of them began to eat.

ACKNOWLEDGEMENTS

This novel is based loosely on events in the lives of Peggy Guggenheim, her lover Douglas Garman, and their respective daughters Pegeen Vail and Deborah Garman, who lived together in Sussex from 1934 to 1937. The characters and setting have been fictionalised, but essential to me in researching this book was Peggy's own outrageous, tantalising, inconsistent account of her life, *Out of This Century: Confessions of an Art Addict*. Among many other useful books were Anton Gill's *Peggy Guggenheim: The Life of an Art Addict* and, for its wonderfully gutsy evocation of life in service, *Below Stairs*, by Margaret Powell.

I'd like to thank Cath Aldworth and Marge Phillips for sharing their fascinating recollections of the mid-1930s with me. Both ladies were wonderful company and extremely generous.

Thanks to Pete Ayrton, John Williams, Rebecca Gray and the team at Serpent's Tail, and to my agent, David Riding, for their commitment to this book. For their advice on drafts, I am grateful to Naomi Foyle, Claire Harries, Kai Merriott and Lorna Thorpe, and I remain deeply indebted to David Swann, who read the first half and convinced me it was going to be all right. Special thanks to my parents for their support, and to my brother Owen for his expertise on every subject. My greatest debt, as always, is to my husband Hugh Dunkerley, who is also my first and best reader.